It was a war-horse,  rider.

"Ahi-a, saaaa, saaa... wrong, Macefoot-Harro...

The mount began to ...less offspring of a non...

Normally no amount of horse-temper would have unseated her; she had ridden since the age of three. But this was totally unexpected, she had to keep a grip on her bow, and war-saddles were not designed for unbroken horses. A huge convulsive twisting leap sent her flying into a low snowbank with a squawk of surprise and a clatter of armor. By the time she had bounced back to her feet the horse was only a fading pounding of hooves, receding at full gallop, reckless of the uncertain footing. That meant it was frightened enough to run in blind panic, risking its legs on roots and hidden bushes.

Quietly, she cursed the whole pantheon and the equine race with the Horse Spirit thrown in.

All the time she had been scanning the area, her back to a thick trunk. It suddenly occurred to her that whatever had frightened her horse might find *her*. And she had only one shaft; the quiver was clipped to her saddlebow. Her mouth turned dry, and her heart beat loud in her ears; the moonlit forest turned alien and hostile, the haunt of Zoweitz-creatures, perhaps even the dreaded demon *mhaigz*. Fear awoke anger. She started out on a cautious search.

There was no warning but a deep heavy creaking, as if a great weight were pressing down on the snow, and when she whirled there was nothing there. A flash of movement; she snapshot, and the shaft went *crack* into a tree, a centimeter deep in the iron-hard frozen wood.

Then it let itself be seen, and the bow dropped from her fingers. A hand fumbled at swordhilt, but it was strengthless. A dim mewing came from her lips. Then there was nothing.

SNOWBROTHER

FIFTH MILLENNIUM NOVELS

Snowbrother by S.M. Stirling
Shadow's Daughter by Shirley Meier
The Cage by S.M. Stirling & Shirley Meier
Lion's Heart by Karen Wehrstein
Lion's Soul by Karen Wehrstein
Shadow's Son
   by Shirley Meier, S.M. Stirling, & Karen Wehrstein

S.M. Stirling

SNOWBROTHER

Copyright © 1992 by S. M. Stirling

A shorter and substantially different version of this novel was published in 1985.

A Baen Books Original

Baen Publishing Enterprises
P.O. Box 1403
Riverdale, N.Y. 10471

ISBN: 0-671-72119-4

Cover art by Larry Elmore

A signed, numbered limited-edition print of the artwork (22 × 27¾") is available from the artist at Elmore Studios, P.O. Box 358, Leitchfield, KY 42754.

Map by Eleanor Kostyk

First printing, May 1992

Distributed by
SIMON & SCHUSTER
1230 Avenue of the Americas
New York, N.Y. 10020

Printed in the United States of America

to Jan

CENTRAL ALMERKUN
LATE 5TH MILLENNIUM

Kommanz
of Paizrar

Kommanz
of Rh'eginz

Kommanz
of Mb'aintab

Kommanz
of Kai-gara

Minztans

NORTHERN NOMADS

Haamraalys-
al-Minztannis

WARZONE
(uninhabited)

NORTHERN
SEA

Granfor

Bemedjaha

Veshra

Minztans

Stonefort Keep

Newstead

SERPENT
SEA

Westwall (World-wall) Mountains

Maznib River

TEN CITIES
LEAGUE

Kommanz
of Ihway

Raddock

Nai
Peri

Kalaab

S'paw

Cbrag

Plainston

Kingdom of
Britt

Darshai

Kresh

Gaald
Marches

The Small
Kingdoms

Whai

Senlaw

Kawnz River

Kingdom of
Zarkis

Free Cantons

Despotate of
Pryil

SOUTHERN NOMADS

PROLOGUE:

*Long ago, in the Before, we were as the gods are,
riding thunderbirds of metal, wielding Break-the-Sky
medicine, smashing whole cities at a single blow. Then,
all the lands were one realm, from the bitterwater of
the east to the sea beyond the Westwall mountains. In
fortresses beneath the earth, or aloft beyond the world
of air our Ancestors ruled, the chosen warriors of the
gods. Weak and sinful, many turned from the honorable path of war, all but the faithful few, and the
ahKomman were angered. So the Godwar came, and
the Year Without Sun; the Ztrateke ahkomman walked
no more with humans, and the world was broken and
changed. But we are warriors still.*

> Kommanz folktale
> quoted in the *Book of Journeys*
> of Anyamarah the Far-Traveled
> preserved in the libraries
> of the Rose Temple, Senlaw
> 775th Year of the Maleficence
> (4720 A.D.)

STONEFORT KEEP
KOMMANZ OF GRANFOR
AUTUMN, 4962 A.D.

"It is good," one of the councilors said, hawking
and spitting in the dirt. The gobbet of phlegm

1

landed near the outland merchant's boot, but his
diplomatic smile never wavered.

Zhy'da Mek Kermak grunted and looked down
at the plow below the low earth dais where the
ruling kin and their wisefolk waited. The Senior of
Stonefort Keep was a tall rawboned woman in her
early fifties, still ropily muscular; except for those
knocked out in fights, she still had all her teeth,
strong and yellow as she grinned.

"Maybe too good," she rasped, taking another pull
at the leather cup of beer. The plow had a wooden
frame, but the share and moldboard were of dark-
shining durcret; that was a southron thing, almost
as strong as metal but far cheaper. In the demonstration two horses had drawn it easily through
tough prairie sod, while six oxen struggled and
heaved at the clumsy Kommanz breaking-plow.

It was a hot day, even though the first night frosts
had come; no sign of a thunderstorm in the cloud-
less sky, which was a good omen. Mustering Fair,
bright noon sun through a harvest-haze of dust, air
heavy with the smells of sweat and dung and smoke.
The angular stone ramparts and towers of the Keep
bulked at their backs, and the close-cropped pasture of the Home Field stretched for kilometers on
either side over land flat as a tabletop. Today it was
crowded. Warriors drilling, the village contingents
come in to show that their skills had not rusted.
Wagonloads of tribute from the dependent territor-
ies, piles of yellow grain, potatoes, whole-cowskin
sacks of sunflower oil, bolts of cloth, milling
herds. And everyone with something to sell, everyone who could be spared in the lands about Stonefort. It was a relief after the tension and fear of
harvest season, when folk took turn and turn-about
reaping and riding guard against nomad raiders or

bandits. The grain and flax and oilseeds were safely cut and carted; potatoes and roots were still to be brought in, but those were safely unburnable.

This was the best time of year; plenty to eat, good hunting—the fall bison herds would be through soon—and usually no more fighting than the soul required. Mostly skirmishing with other Keeps, fighting within the Bans for ransoms and herds. The fair was the beginning of it.

The ruling kinfast had spent the morning handing out judgments; fines and compounding for blood feuds and killings, a few floggings and ear-croppings and nose-slittings for serious crimes like horse theft or blasphemy, one straw-haired head sending rivulets of blood down a pole. That one had killed outside the Bans, cutting down a pregnant freewoman; even someone mad-drunk or *ahrappan* should remember what was peaceholy.

"You, merchants," she said, rising. "Go, over there."

The southlanders bowed slightly and withdrew. They were from the Pentapolis, the League of Ten Cities three weeks' journey to the southeast; odd-looking, in their tight trews and jewel-buttoned silk jackets, with long rapiers at their sides and dart pistols holstered at their hips. They had brought a strong escort down the trade-trail this season, mercenary knights, and armored foot-fighters with pikes and crossbows. Zhy'da did not fear them for that, or for the train of two dozen huge six-wheeled wagons with their ceramic flamethrowers. The merchants were careful to stay within the area marked out by the demon-headed poles; that was peaceholy too, although only with the second Ban.

On the other side of the dais tribute accounts were being handed in, and a tallyman was droning:

"—and it is said that the Thorut's-kin are yeoman-freeholders of Tunbak village. And their clan is Mad Bear and their lords are the Kallak's-kin. And it is said they hold seventy hectares in free of the village and fifty from their lords and grazing right in commons. And it is said their service in peace is the labor of one for one day in every week and two for one day in mainharvest and hayharvest weeks with plow and team and scythe and cartage, and of grain ten horseloads, and one colt in ten and one beast in ten and the wool of fifteen sheep. And it is said their war-service is five lancers fully trained with gear and remounts—"

No, Zhy'da thought. *I fear the southrons' arts of peace, not their weapons.*

"If we buy their plows, we need them to plow at all," she said. "So we must sell more to them, every year."

Her wombchild Zte'vf laughed. "Or take."

She swung an arm without bothering to look around, backhanding him across the mouth.

"Drunk before sundown? Twenty lashes tomorrow." The beginning of a protest; she struck him again. "Shut up, before I remember the dumb donkey I must have fucked to throw a stupid colt like you," she said. "Make obeisance and go, bring your kinsib Shkai'ra to me."

One of the warmasters sighed. "Time was when we raided south to the Great River itself, and the Ten Cities paid us tribute," he said.

Zhy'da shrugged. "Time was when the southrons weren't so many and their cities so strong," she said. Even the rural knights in the south had mostly replaced their brick-and-timber forts with castles of glassfiber-reinforced concrete, and the cities had walls like cliffs and murder-machines to guard them. Too many Kommanz warbands had been caught on their way home, slowed by loot.

"We can beat their war-hosts and kill their peasants, but we can't spare strength to really harm them, not with the Sky-Blue at our backs."

Several of the Kommanza spat off the dais at the mention of the Sky-Blue Wolves of the High Steppe, the cannibal nomads of the short-grass plains to the west.

"A long time since they tried to break the border," the warmaster observed. Nothing this summer but the usual raids; the Kommanz had smashed several, taking prisoners for sale and sending the survivors wailing back to their tents.

Zhy'da nodded; that was the point. Fifty winters ago drought had struck, and half the tribes between the Scarp and the Westwall tried to push east into the tall grass country. The three southeastern realms, the *Kommanz* of Granfor and Ihwaz and Maintab, had called out their levies to meet them: twenty thousand lances. Every second adult in three of the six Kommanz realms had died that year, and the slaughter of nomads in battle and pursuit had left windrows of bones. You still found them here and there, hidden in the long grass and crunching under hooves. Since then both sides in the ancient conflict had had time to breed back their strength.

"With the southron tools . . ." the warmaster continued, shrugging.

Many others grunted agreement; the plow was impressive, but the horse-drawn harvesting machine even more so. Every Keep maintained five-score or so of full-time fighters with no trade but war, and the village chiefs each had their retainers, but the core of a Kommanz warhost was the yeomen. Few of the freeholder kinfasts had more than a slave or so, many none at all; it was not safe to keep many more unfree about, in a land so wild and thinly peopled. Yeomen must train to war and work their fields and flocks as well, and the new machines would spare many hours for drill and fighting. Yet perhaps they were unwise, or unlucky. It was always dangerous to break with custom, an opening for evil witchcraft and bad luck.

"How will we pay?" Zhy'da said, glancing around to the caravanmaster, manager of the Keep's trading interests. The man shrugged, rattling handfuls of tally-sticks.

"We can't send much more south," he said. Slaves were a Kommanz export, mostly nomads, but those were too fierce and flighty to fetch good prices. Then there were wool and leather, dried meat, horses, hides, metals, and pelts traded or taken from the forest peoples north and east. And a trickle of goods brought all the way through the Zekz Kommanz, the Six Realms that surrounded the northern end of the plains of Almerkun like a horseshoe; silk from the lands across the Westwall, along the Mother Ocean; sea-otter furs, walrus ivory, spices, sandalwood, jade.

"Not much more unless we let them build a railroad north, so we could ship bulk grains."

More grunts, this time of derision. Horses could pull enormous loads on durcret rails, but nobody in Stonefort, in the whole of Granfor, was going to let the southrons thrust such a spear into the belly of the Kommanz lands. Not since the Maleficent's day had a southlander army marched into the Realms and lived. That was because the Kommanz would scorch the earth before it and harry its flanks and rear until it weakened and despaired from hunger, and they could overrun and slaughter. A railroad could supply troops through such manmade desert, and the Kommanz Keeps and village walls were built to keep out the wild nomads, not a cityfolk siege-train that could throw ton-weight blocks half a kilometer or more.

"We could send more hired fighters south," one of her kinmates said. Kommanz mercenary cavalry were always in demand.

Zhy'da shook her head. "Too many don't come back. We need those riders. And if we spend more time growing and making goods to sell, that weakens us too. And the southron have reasons of their own to offer such things, when they never have before. Perhaps just gain-hunting, perhaps not. The *Kommand'ahan* in Granfor-the-town has to speak on this, at MidWinter Gathering, but until then we need a way to get wealth that doesn't weaken our warstrength."

The *Kommand'ahan* was sacred, but in secular matters must listen to the Keepholder clans, and Stonefort was among the mightiest of those. She looked up at the sun; in a few hours her children would be back.

"Here's one answer—"

What duty? Shkai'ra Mek Kermak's-kin thought. It could only be an assignment, when the kinmother sent her sib to fetch her from overseeing drill. His words had been few and rough, but she scorned to ask more; they hated each other more than was common, being the youngest of their generation and rivals for succession. A trickle of apprehension stiffened her spine, colder than the sweat that soaked the padding under her armor. Zhy'da Mek Kermak's-kin believed in testing the offspring, sometimes to destruction. Zte'vf's lip was swollen and there was dried blood in his cropped yellow beard. That might have happened in a number of ways, but a kinparent's fist was most likely.

His fault, not mine; if they're angered, it's with him, she reminded herself.

"Take over, Eh'rik," she said to the warmaster beside her. He could handle the inspection as well as she; this was training for her as much as the village levy they were drilling.

He nodded silently. Two of the Stonefort household troopers fell in behind the Mek Kermaks as they left, lances slung and wheelbows in their hands with arrows nocked. That was prudent, although she was full-armed and her sib bore saber and wheelbow. Bandits or outlaws might be about, or skulkers from the high steppe, infiltrating through the broad strips of unbroken grassland between villages. This close to home the steppe was almost tame; she could see herds of longhorns and beefalo and sheep with their herders, and there were patches where the bluestem had been grazed down to knee height. Mostly it was chest-high on a tall horse, a wavering sea of bronze and wine-russet stalks starred with deep purple-blue downy gentians, running to the horizon all around. When they skirted a swampy vale, ducks and geese lifted in clouds huge enough to hide the westering sun. The air was cooling toward sundown, smelling of dry grass and wild rose and horse.

The Kommanza rode at wolf-pace, walk-trot-canter-trot-walk. Soon enough they saw patrols, then the outlying fields of Stonefort's home village, stubble alternating with blocks of potatoes and beets and alfalfa. They passed wagons and pack trains headed in to the Mustering Fair. Dust hazed the eastern horizon, and their lances threw long slender shadows as they rode into the close-cropped area about the castle itself.

Shkai'ra kept her eyes ahead as befitted a noble while she rode through the Mustering Fair, although it was an effort; her concession to curiosity was to clip her helmet to her belt. Noise beat at her. Nothing but a hall-feast or a battle was as loud as a fair; there must be a ten of hundreds of people here. Keep servants and warmasters were setting up the balks and targets for tomorrow's games; mounted archery and lance-work while riding obstacle courses, and there would be unarmed combat and target shooting, too. Booths and tents with wonderful things; shining tools of ceramic or metal, colored cloth—some of real cotton or silk—fine weapons and tooled saddles, things your hands itched to touch. Hawkers dodged near, holding up delicacies; skewers of grilled buffalo-hump and onion, lamb ribs, southland wine or coffee, then dropped back when they were ignored.

The crowds parted before her and her kinsib, like prairie grass before their horses. She swung a fist up in salute and ducked her head as she passed one of her kinfathers buying stock from a dealer. Slaves this time, six fine females and an equal number of strong young males, for the Great Sacrifice at the end of the fair: human, horse, cattle and dog. Then they drew near the dais and its circle of space.

Shkai'ra reached back for the lance in its holster behind her right thigh, pulled it free and stabbed the point into the dirt in token of respect. Zte'vf and she vaulted to the ground together, went to their knees, and pressed their foreheads to the ground between their palms.

"Obedience to you, givers of our blood," the young nobles said.

Zhy'da grunted. "Up, puppies," she said. "Closer."

They knee-walked to the edge of the mound. Four of the ruling generation of Mek Kermak's-kin were there, a few of their senior advisors, and the great shaman Walks-With-Demons. He tapped at the drums slung to his belt, and the circle of emptiness around the dais grew larger.

"I have a task for one of you, punishment and reward," Zhy'da said; the shaman giggled slightly, and she frowned sidelong at him. "The Keep needs new wealth. Wealth that we can use to fee the southron traders for new goods. At least five tens of fingerweights of silver-value, in goods a caravan could take south."

Shkai'ra felt her breath catch behind the impassive mask of her face. *War*, she thought. That was the only way to get goods of great value and low weight quickly.

"Plan a raid to the east, to be carried out before next spring," she said. "Both of you, separately, a plan. You have a week; a raid taking two tens and a ten of warriors, with gear suitable, but no more than one ten of our household fighters. Consult who you will, but if any word of this goes abroad, you both spend another week naked in the stonebox."

Both the younger Mek Kermaks clenched their teeth slightly; that was not a light punishment.

"A good plan, mind; daring but not reckless. Objective, means, supply, tactics, withdrawal, minimal risk. The maker of the best plan commands the raid, reward. The begetter of the worst stays here for their week in the stonebox, punishment."

Or more than that, Shkai'ra knew. It was nearly time for the next generation of the Mek Kermak kinfast to marry and pass on the sacred godborn blood. Like most folk, Kommanza forbade sibs of the same gender to wed, fearing weak offspring. Customs differed; in most lands some or all of the next generation's sisters married together, and then sought out male mates; among others, it was the brothers who wed. Among Kommanza of the *ofzar* class the elders chose, by appointing one child senior.

She looked sidelong at her sib; their glances met, out of the corners of their eyes. He was blue-eyed to her gray, and the ponytail and braids that marked him a warrior adult were butter-yellow to her red-blond; otherwise they were alike enough to be twins. Might well be of the same dam and sire; it was rare to know who your seedfather was. Zhy'da was probably wombmother to them both, but children were swaddled at birth and often passed among whoever of the kinmothers was nursing. . . .

Zte'vf frowned. "Bemedjaka is peaceholy until second snowfall—" he began, then shut his mouth with a snap.

Shkai'ra's face might have been carved from wood, but her mind grinned like a wolf. *He thinks quickly, but too straight,* she chuckled to herself.

Stonefort lay west of the Red River. The Kommanz of Granfor of which it was a part stretched eastward beyond the stream to the beginnings of the Great Woods, two hundred kilometers eastward. Beyond that was Minztannis, the forest-folk country, although few dwelt too near the edge of the grassland; the woodsrunners were no great warriors, and preferred to stay out of reach of raiders from the steppes. But they were rich in metals and great craftsfolk and makers, almost as craft-wise as the southron city-dwellers. Bemedjaka was the nearest large settlement of them. Minztans lived even more scattered than Kommanza; Bemedjaka

was almost a city, two thousand or more, not counting the woodsrunners living around it. A great
prize, too great to loot; there was a treaty, the Minztans of Bemedjaka traded metals and tools and the
services of their smiths for grain, meat, wool, and
flax.

The Kommand'ahan *would never let us sack
Bemedjaka,* she thought; that was a cow better
milked than slaughtered. *There must be a new village within raiding-reach. But the treaty applies—
ah, until second snowfall.*

1

WINTER, 4962 A.D.

It was quiet under the great pines. The cold cut like crystal, through fur and leather and the quilted padding under armor. Woodsmoke drifted on the air and mingled with the clean musky smell of horses and resin tang from the forest, yet each scent was leached to a ghost by the unmerciful chill of predawn. Yesterday's powder snow hung feathery from branch and trunk, blue-white on black, drinking every sound of wind and wood, muffling the clatter and stamp of sixty riders.

The Kommanz warriors sat their horses in stolid silence, long used to worse in the driving blizzards of their native prairie far to the west. All were plains-bred: tall, fair-skinned under tan and windburn, mostly hawk-faced and high in the cheekbones. Long, light hair was braided under helms; pale eyes were slitted in the perpetual half-squint of plainsdwellers. With combat to await, they had shed bison-pelt cloaks for the western battle panoply: round shields of layered bullhide; blunt, conical steel helmets, long-skirted hauberks built up of fiberglass, lacquered leather, and silk cord. Their weapons were lance, wheelbow, curved sword, dagger, and lariat; many added strings of scalps, and all had jagged gaudy designs swirling over shield and breastplate, showing kinfast and Keep.

One outlander was among them: a Minztan forester, sitting his horse with no trace of the westerners' ingrained skill. The marks of fire and blade showed on his body and bound hands. He was the last of the dozen they had captured; the scalps of the others dangled fresh from saddlehorns and belts.

Shkai'ra Mek Kermak's-kin reached across and gripped him by the hair.

"Newstead here?" she asked. Like many of her folk she had learned the forest speech, enough for trade and war.

The Minztan nodded blearily, shuddering with the cold. Shkai'ra released him and raised a hand. One of the troopers behind him tossed her lance up to the overhand grip and reversed it, planting the bone butt knob between his shoulders. She pushed, and the Minztan tumbled to the snow with a grunt of pain.

He floundered to his feet, shivering and drawing back from the figure that crouched before the horses. Alone of the Kommanza that one was unarmored and unarmed, carrying no trace of metal. Blue eyes stared sightlessly from a face made unreadable by looping ovals and tines of scar tissue, scars that had been rubbed with soot while they healed to leave their patterns ink-black against his flesh. On his head was a covering of hide and feathers and bison horns, and the fingers of his left hand tapped ceaselessly at the drum slung to his belt; on one side of it was the sigil of the spirit called *Blood Drinker*, on the other *Flesh Eater*. Before him was a knotted cord spread in a circle; within it was a dried eagle's claw, an ear cut from the Minztan with a flint knife, a scattering of objects Shkai'ra could not have named.

"Well?" she barked, using the superior-to-subject inflection.

The shaman grinned at her with filed and rotten teeth. "Yes, oh, yes," he said in a soft, even voice. He nodded through the screen of trees toward the clearing two kilometers ahead. "I hold, hold their minds within mine." His hand darted out over the circle of cord; he gasped, yelped, chanted words. "Strong witches, much power within those walls. Soon they know I hold them: better you kill, yes. I will eat their hearts, brew magic from their blood, gain their power."

From a pouch he pulled a piece of dried fungus and chewed with bitter pleasure. Then he turned, hand snaking out to touch the Minztan on the throat. The forester stilled, only his chest moving as he breathed, and the frantic motion of his eyes hunted for escape. The shaman drew a stone knife from under his jacket and slashed twice under the angle of the Minztan's jaw. Blood spurted, and still the victim stood, motionless except for shivering. The shaman's head darted forward, mouth fastening on the rivulet of blood, slurping noisily; when he withdrew the body dropped like an emptied sack.

He leaped into the middle of his cord circle, beating again on his belt-drum. Turning swiftly he spat a fine spray of blood to the north, south, east, west.

"Now," he gasped, then began a shuffling dance, chanting:

"Hey-ya-ye-ye-ye-KIAKIA-yip-ye-he-he-he-ya—"

Shkai'ra turned and gave a clenched-fist salute to the warband. No few grinned back, raising lances in salute; the free yeoman-farmers of Stonefort had an easy, unservile respect for their chiefs. Familiar faces from hunts and childhood training were shadowed to a gleam of eyes and teeth under the low brims of the helmets. Many had painted their faces for war, slashing designs of scarlet and black and green in the patterns of their clans; her own Red Hawks from the villages near the Keep, lesser numbers of Gold Dogs, Real Tigers, Running Bison. Shkai'ra wore only the Eagle on her forehead and the thunderbolts on her cheeks, her right as a scion of the *ofzar* class; the mark of Zaik Godlord, Begetter of Victory, Mother of Death.

She felt the band's coiled eagerness as she turned back to her officers. They were mostly older than her nineteen summers, sent along to steady a troop of unblooded youths. *My first raid.*

"No other sentries," she said. That brought a snort of incredulous contempt from the Kommanz officers; hard to believe even Minztan tree rabbits were that careless. "The shaman did his work well. Nothing left now but fighting; we'll be in their village and looting, drinking and fucking before Sun Retreat. Dismiss."

The village in the clearing ahead was not large as Minztan steadings went: a dozen long log kinhalls with their barns, smokehouses, forges, saunas, enough for two hundred adults and as many children. There was a stockade of pointed logs, half-finished; more attention had been paid to clearing the fields. Other clearings would have been made hereabouts, wherever the thin glacial soil would yield oats and potatoes, or hay along the streams.

The Minztans had not come this close to the edge of the steppe for farming; there was plenty of forest farther east, in the huge empty wastes that swept north from the city-lands through swamp, lake, and wood to the tundra. Trapping and hunting were good here too, but they would likely have planted near ore worth mining. Metals were rare everywhere and always precious; the Ancients had taken so much. Travelers' tales told of great circular lakes five kilometers

across that marked the sites of their plundering. But
Minztans were expert at finding old leavings, or ores
too lean for the Ancestors to have bothered with.

"Should be easy," Shkai'ra said to the man beside
her. "Here, take the farlookers." She handed him a
pair of binoculars from a case clipped to her saddlebow.

"We're not here to butcher sheep," he replied dryly.
Thirty years of raid and ambush had left Warmaster
Eh'rik Davzin-kin with a wealth of sour pessimism and
no illusions at all.

Methodically he ran through a final check of the
lacings on his armor and the positions of sword, dagger, bow, and lance. Taking the glasses for a careful
sweep, he pushed his helmet back by the nasal to
reveal a saturnine, seamed face with a tuft of grizzled
chinbeard: balding, he had chosen a shaved skull
rather than warrior braids.

"Old croaker," Shkai'ra said affectionately. "Even
sheep with horns make mutton."

Sent along to restrain a warband where few but the
Bannerleaders were over twenty-five, the Warmaster
replied with a folk proverb: "There's a plowing time,
a harvest time: boast at the funeral feast of your
friend's deeds, for anytime is a time to die. Wait until
we ride under Stonefort gate with the loot before you
celebrate, Chiefkin."

Loot. Well-wrought tools, fine cloth, metals, luxuries
from the southlands, products traded from the cityfolk
manufactories. Lenses for farlookers, paper, drugs,
glassfiber for armor, secrets handed down from before
the Godwar and the Year Without Sun. There was no
knowing what they might find in those squared-log
halls. And there would be captives to sell in the spring
to the Valley traders; the forest folk were always in
demand, being good with their hands and docile.

Fame and glory and booty; success would bring her

the beginnings of a Name, make warriors eager to
follow and share the fruits of cunning and gods-
favored luck; and in the end there would be tablets
and offerings for her ghost, to bring her before the
gods and win fortunate rebirth.

Or she might find death. She had no wish to die,
but all Kommanza were sword-born; better to go with
iron in your gut than in bed of fever or a bad birthing.
And she had done enough, made sacrifice enough, to
warrant reincarnation as a Kommanza. . . .

Yes, with luck (she made a curious gesture with her
sword hand) this could be the beginning of . . .

A giggle from the ground brought her thoughts back
to the present. The spellsmith glanced slyly up out of
eyes no longer filmed with trance.

"The thought in your mind, Chiefkin," he tittered.
"Be careful; for what you desire, the gods may grant."
She jerked a thumb over her shoulder; the shaman
nodded and slipped the cord tight with a snap.

"Released, unbound," he said ceremoniously. "The
veil I take from their eyes, the felt from their ears,
the cord from their tongues." He trotted to the rear
where his pony waited. What came next would be for
the blade and the bow.

Shkai'ra squinted at the sky. "Time?" she said.

Eh'rik nodded.

2

"The Circle turns, the Circle turns,
 —*bird and beast, tree and flower*
Brings Harmony to all we see,
 —*birth and death each in its turn*"

Maihu Jonnah's-kin let her mind wander, freed by
the gentle familiarity of the Litany. The words blended
with the soft flow of the morning lantern, smells of
beeswax polish and oatmeal steaming under goatsmilk
and honey, warmth of her kinmates' hands in hers.
Briefly, her consciousness touched theirs; the butterfly
fidgeting of the neighbor's children, a kaleidoscope of
thought and sense impressions from the adults. It was
the fabric of a winter morning. For a moment, she
frowned. There was a sense of . . . constraint? No, a
blankness, out beyond the edge of perception. She
shrugged it off; in a new settlement like this the Otherworld would be wary, and the folk had not had time
to gain that totality of knowledge of their surroundings
that would warn of any impending wrongness.

A cheerful clatter and babble broke out as they sat;
Minztans were carefree folk by choice. Maihu sipped
thoughtfully at her herb tea, mapping out the day.
Winter was busy for a highsmith: the usual assortment
of broken tools, a half-dozen projects waiting in the
forge to add to the kinfasts' store of trade-barter . . .
and also other duties, she remembered with a sigh.

19

"Dennai," she said.

He looked up, spoon in hand. "Mai'?" he said. "Something on your mind?"

"Doa," she affirmed. "The stockade. We really should get the rest of the upright timbers cut and stacked while the hard snow lasts." It would be difficult to move them after thaw, and everyone would be busy clearing and planting then.

"Doa. And the other kinfasts would be less uneasy if you did the rites."

She sighed again. Even among the New Way radicals who had founded Newstead, it was difficult to arouse much urgency about the details of defense. And of course no Minztan would fell a tree without the proper ceremonies of explanation and apology; such heedlessness had brought the fire down on the Old Ones. The Way of the Circle bred no priesthood, but Maihu was known as one whose meditation had brought her closer to the Harmony than most.

"I'd be happier if the stockade was already finished," she said grimly. "Remember Annelu."

Dennai winced: they had found her hanging head down and gutted over a game trail last fall, with Kommanz runes carved in her forehead.

"Well," he said, "we've surely little to worry about until campaigning season."

She shrugged; Newstead was just a little too far from the steppe for raiders whose horses must carry their own fodder.

"Kinmate, I've lived thirty turnings of the Wheel here in the borderlands; you were born in the deep forest. This is less than two hundred kaelm from the grasslands, and our defense plan depends on the palisade as a base—or so the lakelander expert the Seeker hired said."

Dennai's reply froze unuttered. He was no Adept,

but he knew that wide, sightless stare; it was the Inner
Eye. To use it so here, now, without ritual or preparation, was reckless; it bespoke a terrible urgency.

Maihu had been probing at the constraining barrier
without conscious thought. When it vanished there
was a moment of mental staggering, as if a solid wall
had vanished under her hand. Her awareness flooded
outward, driven by unspoken need; she made no attempt to stop it. An Initiate learned to trust intuition.
Swiftly, she withdrew from the flow of sensory data,
shutting down the upper levels of her mind. She became mind-not-mind, one with the Harmony; into her
flowed the manifold life of plant and insect, bird and
beast, meshing. And there . . . the touch of . . . horses,
far too many. She raised her perceptions up past the
level of instinct, a shadowy awareness of her own reasoning mind returning; an invitation to the danger of
backlash, without the patterning rituals. A wrongness,
blaring, shrilling, hatred and despair and killing-lust,
a coiled-snake readiness to spring. Maihu came to herself with a snap. Training pushed away the savage
throb of pain in her temples; there would be time to
pay the price later. Staggering, she fell against the
wall, threw open the double-paned window and carved
sash. Cold poured into the room, cold and a sound
carrying faint but clear. Echoing, a harsh, deep-toned
baying snarl.

Dennai had heard it before, and the memory sent
the tiny hairs along his spine crawling and struggling
to rise. Kommanz Warhorns, the horns of the giant
wild cattle of the prairie marshes, tipped with walrus
ivory. A child whimpered, terrified by her kinparents'
fear. Maihu's eyes swept her companions, printing the
loved faces on her mind. Nausea welled in a lump of
cold sickness under her heart.

"Shennu," she said huskily. "Get the children over

to the Smoot-kin's hail." *Thank the Circle we didn't bring the youngest.* Many of the Newstead settlers had left their infants with relatives until the village was completed.

Her voice ground on: "Dennai, fetch the weapons. The rest of you, remember the plan; if we're pushed back from the barricade or the walls, we hold the hall and the lanes." A drum began to thud, and she heard the shouts of the villagers. Anger awoke as she saw the white faces of her kinmates.

"We are the Seekers of the New Way," she said quietly and firmly. A part of her was surprised at the lack of tremor in her voice. "We do not seek war. War has come to us. Now we fight!"

"Forest rats didn't think we could come this deep in winter," Shkai'ra mused, and spat. It froze with a crackle before it hit the ground, hard as the pooled blood of the sentry. Angled in her hand, a mirror caught the light of the sun as it rose above the trees and flashed it across the clearing. Somebody loosed a volley of soft curses when a lance tipped a branchload of soft snow on her helmet. No Kommanza liked the shut-in feeling of wooded country, and the eleven-foot shafts were awkward among the trees.

The signal was answered from the opposite side of the opening, where the other troop of the warband waited: *blink!* then blink*blink*, command code for "proceeding as ordered."

From the woods opposite came the sudden weird daunting snarl of the warhorns, an endless bellowing roar that clamored through the trees, across four hundred meters of field to shiver in teeth and bone. The decoys walked their horses slowly out of the woods and paused to dress ranks. An alarm drum began to thud and the Minztans poured out of their homes, sleep-fuddled and half armed but ready to defend their village and moving to some sort of plan. Some dragged logs fitted with spiked stakes, and others over-turned wagons and sleds to make an improvised wall across the open end of the palisade. Edged metal glinted behind it, ramming forward from ranks thick and dark. Binoculars brought them close; they were armed with long spears, or bills and halberds—heavy cutting polearms, with points for stabbing and hooks for dragging a rider down. Most of them seemed to have laminated wooden shields, and many had some sort of body armor; squares of boiled leather or bone on their jackets, or outfits of wooden splints; she saw iron-strapped leather helms, even a few all-steel types.

"Two hundreds of them, maybe two hundreds and two tens," she said. "They're better equipped than I awaited."

Eh'rik nodded, pursing his lips; the enemy were coming a little farther forward than optimum, tacti-cally. Safer to barricade the laneways and force the battle to close quarters; discipline and archery and the terrible shock power of massed lancers would all be lessened among walls and narrowness. The Minztans would still lose, of course, but they would kill more of the Kommanz before they went down. Even forcing the raiders to kill was a victory of sorts; the Kommanza were here for loot and an easy blooding of their youngsters, not slaughter. He smiled coldly; a dead Minztan was dead meat, and beef was much cheaper. Alive, each prisoner was twenty half-fingerweight sil-ver coins stamped with the five stars of the Pentapolis, packed by the hundreds in little oaken kegs . . . coins that would buy strength for Stonefort.

Shkai'ra nodded. "We'll have to storm that barri-cade," she said. There were possibilities: fire-arrows for the houses . . . the picture was satisfying, Minztans screaming in the flames, running out with their hair and clothes burning to meet the arrows. *No. We cannot destroy what we came to take.*

"Truth."

Shkai'ra heeled her horse and the troop behind her walked their mounts into the clearing and began to trot toward the center; four Banners, a hundred and twenty warriors. The Minztans yelled defiance, a deep sound with an edge of fear in it. The Kommanz riders waited in disciplined silence, grinning like wolves. Their commander dipped her lance, brought it around in a circle and jabbed the point toward the barricade.

A snarling blat of horn-call signaled acknowledgment from the other troop. They left their lances in rest and formed in a staggered column of twos, bringing out their wheelbows. Officers' whistles trilled, and they rocked forward into a gallop, nocking arrows. Shkai'ra leaned forward eagerly; now she could tell the reach and number of the Minztan bows. At three hundred meters from the enemy the column turned right and the warriors fired, high arching shots to drop their shafts behind the barricade. Four hundred meters was extreme range for a wheelbow; under one hundred it would punch through even first-quality armor. The Minztans answered with their crossbows and recurves, hunting weapons turned to war. A few Kommanza went down, and more horses; the survivors were scooped up by their comrades, riding pillion as the attacking column bent itself into a circle and then dropping down again when they were out of range.

Shkai'ra drew her lance in a precise arc. Whistles shrilled in the attacking force and it drew back, forming into a single double line facing the village. Her own force drew up before them; she put her own bone whistle in her teeth and trilled coded signals. Two Banners remained mounted; the rest of the force swung to the ground, stacking their lances while they swung extra quivers up to their fellows. Then they formed in three ranks; the first line drew sabers and formed in a shieldwall, while the rear two held lances two-handed like pikes, a row of bristling points.

"Bring in the rest?" Eh'rik asked. There were two more Banners on the other side of the clearing, still in the woods.

"*Nia,*" Shkai'ra decided: no. "When they break, too many could get through or over the palisade and run for the woods." They could never catch fugitives on foot among the timber. "Messenger, have them come out when we close: scale the palisade, fire from the top." There would be a parapet there, and attackers could use it as easily as defenders.

She blew a long descant on the whistle, and the whole force moved forward. Those on foot tramped steadily, slamming their weapons against the hard leather of their shields in an earthquake *wham-wham-wham* that echoed back from the walls and trees. The mounted ranks behind followed with an arrow on the string, reins knotted on the horses' necks. At three hundred meters the mounted archers stopped, raising their weapons. The foot-fighters stepped up their pace to a trot; the sun rose over the pines, ruddy fire on edged steel and the garish lacquer of the armor. Shkai'ra raised her arm and chopped it down, and the archers drew and loosed together. The air filled with the shrill whistle of arrows, and two more flights were in the air before the first landed. Hands stripped arrows out of the quivers at a speed that would empty the forty shafts in minutes ... but the raiders' attack would cover the beaten ground before they reached the barricade.

Few of the Minztans dared rise to return the fire, and many were left writhing on the ground or pinned to the barricade by the meter-length shafts. The raiders charged, screeching as they ran. When they struck the barricade there was a sudden huge noise, thump and bang and rattle. Wood and steel on leather, on wood, skirling off steel or thudding dully into meat; shouts from the Minztans, screams born of sudden agony greater than flesh was made to bear. Over it all the ululating howl of the Kommanz warriors, wailing upward into the insane trilling of the blood squeal. Hands ripped at the barricade as the foresters thrust and hacked desperately to stop them; the attackers stood shield to shield and blocked the metal, striking back with sword and warhammer. Logs and wagons tumbled back, and the plains warriors surged through and over; moments later the defense burst back like glass struck by a sledgehammer. The attackers had better armor, weapons, above all the training since babyhood that made them warriors born.

Shkai'ra grunted as the fight moved back from the barricade. Mounted squads threw lariats over the obstacles and snubbed the braided leather ropes to the pommels of their saddles, dragging them aside as they might a steer. Behind there was a multiple creak and rattle as reins and lances were readied, shields unslung, and arms thrust through the grips.

"Now!" she barked; horns gave a rasping snarl.

The heartbeat was loud in her ears, and she felt the familiar quasisexual tingling up her spine, drawing tight the skin on shoulders and breasts before settling under the rib cage. Dawnlight broke blinding-bright off the lanceheads slanting down around her, silver in a world of white on black. Breath rose like steam from horses and warriors, rich with the comforting scents of equine sweat and oiled leather. Through her gauntlet the rawhide-wound grip of the lance was a familiar weight dragging at her arm as the point came into view beyond her mount's head. As disciplined as their riders, the wedge of horses leapt forward off their haunches, building to a gallop in half a dozen paces. She felt the huge muscles bunch beneath her and then they were flying, weightless for a second at the apex of a leap that took them over a two-wheeled cart. Her teeth clicked together as they landed, hooves tearing out divots of packed snow and dirt.

Beyond, the enemy were in flight, little knots and clusters of them racing back toward the buildings. A few turned to meet the lancers; one threw a javelin, another knelt with square shield up and a broad-bladed bear spear aimed at the boiled-leather chest-plate of her horse. The Kommanza batted the flung spear out of the air with her shield and couched her lance. For an instant she could see the taut white fear-grin beneath the spearman's helm, and then the lancehead slugged home. Punching through the shield with a *crack* like a frozen branch breaking, then into meat and bone with a jarring thump that slammed back from elbow sling through shoulder to braced feet.

She tried to swing the shaft out to drag it free, but the inertia of the Minztan's body levered against the momentum of horse and rider to crack the tough wood across. Then her mount stumbled on the corpse and she had to spend an instant with knees and voice and reins to bring him up again. Her whistle trilled *continue*, and her mount skittered sideways as it swapped ends and killed momentum. The Minztan who had thrown the javelin was still alive, had rolled beneath her shield as the cavalry went overhead. Now she was up and dragging out a short broad chopping-sword, running in at Shkai'ra's horse from the left rear, always a rider's most vulnerable position.

"*Hai!*" the Kommanza shouted, her saber snapping

out with reflex speed; knees and balance brought the horse around, pig-squealing itself and snatching at the enemy with huge yellow chisel-teeth.

The Minztan banged her shield into the horse's nose and stepped in close, cutting back-handed at the rider's knee as the animal shied. Shkai'ra stabbed her saber down and the enemy blade slid along it with an unmusical crash; in the same instant she kicked, and the stirrup-iron broke the Minztan's nose and gashed her face open along both cheeks. The curved plains sword came back until it lay along her spine; Shkai'ra rammed her feet down in the stirrups and clenched her belly in a *huff* of concentration as her fingers milked the hilt of the saber. It came down with the beautiful fluid feeling that meant a perfect strike: this was the *pear-splitter* of the practice yard. Her arm tensed as it landed, thick wrist and strappings taking the jar. The Minztan dropped backward in a huge fan of blood, bright-red against the snow, brain leaking from the split skull.

"*Ehv'kete!*" Shkai'ra shrieked: *I have eaten.*

She stood in the stirrups to get an overview of the fight. Chaos swarmed around the village. Perhaps half the dwellers had run to earth in their homes, too few in each to make it a fortress; the rest were slain or taken captive. Already the Kommanz warriors swarmed around the halls, shooting at any sign of movement. Shkai'ra joined the officers in pulling them back out of easy crossbow range, setting some to breaking up carts to make improvised mantelets. When a band of Minztans tried a sally, whistles brought two Banners out of the saddle to form a shieldwall and smash forward, irresistible. Others rounded up prisoners, kindled fires, stood in the saddle to throw nooses around carved beam ends and swarm hand over hand to roofs, where axes soon thudded on the shingles. The Kommanz hurt were brought under cover, as were those of the Minztans not too badly hurt to heal in time to be useful.

One overexcited rider bent in the saddle to grab a torch and rode toward a kinhall.

"Smoke them out!" he yelled. His squadleader knocked him from his mount with a sweep of her bowstave.

"Burn somebody else's loot, steer-fucker!" she snarled. Shkai'ra saw, grinned, and decided the routine was in capable hands.

She took her whistle between her teeth. *[Identity code], this-building storm, now-if-possible. Consolidate. Commander-FangBanner, rendezvous, fifteen minutes, two hundred meters north-northwest my-present-position*, she signaled. Minztans tended to have concealed doors, from what she knew of them, and Shkai'ra cut between two buildings to make sure none opened on the stockade and the woods. Any who escaped would be a loss, and they might take their portable wealth with them: jewelry, say . . .

"Back, hold them and move *back*," Maihu shouted. "They're trying to delay us."

The knot of Minztans lurched backward toward the wall of the kinhall before the probing Kommanz lances; the riders were keeping their distance, the horses moving light as dancers as the warriors stabbed overhand at the shields. Steel banged off wood ahead of her, and one of her kinmates lurched back. The lancehead jerked out of his face with a grating sound, but someone else stepped in and thrust a spear at the horse's eyes and it backed, shaking its head. People were lurching through the door behind her as she dropped the end of the crossbow to the ground and stamped her boot into the yoke. With a sobbing grunt she pulled it back until the sear clicked, then fumbled the last shaft out of the quiver at her belt and slapped it down in the groove.

"Through the door *now*," she screamed hoarsely, leveling it.

For perhaps three seconds the half-dozen riders hesitated. They whooped and yipped at her, painted faces split by the ridged nasal bars of their helmets; not afraid, but not thinking of this as real combat, either, trying to think of a way to capture her alive. Then they saw the others gaining the door, and two warriors screeched and spurred forward, bent low over the necks of the horses with their lances thrust forward; two more behind were slinging their spears and readying bows, while another swung his lariat overhead.

Tunng. The crossbow spoke, and the feathers of the short bolt seemed to sprout from the throat of one horse. It screamed, heartrendingly human even then, missed a stride and went down shoulder-first. The rider leapt clear with inhuman skill, but the other lancer had to draw up to avoid overriding her. Maihu used the instant to leap backward, stumbling over the doorsill into the entranceway. Blackness fell as the thick door slammed shut and hands threw the bar home. Seconds later metal began to hammer at it from the outside, then thunderous hooves as a Kommanza backed his mount up to it and made the animal kick.

For an instant all Maihu could do was sag against the planks of the inner chamber, blank-eyed and mouth gaping as she hauled breath into fire-tight lungs. Her kinmate Tomlu stepped up to the narrow slit window beside the door, poised her spear and thrust. Shouts and screams outside and she dodged back; lanceheads probed in after her, but Dennai swept down a two-edged sword made for export to the country of the Inland Seas far to the east. Ashwood cracked; the other lance withdrew, but stayed poised just outside as a glittering threat if anyone should step up to the slit to shoot. Axes splintered at the door.

"Got to get moving," Maihu croaked. Dennai stood beside her, uneasy in his unfamiliar leather chest armor.

"What do we do?" he cried.

Maihu took a deep breath; a hand pushed a dipper of water at her and she gulped it. "Run. Run for the woods and get winter-travel gear from one of the caches, then go east for help. There are people of the Seeker's at Garnetseat. And an Adept."

"But the children!"

She took his head between her hands. "Love, *I know*. But we can't take them with us, and the faster word gets back the more hope of stopping these animals short of the steppe. And there is the Summoning."

He bit his lip until the blood came, and nodded. The ten adult members of the Jonnah's-kin ran through into the main ground-floor chamber. The tall doors were barred, and through the thick log walls came screams and clashes and the shrill neighing of horses. Maihu smelled her own fear, tasted it flat and metallic on her tongue. Her wombchild Taimi burst into the hall, gasping, his eyes glittering with the heedless excitement of his thirteen years.

"The back—" He paused for breath. "The back is clear, right to the stockade, and the field beyond to the woods."

One of her kinmates yelled from a window slit. Seconds later a tremendous splintering crash slammed against the door, shaking the boards beneath their feet. Dust flew up from crevices, choking. Somebody sneezed.

"They've got a log slung lengthwise between horses!" Zimdi called, and fired his crossbow. "*Got* one!"

Almost instantly a long arrow slashed through the narrow opening and took him between the eyes. The narrow pile head was driven by a hundred-pound wheelbow less than twenty meters away: it punched through his forehead and out the rear of his skull, the force of the impact picking him up and throwing him back three paces.

Maihu understood the westerners' tongue, heard a man screaming out in its ripping gutturals:

"At the middle! At the middle where the doors join, you sheep-raping pigs' arseholes! You, you, you, give them some covering fire next time; if we lose another horse I'll have your pubic hairs for a scalp!"

Jannu, her eldest kinmate, gripped her arm. "We'll hold them," she said. A sweep of her arm took in half the kinfast, the elders, the lame, a man recently recovered from a fever. "You can make speed. Now go."

Maihu hesitated for an instant. "Go in the Circle," she said, and led the others out at a run.

Seconds later the ram hit the doors with a massive impact that tore loose the brackets and broke the bar holding it shut. Arrows whipped through the windows with a whining *whup-whup-whup* and a blast of frigid air blew past the shattered leaves of the entrance. A Kommanza hurdled the body of the dead horse outside and leaped through the narrow opening. He landed lightly on his feet, moving with a beautiful fluid grace. His shield was painted in the likeness of a gaping scarlet mouth ringed with fangs, and the long saber made a sound like ripping silk as it whickered through the air. Two Minztans rushed him. He threw himself forward and down, curling into a ball and rolling under their feet. The foresters went over in a thrashing tangle from which the Kommanza somehow bounced erect. The saber took one Minztan across the spine even as he pirouetted to kick the other precisely behind the ear. Another Kommanza pushed through the door, and another. One raised her bow and shot, filling the room with its great bass throb. Jannu braced to meet the first as he stalked her. Fascinated, she saw the downy black beard of youth on his cheeks, scars, a short gold bar through his nose, narrow green eyes lynx-steady. Her axe stroke bounced off his shield. She heard the clatter, felt a sudden intense cold. Looking down: the curved sword sliding up through her stomach, withdrawing red-black; a sudden foul smell.

"Ah," she said, falling to the floor and curling around herself, then: "Ah!" as the pain began to seep through. A hand gripped the hair over the crown of her head, pulled back until her neck creaked. The young Kommanza laid down his sword, drew his knife, and traced a palm-sized patch. With a grunt of effort he wrenched the scalp free and held it before her eyes. Fading, it was the last thing she saw as the knife slit her throat, neatly, from ear to ear.

Being preoccupied, Shkai'ra failed to see the rope lying across the lane before it snapped up under the forefeet of her horse. The animal went over with a scream of pain and fear, cut short with a sickening snap of neckbone. A lifetime's drilled reflex brought her feet out of the stirrups, curled her into a ball in midair. The hilt of her saber caught her a painful thump under the armpit, but she ignored it and the taste of blood in her mouth as rage and sorrow washed over her. Spring-Foot-Among-Wildflowers had been not only a trained warhorse and thus valuable, but a friend raised from colthood. By Baiwun Thunderer, someone was going to die for this!

She came to her feet and sprinted back for her bow. That turned into a frantic dive as a crossbow bolt whirred by her head and thumped into the logs. She pulled the bow free of its case, yanked a shaft out of the quiver, nocked, turned, and loosed in a smooth, flowing curve. The Minztan archer on the roof threw up her hands with a grunt no louder than the meaty thud of the arrow striking home and slid with her weapon to land at Shkai'ra's feet. She had used a broad-headed hunting shaft, better than a needle-thin bodkin point against an unarmored enemy, and it had driven up under the breastbone to sever the spine. Blood flowed out red as sunlight on the snow. There were only three unbroken shafts in the quiver. Shkai'ra mumbled a curse as she clenched them between her teeth and looked around for another target. She did not have long to wait: a section of one of the walls fell outward, and five of the enemy poured through. She was between them and the only hope of escape. They charged.

She dropped to one knee and shot three times in as many seconds, killing with every shaft; at that range shock alone would kill from a wheelbow as heavy as hers. The leader was a big man in a leather breastplate, swinging a long sword. Her shaft sank to the feathers in his chest, knocking him backward to trip the spearwielder following. Her second arrow slammed through that one's neck and nailed them together. The third paused to aim her own weapon, and waited a moment too long: hunters had less reason than a Kommanza to learn close-range snapshooting. The last two checked, long enough for her to shift the shield slung across her back to her left arm and snap out her saber.

For a moment they stared at each other, the Minztans stunned by their comrades' deaths, the Kommanza considering. The two remaining were a woman in her thirties, with a wooden shield and spear, and a slight youth with a spike axe that looked too heavy for his wrists. Shkai'ra made a swift decision. She had been standing in the standard footfighting position, crouched with her feet at right angles, left forward and shield up under her eyes, saber held high with the hilt toward the enemy. A vast lighthearted calm possessed her as she filled her lungs and charged with an earsplitting scream.

"AAAAAAAAAAiiiiiiiieeeeEEEEEEEE—" she shrieked, an endless saw-edged wailing that clawed at the nerves. Charging, she ran crabwise with her blade whirling to distract the eye; it was a reckless move against an experienced opponent, but a thousand subtle clues of stance and tension had told her that these were no warriors she faced.

The other woman lunged with her spear. Shkai'ra went in under the point, crouching and driving upward with all the strength of leg and thigh added to her momentum, bracing her shoulder against her buckler. The shields struck with a gunshot crack and the Minztan reeled backward. Shkai'ra followed, ignoring the spear once she was inside its reach. Levering the other's shield aside with the edge of her own, she struck with her swordhilt to the temple. The villager crumpled. Turning, Shkai'ra caught the boy's axblade. It thumped and banged off the hard curved leather of her shield, and the weight of it pulled him around, wide open for a thrust. She grinned and moved in, trying to pin him to a wall with her shield.

"Better put that down before you cut yourself, pretty one," she said. "Nice little stallion, come lie down for my saddle and we'll ride—"

Through accent and clamor, the youth understood

her. "I'll, I'll kill you!" he screamed, his voice breaking in mid-shout. He was slender, early teens, she judged—although Minztans matured later than her own people, eating less meat.

He swung his weapon up in a clumsy overhead stroke that left his midriff exposed. Shkai'ra leaned over at an impossible angle and kicked him neatly in the solar plexus, pulling the killing force from the blow. His breath went out with an agonized whoop.

She ran her gloved fingers down the edge of her saber: no nicks, praise be to the Steel Spirit and Zailo Protector. Snapping it back into the scabbard, she bent to tie her captives with belt thongs. The woman was stirring, slack-faced and retching with the effects of mild concussion; the boy was glaring at her as he struggled for breath. She hesitated, gripping his shoulders, then pushed back her helmet by the nasal.

"Later," she said, and gave the furious face a bruising kiss before dropping him back into the pooled blood and vomit on the trampled snow. A trooper rode up. "Get these out of the cold," Shkai'ra said, jerking a thumb. She vaulted easily into the saddle of the remount.

"Gather my gear, and see these two are hale when I send for them."

It was noon before the last holdouts yielded. Shkai'ra stood before a braced door, boots astride a fallen timber the warriors had been using as a ram, and hailed those within.

"*Ahi-a*, parley!" she shouted, resting her hands on her belt, stance casual and face an unreadable mask. They were desperate in there, and her armor would not stop a crossbow bolt at this range. Vividly she felt the cold air curl over her greased skin, smelled smoke and sweat, blood and the latrine stink of ripped bowel that went with violent death. The sun glittered on the bands of painted carving that ran along the walls of the house.

"What do you want, bandit?" called a hoarse voice from behind the battered doors.

"To offer terms," she answered. "Will you listen?" There was a murmur, too swift and faint through thick wood to follow in a foreign tongue.

"What conditions?" he finally replied.

"I'll spare all too old, too young, or too sick to be worth keeping. They can stay, with enough food to keep life in them till your folk from the eastern villages come. Come spring, you can bid against the southrons for those we sell."

A bolt flashed out from a slit and went over her head with a sharp *zhip!* of cloven air. She flung up a hand to stop the storm of return fire: unlikely to hit, and an arm had struck up that weapon. Still, the answer was loud with rage.

"Those are no terms! We've supplies in here. We can hold out until help comes, or you starve."

Shkai'ra laughed with pure contempt. "What, three weeks?" she gibed. "Those are good terms, *eh'kafrek*," she said, using an insult so old the meaning was lost. "Zaik godlord hear me, if you don't make submission now, I'll have the children and oldsters we've taken flayed here before your eyes."

A wail came from within, and the sound of voices raised in furious dispute. From one of her breed the threat was believed. Minztans had bordered on the Zekz Kommanz, the Six Realms, long enough to know that.

"What surety do you give us?" the Minztan answered at last. Shkai'ra fought down anger at having her word doubted speaking under a truce lance: what else could you expect of outlanders? They were brought up without honor, like moles without light. She stripped off a gauntlet and held the blade of her dagger to the skin.

"Baiwun Avenger of Honor hear me: my oath on the Steel Spirit, may it forsake me if I lie." No Kommanza would break that pledge; a forsworn warrior's own weapons would turn on her and bring an early and dishonorable death.

The minutes stretched. At last the door scraped open and the Minztans shuffled forth. Kommanz warriors pounced to disarm and bind. Shkai'ra relaxed at last. Now they could post a guard detail, tally the loot ... and yes, it would be best to give the gods somewhat, soon. They had been generous enough, and it was never wise to stint the Mighty Ones. And it would soothe the nerves of those who feared ghosts and foreign magic. A Kommanza was not permitted to fear anything but spirits and thunder ...

The trooper prodded Maihu and Taimi to their feet with the butt of her lance. Taimi started a blundering dash for the fields; the ceramic knob smacked down on his elbow, driving him to his knees with a cry of agony. The Kommanza slid her lance back into the boot at the rear of her saddle, uncoiled a whip, and waited blank-faced as Maihu helped her kinchild to his feet. Her bound hands were awkward, and the side of her head was still a throbbing ache. The plainsdweller methodically slashed each of them a half-dozen times, across the legs rather than the embroidered Minztan winter jackets they both wore. Maihu bent her head and kept silence, whispering to Taimi as he struggled not to cry out.

"Chiefkin say, not kill," the westerner said in a slow, thickly accented Minztan. "No say, no whip. You come."

Their guard shepherded them across what would have been the main square of Newstead, amid trampling hooves and raucous shouts and a growing pile of limp scalped bodies, through the shattered doors of their kinhall. There were bloodstains on the polished floors, and hoofmarks, and someone had kicked a severed hand into a corner. An officer was directing repairs. From somewhere nearby came a rhythmic screaming that trailed away into sobs.

"Honorable, the Chiefkin said to put these two away somewhere," the trooper said.

The man looked at them, tugging at his short brick-red beard. "*Yoi,*" he said, stabbing a finger into Maihu's chest. "*Kommanzanu dh'taika i'?*" Watching her closely he repeated the query: did she understand Kommanzanu?

Her face remained carefully blank. "*Gakkaz ot ufuazi,*" he said to their guard with a shrug. She understood that: "The slaves/animals/foreigners are ignorant."

"The Chiefkin may want to interrogate them; she understands their sheep-bleating. Or fuck them, or whatever. Put 'em in a room, give 'em water."

Maihu waited until the pantry door swung home before picking up the dipper and washing the taste of bile out of her mouth. She winced as she touched the swelling bruise and remembered the brief fight. *Circle,* she thought, *how could she be so quick?*

"Are you all right?" Taimi asked. She looked up at him and tried to force a smile, he was near breaking, skin white and pinched around his mouth. Suddenly he was weeping. She pulled him into her arms, rocking him.

"They're dead," he gasped. "I saw . . . I saw . . ."

"I know," she soothed, "I know." It was comforting to give comfort: it was the Minztan way, to accept grief. There was no shame in it, the Way of nature

and the Circle. As shock receded her own loss came
through, cold pain buried under a knot of fear and
hatred. And the tears would not come. At last he subsided, recovering with the resilience of youth.

"She . . . that one . . . she said she'd . . ."

He stumbled over the words. "What can we do?"

"Stay alive," she said. "Do what we must. Listen:
this is not their land; it will fight against them, all the
Life." The word had a broader meaning in their
tongue; it meant Totality, rock and soil and water, tree
and beast and unseen spirit. "We are the Guardians
of the Way. Remember that!"

Maihu began to whisper the Litany, and after a moment Taimi joined in. The ancient words flowed
through them; they fell silent and withdrew into in-
wardness. Hours passed, unnoticed. It was after dark
when the warriors came, and they paused, muttering
at the sight of the two immobile figures.

One of them made a sign with her fingers. "Spirit
talk," she grunted. "The *gakkaz* send their souls out
to talk to woods demons."

The squadleader hawked and spat. "Sheepshit," he
sneered. "Minztans always run; these are penned, so
they run away into their heads." He planted a boot
against Maihu's shoulder and pushed her over roughly.
"Up, you. The Chiefkin calls."

Shkai'ra ignored the captives as they were brought
into the upper chamber she had taken as her own.

"—fast, on ski," the warmaster was saying. "Say,
hmmmm, a day until hunters and trappers get back,
see what's befallen, and a week to the nearest Minztan
stead. Then they'll run around like headless chickens
for a while, before they can mobilize a band and return here. Still, with time they could overfall us with
numbers."

"Plenty of time, though," she said.

Eh'rik shook his head. "Not if they come up to us on the trail: we'll be slow, with slaves and plunder. And it's one thing to ride these rabbits down in the open, but skulkers along the forest trails . . ."

He raised his hands palm up, then flipped them down. "Losses, Chiefkin."

"Ahi-a," Shkai'ra mused, tugging at her lower lip. "The wounded would be better for a time under cover."

"True, true . . . I'd not like to lose any of the lads and lasses without need." Those warriors were the future of Stonefort. "We'll need them all come summer and the nomads."

Fighting Minztans was nothing more than a profitable and mildly dangerous blood sport, but the wild raiders from the high plains were deadly serious business.

"Say, four days here, Chiefkin?"

"Ia," she said. "And send out some scouts; see if we can cut cross-country on our way back. The rivers will carry us, and from the lie of the land, there should be drainage through here."

She turned to the prisoners. The second-story room she had chosen was broad, with walls of smooth squared logs. The wood was stained and carved, hung in places with bright fabrics; racks held enough metal in weapons and tools to bring a smirk of satisfied greed to her lips. On the floor was a mass of pelts, wolf and bear and snowtiger. A pottery stove kept it far warmer than the rammed-earth farmer's huts or bleak stone Keeps of the prairie. She gestured dismissal at the guard and stalked closer. The Kommanza pulled on a thong that hung around the other woman's neck. A silver hammer was strung on it: it said much for Kommanz discipline that so valuable an ornament had not vanished when the Minztan was searched for weapons.

"Nice," Shkai'ra said. The Minztan recoiled from the wave of smells that came from her: old sweat soaked into wool, the rancid tallow on her skin, and the sunflower oil on her hair. She had stripped to wool tunic and baggy trousers in the unaccustomed heat, and fresh moisture stained armpits and neck. Once out of hauberk and gambeson she looked nearer to her twenty years, tall and light-complexioned in the manner of her folk, gray-eyed, her hair an unusual coppery gold under dirt and oil.

Maihu pulled her awareness in. There were things one could do with the Way, but this was too hideously dangerous. She could sense the other's roil of emotions: desire and anticipation and a bright, almost innocent cruelty, like a cat's with a crippled bird, and purpose behind that. At best, she could expect savage abuse, at worst . . . once the killing-lust was aroused even her usefulness would not protect her; she was no more than a flickering whim away from bleeding out her life on the rugs, and so was Taimi.

"This means you're a smith, doesn't it?" Shkai'ra asked. Nearby a bottle of southland grape brandy stood on a shelf. The Kommanza grabbed it, wrenched the cork loose with her teeth, and took a long experimental draft that brought a gasp of appreciation.

"You didn't answer," she said calmly, and caught the older woman a backhanded crack across the face.

Maihu gasped involuntarily, and nodded. When the Kommanza raised her hand again, she added, "Yes."

"Chiefkin."

"Yes, Chiefkin," she replied, looking at the floor. A detached part of her mind studied the tips of her captor's boots, and wished she had scraped the horse dung off them before coming inside.

"Highsmith," Shkai'ra continued, punctuating her words with long pulls at the bottle. She roamed the

chamber. Maihu cringed inwardly as hands left greasy
fingermarks on the tapestries. "Of the richest kinfast
in Newstead. You'd know where the best of the loot
was hidden."

She brought her face down to the shorter woman's
level, head tilted to one side. Her face was calm,
empty of emotion, the expressionless mask that Minztans found so alien. Maihu found what lay beyond
equally alien, in its way, and focused on detail: harsh
hawk-handsome features, wide thin-lipped mouth,
squint lines beside the eyes, a tiny gold ring through
one nostril of the aquiline nose . . .

"By the Mighty Ones, I think you think you won't
tell me." She shook her head and took another drink.
"Sooo foolish." Suddenly she giggled, a shrill high-
pitched sound. Maihu swallowed convulsively.

"Ahi-a, let's see . . . " She ran her hands over the
Minztan's bowl-cut black hair, down her shoulders,
then undid the lacing of her shirt and trouser belt.
The fingers kneaded and probed, half caress, half
stockbreeder's appraisal.

"But I can't threaten you with what I'll do anyway,
can I?" she said. "But this, now . . ."

She worked her thumbs into Maihu's armpits, felt
for the nerve clusters, began to press. The Minztan
braced herself, her eyes seeming to turn a darker blue
as the pupils contracted; she was preparing to ride out
the pain with the withdrawal technique.

Shkai'ra shook her head and stepped back. "I hear,"
she said conversationally, "that you're called Maihu."
She pointed to the boy. "That's Taimi. Your kinchild.
Wombchild, too." She drew her knife and stood for a
moment tapping the flat of her blade against her
knuckles. At her nod Eh'rik surged erect and gripped
Taimi by the upper arms, digging thumbs into his
shoulderblades until his chest arched out painfully.

His lips quivered. Suddenly she turned and slashed. Maihu bit back a scream as Taimi's shirt floated open, cut cleanly from neck to hem. She slid the point between waistband and skin and slit downward to drop the trousers. Then, very gently, she touched the edge to his testicles.

"Careful, 's sharp," she giggled, watching the eyes grow enormous in the freckled face. "In the southlands," she continued easily, "they'll pay more for a well-gelded boy. Gods alone know why! I've never cut a human, but with a horse or calf you make a slit here . . ." She gripped him in one hand and prepared to slice.

Maihu closed her eyes and spoke rapidly, sweating. "We . . . found copper here, and a little gold. And ruins of the Old Ones; iron, still in the concrete, and other metals. The ingots are . . ."

"Good, good," Shkai'ra laughed. The Kommanz did not touch old buildings; there were few left, on the steppe. But forge fires would remove the deathcurse that rotted your bones and made the hair fall out.

"If 'tis as you say, y' sprat here can keep his jewels. Wha' you think, Eh'rik?"

The warmaster released Taimi, who sank to the floor, trembling.

"I think it's fortunate you made the band drink in relays, not all at once," he said dryly.

" 'Course," she said smugly. "Mus' have discipline. Strong discipline. Can' fight withou' you have discipline. Look a' these steer-fuckers—got no discipline, so can' fight."

The level of the brandy was dropping fast. Shkai'ra walked backward into a chair and sat, cradling the bottle in her arms and feeling wonderful, letting the pleasant buzzing hum in her ears. Like bees in clover, she thought. Like bees in clover in the spring, by the river, lying watching the wild geese fly north.

My luck is tremendous! she thought happily. *Better than the loot of ten caravans, and so few losses* . . .

"Yo' wan' one to play with?" she asked Eh'rik expansively. "Boy's prettier, bottom like a peach, but t' dam is more inter-inter—" She slapped herself on the cheek. "Interesting."

She wet her lips and looked at the Minztans. Not like the thralls back home, who were too meek to be worth the effort. Rape was magic too, strong warmagic to take an enemy's strength. She had been taken a few times herself, of course; by older siblings between puberty and the time she could fight back effectively, by instructors, once or twice by a kinparent sober enough to catch her after a feast; and last year after a rustling party she rode on lost a skirmish with Buffalo Gorge Keep. That was fighting within the Bans, of course, against other Commands—Law said you had to surrender if surrounded, to keep too many of the People from being slain untimely. It was deathcursed to kill or cripple or torture a Lawful captive awaiting ransom, but nothing said you couldn't fuck them. She winced mentally; that had been *hideously* embarrassing.

He jerked a thumb toward Taimi. "Zoweitz carry off interesting, Chiefkin," he said. "I don't want to *talk*. I'll take that one."

"Otta gi' me first choice," she said, frowning with concentration. "On account takes longer an' harder for me."

"Blame Jaiwun Allmate for that, Chiefkin," he said, taking out his dicebox. "*It* made us male and female. High gets the choice?"

Shkai'ra paused in the difficult business of taking off her boots. She threw an eight and crowed with delight. It seemed she was victory-sure tonight.

"Throw again f' both?" she asked, pulling her tunic over her head and rubbing her breasts.

Eh'rik hesitated, agreed, and lost again. *"Tuk t'hait whul-zhaitz!"* he swore. "Chief, throw away something you value. A run of luck like this makes the gods jealous!"

He glanced at the prisoners. "Don't untie the woman," he added thoughtfully.

"I'm drunk, no' stupid."

3

In the darkness, a figure moved between the silent halls of Newstead. Naked to the waist and barefoot, the shaman scarcely felt the savage cold of the midwinter night; training made it a simple matter to draw on the inner power to burn the body's reserves of fuel more rapidly. That was one reason the hide stretched so tight over bony ribs, hide scarred and patterned as thickly as his face, with runes graven by flint knives, or the marks where rawhide bands had been driven through flesh to support him as he hung from a tree.

As he loped he snuffled, now bending low, now thrusting his face upward toward the stars. Ceaselessly, his fingers thuttered on the drumhead slung from his waist. Senses scanned, many-leveled; there was nothing but the lingering stink of outland magic, soaked into the carven timbers around. He touched one wall gingerly, thinking with pleasure of the blaze of burning; the Chiefkin was an able killer, but soft, not to raze this place to the ground and give all the ones not useful to the gods. The council of *dhaik'tz*, the shamans, would hear of it . . .

47

Yet he remained uneasy. This had been too easy; so simple, to blind the Minztan sheep. There had been no strong counterspell, barely a flicker of resistance. And he could detect nothing moving in the world beyond the world, thin though the Veil was here. He thought of the sack of skins in his saddlebags, wolf and glutton and otter . . . No, that was too dangerous, better to wait until there was need.

The guard had hardly sensed the shaman's approach; the sound of the drum had become too much part of the alien night. Warrior training strained familiar sounds out, to concentrate on the unusual; and the sound was comforting, here. At home a shaman was half feared and half despised. Amid the foreign buildings and the overshadowing trees, among so many hungry ghosts, it was well to have protection. Still, he started when the shadow of the bison-horn headdress fell across the snowdrift. Rising, he lowered the arrowhead and inclined his helmet.

"Ztrateke ahkomman yh'e-mitchi," the guard said formally: "Gods with you."

Inwardly, he shuddered at the other's near-nakedness; he knew himself for a hardy man, but even with full armor, padded undercoat, and wool cloak the cold drove knives into his joints. And even in this weather he could smell the rotting human meat and sour herbal stink on the man's breath.

"All goes well?" he continued politely.

The bare-chested man wrapped around himself arms of skin and knotted stringy muscle over bone.

"Witches," he muttered, reaching for the bag of dried fungus at his waist. With an effort, he stopped himself; too much could dull the wits. And the magic growth was rare and precious, traveling through a dozen hands from the deserts and mountains of the far southwest. He smiled up at the warrior, enjoying the man's fear. "Witches, powerful ones. I smell them."

Suddenly, he giggled and began to prance, beating out the time on his drum. "I will smell them out; then I can eat!" The homed shadow jerked away between the nightgray walls, the sound of the drum fading after him. The guard stared, spat, and resumed his pacing.

Shkai'ra kicked off the rest of her clothes, stretched, emptied the bottle, and tossed it into a corner. Naked, the fullness of her figure showed, and the hard flat sheaths of muscle that rolled over shoulders and stomach and back. There were faint scars on her left side and back, even fainter the stretch marks of childbirth on the ridged muscle of her belly. She rubbed her breasts again as she walked over to the Minztan woman, pushed her onto the bed and examined the bindings: tight leather, no way to undo the knots.

"Wouldn' wan' have you bust my head whil' I come," she said, using the Minztan's belt to strap her hands tight to the headboard. "But y'can watch. You're next.

"You first," she continued, turning to Taimi. He came clumsily to his feet; she watched him, caressing her own breasts and then putting a hand between her legs.

The boy closed his eyes and staggered back as she pressed against him, flinching from her rank smell and the rough hands scraping over his body. She cut his bonds.

"Here," she said, extending her dagger hilt first. It was heavy in his hand, long, double-edged, the grip wound with rawhide. He looked at her warily.

"I'm drum—" She whistled, shook her head, and continued. "I'm drunk, an' unarmed. I killed your kin and sacked your village. If you don' stop me I'm going to fuck you an' your dam both. Come on, try an' kill me."

She weaved on her feet. Taimi felt rage welling up under his fear, like a cold bubble swelling up past his breastbone to burst in his throat, acid and bitter. With a shout he lunged, throwing his body behind the blade. A part of him knew he could not kill her, but he hoped against the odds to inflict some hurt.

She swayed aside; a palm edge cracked into his wrist, and the knife skittered off as his fingers flew open in reflex. The floor rushed to meet him as her shin swept his feet out from under him.

"Never *that* drunk," she said, standing over him and counting on her fingers, laboriously.

"Good, don't have to take tha' pig-piss potion the shamans make." She fell on him. They rolled over the furs grappling and straining as he tried to throw her off, she laughing and nuzzling at his face and neck and licking at his nipples. When he realized she was stronger and heavier, and enjoying herself wholeheartedly, he stopped and lay stiffly.

"Hmmmm," she murmured. Her hand groped downward, found his penis, began kneading rhythmically. She chuckled softly at the look on his averted face, remembering hands pulling her legs apart and the stinging pain. "You get it easier . . ."

"Come on, little stallion . . . *Ahi-a*, good." She bent and took him in her mouth, holding a wrist in each hand, savoring the familiar sensation. He began to sob quietly as he hardened.

Taimi lay tense but unresisting as she slid forward, drawing out the moment as she straddled his hips. She closed her eyes, feeling the rough fur under her knees, her hair plastered to the sweat on her back, the warm whole-body glow of anticipation. Then she enclosed him and began moving her pelvis steadily,

her small panting grunts of effort mingling with his
weeping as she clenched and relaxed. Unraveling, her
red-blond hair fell across his face as she leaned forward on her elbows and rocked.

Maihu woke. For a moment she struggled with bewilderment, before memory returned. The barbarian's
weapon belt hung from the bedpost within reach ...
No, that would be playing into her hands. And even
if she succeeded by some miracle, the revenge would
kill her and her fellow villagers, slowly. A steppe savage might be content to kill and die for vengeance,
but the Way of the Circle counseled patience, and
justice ... justice precise and exact. She took stock,
using the lesser Litany to force calm. The bruise on
her temple was still tender, but there was no blurred
vision or dizziness that might mean serious trouble.
For the rest, bruises and scrapes, a few bites and
scratches, nothing too bad. She shuddered as she remembered the shaven-skulled animal who had almost
gotten her. The woman had been easier, rough but
not out to cause pain as long as she was obeyed. The
customs of her people being what they were, the night
past was simply an angering and humiliating episode
of coercion rather than anything soul-searing. For a
mature adult, at least, she thought. Taimi worried her.
He was young, a gentle boy, almost a virgin. It was
not good for the young to have one of the best things
in life linked with hatred and pain.

Her lips quirked. She was assuming they had a future, other than as slaves in Stonefort. Hugging her
knees, she looked down on the Kommanza. She was
lying on her face, arms curled around her head and
her long hair bright against the brown linen of the
mattress cover; the jagged paint on her face had run,
smearing with sweat and drying in new patterns. Her

skin was very white where the sun and wind had not touched it, lightly dusted with freckles across the shoulders. There were scars there too, and all down her back to the buttocks in close-spaced rows. It took her a moment to realize, with horror, that they were whip scars. Old ones, and they must have been very deep.

Shkai'ra's eyes opened, pale mist-gray. Drilled reflex sent one hand out to touch the hilt of her saber. She saw the direction of her slave's gaze.

"I was a disobedient child," she said, and sat up. She winced, gripping her head between her hands. "Agggg, that brandy has a hit like Eh'mex Hammer of the gods!"

The door opened at her call, and a helmeted head looked in. Shkai'ra swung erect and clutched at a bedpost.

"Good light, Chiefkin," the guard said cheerfully. "Have you tried raw eggs?"

"Silence!" she growled, and winced again, frowning in concentration. "Wait—take this one out." She pointed to Taimi. "Get him some clothes, and put him to work. Tell the officer of the watch that he's mine." She considered. "Get me a bowl of milk. Hot. And some eggs, three."

Taimi rose uncertainly, still muzzy from exhausted sleep. Maihu helped him to the door, whispering in his ear. She doubted he heard: there was a disquieting blankness in his face.

The Kommanza threw herself into a series of exercises, starting slowly: tendon-stretching, knee bends, press-ups on her fingertips, palms, knuckles, one-handed. Rising, she went into the attack-defense patterns of rh'Ukkul, her people's fighting art. Whirling, blocking, stroking with palm edge and fist and feet against imaginary opponents, soon she was breathing deeply, the stiffness fading from her joints, and muscles moving and sliding freely under the skin. Her headache faded to a dull throb, and her stomach settled a little. Sweeping out her saber, she began a series of drills, single-hand cuts and thrusts and then the two-handed grip used for foot fighting without a shield. The warmasters claimed that the long blade was the most versatile of all weapons, combining the virtues of spear, lance, dagger, and ax.

She finished with a flourish whose speed shocked the Minztan, then raised the guard to her lips in the ritual gesture of respect and cleaned the blade reverently before returning it to the sheath.

"You have a sauna here?" Shkai'ra asked.

"Yes, Chiefkin," Maihu replied. *Circle unending,* she thought. *We'll never have fighters to match that.* She remembered the whip scars. *The Seeker was right, we'd have to become like them to do it. But there are other ways. . . .* The door opened, and the guard entered with a bowl. Shkai'ra took the milk in her left hand and deftly broke the eggs into her mouth with the other, tossing the shells on the floor. The milk followed, and she wiped her lips with a grimace.

"Tell the warmaster I'll be with him in an hour," she said. "Have food ready. Staff meeting at noon-meal, all the bandcouncil."

The trooper ducked her head. "The Chiefkin wishes," she said formally. A Mek Kermak with a hangover was nothing to provoke.

"You do massage?" the Kommanza asked Maihu. She nodded warily. "Good, I thought so." It was a common art among the forest people. "Come along to the baths, then."

She saw Maihu's surprise and, astonishingly, grinned. "Thought we never washed, nia?" Impatiently: "I won't hit you for telling the truth!"

"Well . . . yes, Chiefkin."

Shkai'ra sniffed at herself. "Doubt you'll be too fond of taking the oil off yourself on the steppe, either: too much wind and nothing to stop it. But I take a bath every month, whether I need it or not, even in winter. And scrapes heal faster if you clean them. Bring my gear, that box there."

Then: *"No!"*

She swooped and grabbed the weapon belt. *"Nobody* touches a Kommanza's weapons except her kinmates!" She relaxed. "Well enough, you didn't know. Lead on."

Shkai'ra spent a half-hour in the steam bath, while Maihu poured water on the red-hot stones and switched her with the traditional birch twigs; the sauna was one of the few customs the two peoples shared, although the plainsfolk added a final scrubdown with snow. The warmaster met them in the eating hall. That was half the kinhall, rising three stories to the shadowed rafters above; a space not alone for meals, but for play, work, ritual, the shared life of the kinfast. Now the tables had been pushed against the walls to hold loot for tallying, their inlay of flowers and birds scarred by careless hands. The hearth was fireless, and the former owners struggled in under bundles of their own property, encouraged by steppe warriors with riding quirts. By unspoken pact they avoided each other's eyes; Maihu found herself grateful for that.

"Much?" Shkai'ra said, nodding at the growing piles of booty. Scooping fresh protective grease from a pot, she began smearing it thickly over face and neck. A platter of blood sausage and hot rye bread stood on a bale of white foxskins; she seized a handful of each and began to eat noisily. Maihu's stomach rumbled at the smell; she had not eaten since last dawn. . . . Eh'rik gestured at the heaps on the floor. It was im-

pressive; Maihu saw that the raiders had missed little.
There was a keg of precious metal, as much as a strong
man could lift, Minztan work, and Southland coins;
stacks of loaf-shaped ingots of copper and iron; bolts
of cloth—linen and wool, imported silk and cotton;
bale after bale of furs and pelts; crates of tools better
than any the Kommanz smiths could fashion.

The warmaster plucked a sword blade out of a bundle; it was much like the one at Shkai'ra's side, long,
slightly curved, with a slanted chisel point and the
waving patters that told of a weapon worked up from
thousands of strands of iron and steel to give strength
and suppleness. The arc of the blade was a segment
of a great circle, the cutting edge hardened and polished to a mirror finish, while the thicker back was
left springy and resilient; but for the elaborate knuckle
guard it was the same bleakly efficient killing tool that
the warriors of ancient Nippon had called the *dai-
katana*, three thousand years before. Maihu flicked a
smith's practiced eye over it: Minztan made to a Kommanz pattern for the western trade and worth . . . the
thought trailed off in calculations of grain and cattle.

"And this is only the best," Eh'rik enthused. He
opened a small wooden chest with one toe. "Resin
blocks." That was a real prize; really first-class armor
needed glasscloth heat-set in resin, and only the southland wizards would make it. The secret was guarded
closely, and the product itself sold for as much as the
market would bear. Steel-plate armor would have
been even better, of course, but who could afford it
save an emperor?

The shaven-skulled man cocked an eye at the Minztan. "Was told," he said slowly, with a heavy accent,
"that you *eh'kafrek* had found the secret of this."

Maihu shook her head nervously. "No, Great
Killer," she said, translating the Kommanz honorific

into her own tongue. "We tried, but there's more than craftskill in it."

"Shouldn't stop you," Shkai'ra said. "Minztans are known for witches as far as the Lakes and the Great River."

"I'm not an Adept," she said hastily, which was true enough. The better preparation for the lie to follow. "I know nothing of their arts." No quicker way to die than arousing their superstitions, she thought. But the truth would serve after that. "Our Wreakings . . . they deal with living things, the earth, the weather . . . not that."

"The witch lies," a soft voice said.

Maihu started and swung around at the sound. She recognized the figure of the plains shaman at once; the physical signs were unmistakable, and to an Initiate there were indications more subtle than that. Instantly the warding song began running through her mind, covering the surface of thought with an impenetrable flicker. Then she looked down to the lump of flesh he held in one hand. It was not until he raised it to his mouth and worried off a shred with pointed teeth that she recognized the shape of a human heart. She barely managed to turn away before the sour bile of an empty stomach spattered out of her mouth onto the floorboards. The sharp stink of it was heavy as she bent, heaving dryly. It cut through the other smells, of fur and cloth and food and the rank Kommanz bodies. The two warriors laughed, the shrill mocking giggle of their folk. Not that they ate manmeat themselves; only the high plains nomads did that by choice, and shamans for the mana power. The display of Minztan weakness brought mirth; it went to show why the bark-eaters made good slaves.

Maihu wiped and spat away the last threads of vomit and struggled for control. The shaman had not joined in the laughter. His eyes stayed fixed on her ... scars, stink, weird accoutrements were forgotten until there were only the eyes, like windows into nothing. With an effort she tore her gaze away and huddled back against Shkai'ra. Outright violence was nothing next to this.

"Give her to me," the shaman said. He moved, a rustling of feathers and horns in the gloom. "This one is witchborn; give her to me, and I will brew strength from her blood."

Shkai'ra bridled. "No," she said curtly. "You've had your meat, spook-pusher: go talk to the ghosts, keep us safe. This one's mine."

The shaman scarcely seemed to hear her. "Give her to me," he repeated dreamily.

That was an error. Shkai'ra stepped forward, brought up a booted foot, planted it in his chest, and shoved; not hard, just enough to send him sprawling back to the floor. The warriors nearby stopped, shocked.

"You break custom!" the scarred man said, bouncing back to his feet. He crouched and snarled. "I am Walks-with-Demons, peaceholy!"

"I lifted no steel against you," she said. He paused, checked. That was the wording of the law. Glancing around, he saw faint smiles; the shamans were feared, but not popular.

"Luck will turn against you," he warned.

Shkai'ra made the warding sign, but stalked forward. "My steel and the gods of my foremothers are all the luck I need," she barked.

Suddenly her face went very white. Lips peeled back from teeth, and her eyes widened until the rims showed pale around the smoky gray of the iris. The usual low tone of her voice swelled, to an astonishing husky roar:

"And who are you to come between me and my victim?"

The sound of the shout echoed back from the walls, filling the great room. "*WHAT AM I? WHAT AM I, DOG?*"

Unwillingly, the shaman went down on his haunches and stretched out a hand. His person might be peaceholy, but no law could restrain a warrior gone *ahrappan*, berserk, kill-crazy.

"You are *ofzar*," he said. "*Ofzar*, godborn."

He backed away, then turned and lurched out into the brightness that showed through the slit of the opened door. It had been many years since any had dared to put him in fear. Shkai'ra turned back to a shaken Eh'rik.

"That was reckless, Chiefkin," he said.

She shrugged. "They'd have you asking instruction on how to wipe your arse, did you let them. If he'd asked well, I might have given him the scut, but to command me—"

She paused, took deep breaths to win back calm, shaking her shoulders. Leaning close, she whispered: "Besides, come the time when the next High Senior is chosen, more will remember this well for the boldness than with fear."

She turned and prodded the huddled Minztan with her toe. "*You'd* better be worth the trouble."

Then Shkai'ra turned her attention to the newly gathered booty. "So, a good haul," Maihu heard her say. "Enough metal to give every killer in Stonefort twenty new arrowheads; ten good swords; all this caravan stuff . . . and as much woodwork and inlay, furs and suchlike as we care to carry back. The highsmith there gave us good redes."

"Ahi-a, for a village this small, quite a bit." She finished the last of the sausage and belched. "Hoi, Minztana, if you've such wealth, why did you come this close to the steppe?"

"We ... were crowded in the deep forest, Chief-kin," Maihu said slowly, looking down at the table that ran the length of the thirty-meter room. It was inlaid with bright flower patterns in colored glass and stone; Maihu could have told the legends behind each one, nothing without meaning. *I must be clever*, she thought. *Answer with truth, but not all of it.*

Eh'rik grunted skeptically. "The Minztan ranges are big enough, and they live even more scattered than we do," he said.

Shkai'ra sighed. It was exasperating, how even intelligent ones like Eh'rik did not *see.*

"What do the Minztans buy at the fairs?" she said.

"Buy?" he asked, surprised. "Wool. Hides, flax, grain, salt meat ... sssssa, yes."

"Right. Piss-poor land, sour and rocky, so it takes more hectares to support a person. Hmmmm?" She glanced at Maihu.

"Yes, Chiefkin," she replied. The politics of the New Way were a result of that basic pressure. This savage was almost perceptive. She would have to be very cautious.

"After a while, the fields have to rest, and we live as much from trade and hunting and crafts as farming; if we're too crowded it injures the *halassia*, the Harmony. Cutting more trees than grow, or hunting more beasts than are born. We had wealth, but it couldn't buy more than the land will yield."

Shkai'ra nodded. "But stupid, to try expanding into land we claim. We don't live here, can't, not enough open space and grass ... but we need the timber and the trapping."

"You raid farther east anyway!" Maihu snapped. Then added, appalled at her outburst, "Chiefkin."

To her surprise, both the Kommanza snickered. "Of course, when we want to. But on land we claim we'll kill anyone who sets foot." Shkai'ra turned to the war-master. "How many of the prisoners are worth slaving?"

"Hmmmm, about a hundred and fifty, Chiefkin, including walking wounded and hale older children. They'll all bring good prices when the caravans come after snowmelt. We could swap a few with Ardkeep and Highbanner before then, depending on what skills they have. Best you take a look at them, Chiefkin."

She shrugged, stuffing more of the food into her mouth with her thumbs and swallowing with a grunt before buckling her coat. Not awaiting a fight, she had donned the fleece-lined trousers and long hooded coat that were standard winter wear. The coat was of snow-tiger tanned cloth-supple, with embroidery at the cuff and hem, and carved walrus-ivory latches down the front. Her belt bore the weapons no freeborn Kommanza was ever willingly without; she had added a bone flute and many-armed lucksprite. As one of the godborn *ofzar* class, the buckle of her belt was of silver, shaped in the holy sunburst.

Maihu followed silently as they left, willing herself to the invisibility of obedience. Outside the wind bit chill but clean, and there was astonishingly little damage evident: the bodies had been cleared away, after the ritual scalping that prevented haunts. A few of the conquerors were about, seeing to the horses, that being a task too important and sacred for untrained slaves. Most of the rest would be indoors, resting or working on their gear; others would be ranging in a broad loose-meshed net of scouts around the settlement.

Shkai'ra looked back at her, then offered a hunk of bread. "Hungry?" she said.

Maihu hesitated, then accepted and began tearing at it eagerly. She had not eaten for a full day—and it was her own grain, after all.

"Ever seen the steppe, Minztana?" Shkai'ra asked.

"Yes, Chiefkin: Ardkeep for the trade fairs, and Highbanner to arrange ransoms."

"Good," she said. "Ever studied chickens?"

Warily, Maihu shook her head. "You. should. In every flock, there's a lord chicken who can peck everybody—then a number two who can peck everybody but the first, and only be pecked by the first, and so on down to the last one. That one gets it from everyone and can't fight back.

"Now, normally a smith like you would be kinfast common property. Stonefort works like a chicken herd: the High Senior kicks somebody in the arse and the low chicken gets it seventeen times over at tenth remove. You're low chicken."

Maihu could not hold back a slight shudder. The outlander's tone was light, but Maihu's imagination pictured the reality behind the words. She braced herself and turned her head aside to conceal the flare of anger. *When the Summoning is made,* she thought, *we'll see who is put in fear.*

"So," Shkai'ra continued smoothly, "if I were to keep you as part of my loot share, and your tools and—" she glanced sidelong at her captive—"perhaps such of your kin as live, instead of letting them be sold off, you'd do better. I guard my own, and know better than to expect good work without proper care. Here, have some more bread."

Maihu breathed deeply, struggling for control. "You'll feed me well, on grain I worked to sow and reap? Chiefkin?"

The westerner stared blankly, then blinked as the meaning of the words filtered through. "It isn't yours if you haven't the strength to ward it," she said in the calm, matter-of-fact tone used for truths so obvious they are seldom spoken. She might have been observing that horses had four legs.

How can they know the world's Harmony? the Minztan thought. *She expects—she actually expects—me to fall down in gratitude, after what's happened.*

It brought home how alien these folk were, in their inward selves. The Minztan Way was to keep the Circle, taking nothing from the world without return, killing only to live and with sorrow. The Kommanz had been bred to war for generations, since the fabled Before, against the cannibal nomads from the high plains who would burn their crops, against southrons and Minztans, and in their own blood feuds. War was their life, an avocation, an obsession, religion and sport and pastime, woven into the fabric of their being.

Savages, she thought fiercely: *steal, kill, burn, rape, it's all a filthy game to them.*

Shkai'ra stopped and shot out a hand to grab the Minztan by her jacket.

"*Zaik-uz, Minztana, mok ah-zhivut to-a junnah-na!*" she laughed in her own tongue, then dropped into the forest language: "You folk don't get much practice in hiding your thoughts, *nia?* Did I have a face that naked, I'd not have lived to grow warrior braids."

It was true enough; there was little need or point in concealment among Minztans, when the ability to see with the Inner Eye was so common. Maihu sensed a remorseless willingness to kill, oddly impersonal, without real anger.

Shkai'ra drew her knife and brought the point up to rest under the other's chin, pressing steadily until her head was craned back to its limit and a single drop of blood appeared to freeze on the etched steel.

"Now, tell me, what use are you to me if I've to worry about you knifing me every time I turn my back? I need you *bh'raikkun,* or dead." The word meant tame, domesticated.

Maihu looked about wildly. Nearby there were none

but a work party of Minztans loading a row of long slender steppe sleds under the eye of a Kommanz warrior. Shamed, they refused to see her, fusing their eyes to the task; the guard leaned on his lance and watched her with idle curiosity, breath puffing white under the faceshadowing helm. A painted skull glimmered chalk-pale on the shiny black leather of his breastplate, drooling redly from fanged teeth. A string of fresh scalps clattered frozen at his belt.

"Go ahead," Shkai'ra purred. "Convince me I shouldn't slit you open right now, for the pleasure of seeing your blood run out on the snow. Or why I shouldn't starve and beat you into meekness."

Maihu forced her body to relax and dropped her eyes. The knifepoint slid away. "The Chiefkin wishes," she whispered softly, crouching in the snow and reaching out to touch the other's knee: the gesture of submission, among the plainsfolk.

"Good," Shkai'ra said. Pulling the Minztan erect she spoke again, slowly, their faces scant centimeters apart. "Don't try to fight me, ever, Minztana. Or tell yourself you'd rather die, because we both know the truth." She brushed chapped lips against her captive's mouth. "Remember that, and we'll suit well. And learn our ways quickly, because you'll spend whatever days are left you among us."

They came to the barn where the Minztan captives had been herded. The guards rose from their heel-squats and saluted, raising weapons or bowing over crossed hands.

"Any trouble, Bannerleader?" Shkai'ra asked.

The man grinned wolfishly. "From these skinned rabbits?" he asked with contempt. A long-hafted war-hammer was slung from his wrist, the stone head clotted with blood and brains. "A few tried to scamper: we pinned one and brained another. Quiet as mice, the rest of them."

He turned to the door and shouted: "Hoi, in there, the Chief comes!" The doors swung open. A body was nailed to the boards by knives through its wrists and ankles. It still twitched and whined thinly.

Maihu retched once and forced herself to speak. "Chiefkin?" Shkai'ra looked around at the touch on her arm. "Please . . . could you . . . " She glanced at the figure. It was Sharli. She remembered how skillful he had been with his trapline. Shkai'ra thought for a moment, pursed her lips, and signed to the officer. He turned on one heel, the warhammer flung out in a sweeping circle. There was a thick, wet crunch and the crucified Minztan was still.

Within, the huddled captives flinched and gripped each other more closely for the animal comfort of nearness. There were enough of them to keep the barn too warm for frostbite, with straw and blankets; also enough to raise a powerful stench, given their captors' ideas of cleanliness. The uninjured shuffled to their feet, clutching at friends, kinmates, children in their forlornness.

"Line up!" barked the red-haired Bannerleader. "Not a bad lot, Chiefkin, but sullen."

"Ahi-a, can't expect them to like us, Kh'ait," she replied reasonably, spreading her hands. She reached out and gripped Maihu's neck. "Now, Maihu Jonnah's-kin highsmith, show me your usefulness. The name and skills of each."

4

Ingrained habit saved the trappers. They had been out walking the woods, not merely for what they might gather, but to know them, that Newstead might grow into this stretch of earth. For that it was needful they spend much time traveling about, sampling, exploring game trails, noting the types and manner of plant growth, perhaps waiting and meditating by this oddly shaped tree, that solitary rock, for the vision that would tell them how this particular guardian-spirit aspect of the infinite Harmony wished to be known and served.

It had been some weeks since they had left. With sleeping bags, firelighters, the experience of generation upon generation, even the winter woods were home. Any Minztan could survive there, and specialists such as they could be safe, even comfortable. Still, their kinhalls beckoned and their pace increased as they came within the last few *kaelm* of the village. But eyes, ears, skins were sensitized; the holistic sense-awareness field that their way of life demanded scanned about ceaselessly.

The elder braked to a halt and thrust her ski poles upright in the snow before she crouched.

"Horse!" she hissed in surprise. Her companion moved up beside her, stared wordlessly, then began to backtrack while she cast about.

He returned. "One only," he said. "Big, and shod." Even durcret horseshoes were expensive, and their people rarely bothered to so equip the few ponies they kept. He held up a few russet hairs that had caught in the bark of a tree. "No forest pony, this!"

She nodded and pointed ahead. The trail passed beneath a leaning pine: several of the lower branches had been cut. Hacked, from the look of them, and with something knife-sharp. Her mind computed angles and heights.

"Kommanz," she said, touching the sheared end of one limb, muttering a silent apology for the needless destruction. "That was done with a saber."

Their eyes met, shared a great sickness. "We should head for Garnetseat?" he said.

"No. We check first. This could be the screen for a raiding part looping around to strike from the east."

"Do you really think so?"

"No."

This was climax forest, huge trees and more open space beneath them than was comfortable. But hunters learned the arts of concealment perforce, and they slipped through the scout mesh with silent contempt for all clumsy hearthdwellers. It was bad luck and a shift in the wind that carried their scent to the hounds that the raiders had brought along, and unlike their masters those could outpace humans on skis. The westerners followed, but their quarry led the way through ground too barren to carry the tall trees, and therefore thick with undergrowth, tangled and spiny. They tried to ride into that as well, by sheer instinct:

shrieked curses and crackling and neighing told of how well *that* fared. Luckily for the Minztans there were only a few of the tracker dogs. Huge gaunt beasts with the blood of the giant man-high steppe wolves in them, they were trained to kill as well as follow.

For a moment combat ramped through the bushes, while the raiders sent shafts plunging blindly into the melee before thinking to dismount and force their way through branch and thorn. By then it was too late: the Minztan crossbows had spoken, and the trappers were away on a swift zigzag route through ground chosen for low visibility and deep snow.

Hours later they lay up in a thicket and watched one of the pursuers ride by. The horse came at a slow trot, plunging through drifts with a heaving leap; the rider sat relaxed, bobbing and swaying with awesome, unconscious skill, bow in his hands and eyes scanning restlessly. He was close, close enough for them to see the patterns enameled on his armor, the ribbons wound in his forked beard, to smell horse and leather and sweat. They lay very still with their breathing controlled to shallowness; Kommanza from the border villages hunted the forest and had some woodcraft. The Kommanza stopped, backed his horse. It was restless, whickering; his eyes swept methodically over the bushes.

The elder Minztan drew a deep, controlled breath. Fingers drew a tiny pattern in the snow before her eyes; with a straining effort no less real for the stillness of her body, she sent her consciousness plunging through it into the totality of the woods around. She did not attempt to spin illusion, or turn the hunter's mind; such was work for an Adept. Instead, she pulled the patters of the wilderness around her, made it fit like a seamless web that left no telltale detail to disrupt and catch the eye. The plains warrior shook his

head, muttered, heeled his mount into motion. The
Minztan could feel his unease. But no steppeddweller
was at home in the deep woods; the strangeness
played on their nerves, until the true hunter's sense
was lost as imagination put a lurker behind every piece
of cover.

After he passed, the young man raised his crossbow,
It was an easy shot, and the armor would be no protection this close. His companion touched his arm and
shook her head. Seconds later a whistle call came from
their left, faint but clear in a rising-falling four-note
pattern. The man repeated it through the bone whistle
in his mouth, the sound loud and piercing through the
trees. And faint and far, to their right, another echoed
it. Just then another horse came up: the squadleader
riding the line of her section. Passing at a canter, she
shouted at the lone scout and plunged on into the
woods.

Silence fell. When it was safe the younger Minztan
whispered: "Did you hear that one"—he nodded toward
where the noncom had disappeared "—coming?"

She shook her head. "They scout in a grid, like a
diamond-mesh fishnet. If you'd killed that one they'd
have spotted the gap and had a troop on the way here
in minutes; each one keeps in touch with those little
flutes."

Bitterly, she pounded her fist into the snow. "Why
didn't they get the stockade finished? With that and
the pigeons, the Seeker's people in Garnetseat could
have come up, we would have swamped them with
numbers. Fools! Why did the New Way give us aid in
goods and food, if not for that?"

"Can we do anything?"

"Perhaps. Perhaps. It depends on how soon the
raiders leave, how fast they travel, how quickly we can
alert the relief. They won't be counting on our having

a force ready to move on short notice. But we didn't think so many could come into the woods in winter, not the full hundred we have seen."

She bit at the knuckle of her mitten. "Of course, if they go the right way, It could come, if the right people survived the first attack."

She looked to where the westering sun threw red light on the treetops. That was a huge flock of *ifs*, though. "We'll wait for full night, then travel. Best we try to get some sleep; you nap first. Safe enough, now their first line is past us."

Curiosity prompted him as he curled into the snow. "What did she say, the one who went by?"

For the first time that day the woman smiled, hard and sour. "She said, 'Be careful, they may try to turn in the dark.'"

Taimi was glad of the work that morning, and gladder still of the enforced silence. Hours went by as he helped empty the village granaries, heaving wicker baskets of oats and rye from the barns to fill a long train of slender steppe sleds. The task was not heavy; there were plenty of hands, and the Kommanz were in no hurry. It was near noon before he began to notice detail: grain dust coating the inside of nose and throat, hunger, the number of empty sacks in the sleds the enemy had brought . . . It was a moment before the meaning of that struck him. His folk fed the stock they kept over winter on hay, not having breadstuff to spare. But the Kommanza had brought hundreds of war-horses and draft beasts many days' journey into a land where the winter snows hid only pine needles and weeds. The animals had traveled fast and kept in condition on grain, and the raiders had been so confident of victory that they had brought only enough to last until the village was reached; that

was what had enabled them to strike so fast and deep
in the cold season. It was a gesture of purest
contempt.

Anger was healing, gave him energy for the oatmeal
porridge and cheese dished out to the working detail.
He took the opportunity to glance around and take
stock. Much of the clearing was covered by the horse
herd, bounded by leather ropes slung from poles; no
more was needed, with mounts as well trained as
these. Taimi remembered hearing that every Kommanza of the freeholding yeoman-farmer kinfasts had
as many as half a dozen war mounts. Surely they had
not brought so many here, but there were still more
animals than he had ever seen in one spot before.

Ten warriors squatted nearby in the lee of a building, wearing full armor and holding the reins of their
horses linked to their belts. A small fire and the bison-
pelt cloaks must be giving them scant warmth, but
they sat immobile and uncomplaining for the most
part. Some chewed stolidly on iron-hard strips of
jerked meat, and one was sharpening an ax. It was a
lighter weapon than those the Minztans used, a simple
wedge of steel with a slender triangular spike on the
reverse, hefted on a limber shaft of laminated wood
and horn with a loop for the wrist and a grip of plaited
rawhide shrunk on. The metal went *wheep-wheep*
across the hone, steadily and methodically. At last the
Kommanza tested the edge on a thumb, grunted satisfaction, and rose to slip on the sheath that covered
the edge before hanging the weapon from his saddlebow. There he paused, unhooked a canteen, tilted it
to pour a stream of whitish liquid down his throat.
One of his companions looked up and snarled something at him when he prepared to take a second drink;
Taimi recognized the speaker as an officer from the
spray of eagle feathers clipped to his helmet above the

nasal. The trooper shrugged and swallowed more of the *naikbuzk*, fermented mare's milk.

The officer moved without warning, snatching a burning branch from the fire and swinging around to scythe the offender's feet out from under him. Surprised, he hardly had time to break his fall before the other was on him, swinging hearty full-strength kicks to his midriff and beating him over the head and shoulders with the stick; neither was very serious to someone in full armor, but it was enough to prevent him from rising. Especially since he doggedly refused to let the *naikbuzk* out of his hand, or even to let a drop spill as he rolled over the packed snow of the lane. The rest of the two squads watched, most with their customary lack of expression, a few with smiles, slight feral barings of the teeth. One of these called out a short sentence, and a rippling chuckle flowed down the line.

The commander stopped, panting, and spat into the fire. But before he had time to gather momentum for his tirade, a sound came from the woods. To the Minztans it was merely music, hardly loud enough to separate the notes. Hunting-trained ears determined the location as southwest of the village, in an area of scrub wood and thickets. The Kommanz fighters froze, heads turning to the whistle trill. Seconds passed, and they dissolved into movement. The ten by the wall threw themselves into the saddle and kicked their horses into a gallop, thunder and clatter as they pounded over the frozen ground and looped around the horse herd to gain the woods. One of the guards watching the prisoners pulled a horn from her belt and sounded a sharp, raucous blast. Doors burst open and warriors spilled out, lacing up pieces of their armor and running to duty stations. One paused near the Minztans to question the guards.

"To a-paizu nikkin i'?" Taimi could follow that:
What was happening? The reply was too fast and complex for his limited knowledge of Kommanzanu. Tense
with excitement, he strained to listen. Could this be
the start of a rescue? On second thought, that was
unlikely. There had been too little time, and the nearest settlement of his people was far away. But *something* had happened. He thought of the empty grain
sacks and reflected grimly that the steppe people
might learn to take his folk less lightly before they
returned to their homes.

"Ia," the first Kommanza said: Yes. *"Fy-uzh'buttik
a-kot."*

Slowly, he puzzled out the unfamiliar words, struggling to remember what he had learned of the tense
system. Get the *something* dogs, he thought, and saw
it confirmed when three huge gray hounds were
brought forth, snarling and tugging at their leashes.

Emboldened, he whispered to the woman next to
him: "Some of our people must have come."

"Ewunnu and Sasimi were out on the Knowing,"
came the low-voiced reply. "Circle grant that they
escape."

One of the remaining guards turned and slashed the
woman across the face with her quirt, slicing deep.
She fell back with a cry, holding her cheek. The Kommanza flicked the whip in front of Taimi with a crack;
blood spattered on his face and lips, warm and salty.

"Up," she said, and stared blankly into his eyes for
a moment. "In house." The others were roused with
kicks.

Most of the Kommanz trickled back to the village
within an hour or so. Taimi was surprised at how many
crowded themselves into this one kinhall; their folk
were accustomed to close living when they were between walls. The tall-grass prairie of their homeland

was wide and empty, but village and ranchhouse and
Keep alike huddled densely packed behind defensive
walls. Even a day had altered the Jonnah's-kin hall
strangely. Broad rooms, tile floors, woodcarvings, and
rugs remained the same, but most of the furniture had
been cast out or broken up for firewood. The Kommanza did not use chairs, preferring to squat or sit
cross-legged in nests of pillows. The air was colder
than his mother's kinfast had kept it, to suit the habits
of a folk whose lands were poor in fuel and lacking in
the skill needed to fashion efficient airtight stoves such
as the forest people used. And the smells were
strange. A feast was being prepared in the kitchens
but underlying that was an odd taint. It was not just
uncleanliness, or the scent of leather and oil and
horses that seemed a part of the Kommanz essence.
The underlying smell of their bodies was different,
perhaps a rankness born of a diet heavy in milk and
red meat.

Now that they were out of their armor, it was plain
that few were more than a hand of years older than
Taimi. That made the lack of such chatter and laughter as Minztans were used to even more obvious. And
when they did laugh, it was in a high-pitched breathless giggle that plucked rawly on his nerves. Most sat
quietly working on their gear, or simply staring into
space with disturbing intensity, leaning their chins on
their swordhilts. Others sat over games, dice or chess,
or a buffalo hide marked into polygons with a dozen
players crowded around it. Edging nearer, he saw a
map beneath the lines and scores of carved plaques;
the players pushed the miniature units of fighters back
and forth, casting dice to determine random factors.
An officer with a tally stick supervised, ready to allo-
cate victory or defeat.

In one of the larger rooms some passed the time

with the interminable round of combat practice, drill with double-weighted weapons or unarmed bouts. Fascinated despite himself, Taimi lowered his bucket of water to the floor and watched. One young warrior stood in the center of a circle stripped to the waist. A slight smile was on his face, and the long black braids fell swaying to his shoulders: he was tall even for the western race, slender and long-limbed, muscle moving smoothly under his skin, hard as tile. Two others attacked with ringing shouts. One leaped high to kick for his face. The other threw herself forward feet-first at knee height, legs crooked for a bone-shattering blow. Both attacks looked fast, to Taimi's eyes faster than the tall Kommanza's response.

That was smooth, almost leisurely, and oddly the attackers seemed to be cooperating. The first found her target gone; the man sprang sideways and landed on crossed forearms. At the same time his body was coiling, legs shooting up to grip her around the waist and add horizontal momentum with a powerful wrenching twist. She began to roll in midair, hit the wall with a crash, slid to the floor, and staggered away on all fours, shaking her head as a trickle of red seeped from her nose. The second flew through the empty space where the defender's knees had been, landed, and began to come erect in a flickering shoulder roll. Before the motion was complete the first man had back-flipped to his feet, using the follow-through of his throw to lever himself up. He flowed forward and caught the second attacker before she could regain stance. A foot sweep sent her down again, a hand fastened in her hair and another whipped down clenched in a fist to halt a millimeter behind her ear.

The watchers applauded in the Kommanz manner, hissing and snapping their fingers. The victor was sweating lightly, breathing deep and slow. Turning, he saw Taimi watching, giggled, and made a thrusting motion with his hips, giggling again as the Minztan flushed and glanced away.

That was unfortunate. His eyes fell on Shkai'ra, leaning against a wall. The flush faded to a white pallor, and he began to shake. Water slopped out of the bucket as he stumbled from the room.

The Kommanz leader undid her coat and belt, calling out. "Nice kill, Dh'vik," she said.

Dh'vik's green eyes narrowed to slits. Shkai'ra moved forward easily, light on her feet and keeping her balance centered as they both crouched and circled for advantage. Advancing, she snapped off a series of front kicks. Dh'vik parried easily; the slap of leather on flesh sounded as he deflected the blows with sweeping motions of forearm and shoulder backed by an odd flexing snap of the hips that put power behind the parry. Then he attacked with a looping side kick that brought him whirling around, aiming for the throat.

Shkai'ra had been standing with knees bent and feet at right angles. Moving, she relaxed the left knee and let her weight move her down and back out of the path of the boot. Calm and detached, her mind calculated the angles and possibilities; on another level, it admired the skill and speed behind the move. With a little more experience, Dh'vik was going to be very formidable, especially with that reach. For the present, he tended to overconfidence, as witness this follow-through, which—

Even as he settled back into stance she was moving, lunging with arm locked and fingers stiffened into a blade that had the whole mass of her body behind it. The man's hands flashed up, crossed, to catch the strike. Wisely, he made no attempt to oppose the force. Instead he threw himself backward and down, using the combined weight of their bodies to overbalance the chieftain and lashing upward with a foot as they fell. That would have been a killing stroke if it had landed with full force, and if Shkai'ra had stayed to receive it. For she had gone *with* the movement, throwing herself forward and up and turning in midair in a superb display of gymnastic skill. That brought her a complete one hundred eighty degrees, the immense leverage breaking his hold as her body rotated around the pivot of their joined hands. She landed on her feet, feather-light, turning and lunging in the same instant to land on his back. Her right arm whipped around his throat, locking it in the crook of her elbow. The palm slapped home into the angle of her left arm even as that hand buried itself in his hair—a breaking hold. She wound her legs around his to hold him for the instant needed to pantomime the brief wrench that would crack his neck across.

They rolled away from each other and to their feet. For seconds he glared at her before they slapped palms.

"Not bad at all," she said. "But you fell well and true on the handstrike."

"*Ia*," he said ruefully.

Down the corridor Taimi halted, shuddering and gasping. A hand fell on his shoulder, and he jerked convulsively.

"Easy, kinchild," a familiar voice soothed.

"Sadhi!" he exclaimed. There had been no hope in him that any other of his kinparents had survived.

"Are—"

"Dead," Sadhi said bleakly. His eyes turned to the door. "That black-haired one, he killed Jannu. He scalped her before she died, then cut her throat."

Taimi made a small sound in his throat. "I wish—

I wish—I wish we were witches, what they say we are! If I could call ghosts out of the woods to eat their souls, I would!"

"Are you hurt, child?" his kinfather said gently. It was disturbing to hear his kinchild speak so; Minztans had little liking for the merciless superstitions of the steppe. Yet it was a relief to hear too; none of his folk could feel such hatred and rage without guilt, and to see another share it eased the feeling of sin. He put a protective arm around Taimi's shoulders.

The boy wrenched away fiercely.

"No ... I'm all right. And you?"

"Nothing worse than the old limp," the man replied.

Seeing his hurt, Taimi embraced him. "Maihu? Dennai?"

"All gone, except Maihu and me," Taimi said. He lowered his voice and glanced around. "The leader, she was waiting in the laneway. We were captured, and—"

He sank down and sobbed. Sadhi tried to comfort him, but sensed the boy's withdrawal. Inwardly he was stunned. The Jonnah's had been a small kinfast, only ten full mates. With two adult survivors the continuity of the kinfast was shattered, the family gone, the sense of all-encompassing *belonging* that was the core of his life seeping away. Individuals came and went, but the bloodline went on forever; the Jonnah's-kin had endured since the time of the Old Ones, when history faded into legend. He shivered to the knowledge that only three lives stood between it and extinction; and the little ones, but they had not learned the traditions, the essence ...

"Taimi," he whispered. The boy looked up through swimming eyes. "We can't stay here talking ... they've got me working in the kitchen. Try to get word to Mai', she'll ... she'll know what to do. She's the Initiate." His voice went quietly fierce. "And *don't you dare die, boy!*"

Taimi wiped a hand across his face as the man limped off. There was a hollow emptiness inside him, as if the bottom of his world were sinking downward and a chill blowing across the back of his neck. The Kommanz turned their children over to the warmasters as soon as they could walk, but the forest people did not believe in forcing adulthood before its time. For all his thirteen years Taimi had been surrounded by a love and caring that came equally from all his ten kinparents. There had been nothing they could not do, no trouble they could not help. How could they, the older and wiser, be as lost as he, as frightened? Turning the emotions over in his mind, he realized that he felt ... betrayed. He recoiled at the disloyalty, but the feeling remained, a curdling in the pit of his stomach.

Mind whirling, he scarcely noticed when Shkai'ra came up behind him and laid proprietorial hands along his flanks. It was the smell that brought back the memories, made him tense and quiver and press back against the wall. The scents of oil and tallow and musk, and the rough long-fingered hands.

"Good," she said. "I was beginning to think it was your *blood* I'd been draining." She ruffled his light brown hair and gazed into the hazel eyes. "You look like a fawn caught in a trap." Which, she reflected, was true enough. She gave him a playful swat across the buttocks and continued:

"Run along. I'll find time for you tomorrow. Today's too soon. Even at your age, males have no staying power."

5

It took the Newstead hunters three days to reach Garnetseat; the outlying sentries met them a full day out. No Kommanza could have covered that ground so quickly, or even believed it possible to make such speed on foot through wooded country. Even for those used to long treks on skis, for bodies tempered by a lifetime of such effort, the toil was grim. Little strength was left in the pair by the time the broad clearing came in sight. That land was the best in the eastern reaches of the Haaniryls-an-Minztannis, being the bed of an ancient lake and free of stones. Around were wide stretches for hunting, timber, mining. The settlement had prospered in the century since its foundation, and over five hundred souls dwelt there. Yet it also bore the marks of the borderlands: earth rampart, log stockade, blockhouses at the corners, and a ditch planted with sharpened stakes. Many from the heartlands of the deep forest would have winced at that, considered the ways of the frontier folk tainted with the un-Circled customs of the outlanders.

Yet more than one raiding band had retired baffled

from those walls, and a few had left their dead impaled on the stakes or twitching under the high walls. Siegecraft was not an art in which the steppe peoples excelled; they preferred skirmish, ambush, the vast swirling campaigns of the grass sea that ended with the boot-to-boot charge of armored lancers. And this was the main trade route to the east, south of Bemedjaka. Garnetseat stood as a barrier against the Kommanz. Thus it held many adherents of the New Way, and had sheltered the Seeker herself from time to time. And it had contributed in goods and people to the effort that had colonized Newstead.

The news of the fugitives' arrival brought the folk murmuring into the streets, calling out questions and then falling into silence at the sight of gaunt, shuttered faces. But to Ewennu and Sasimi it was a return to sanity. Seeing the faces of Minztan folk, hearing the singsong lilt of their native tongue, the fearless *closeness* gave them strength. Still more were their spirits lifted by the sight that awaited them in the central square, before the round meeting hail and chapel that was the prime feature of any Minztan garth. The cone-shaped roof stood serene against the bright winter sky, supported by pillars carved and painted in the forms of guardian spirits human and animal and abstract. Before it stood something new.

In any other land, the twenty young men and women would have been commonplace enough, dressed alike in round helmets and leather back-and-breasts, shortswords and daggers at their belts, crossbows or billhooks in their hands. To a Minztan it was revolutionary to have full-time fighters of their own people, forest folk who had no trade but war and weapons training. The leader was a tall man, lanky, at age thirty older than his troops by a decade. He wore a knee-length chainmail hauberk and steel strips on leather

armguards, a plain double-edged sword at his waist.
Rare and precious and hideously expensive, the armor
marked him as one of the Seeker's elite cadre, one
high in the ranks of the New Way. Still more unusual
was the weapon he carried, a dart rifle with a six-shot
magazine, powered by a coiled spring in the stock.
Imported from the fabled eastern realm of Fehinna,
on the shores of the Lannic Ocean, it was almost as
costly as a firearm would have been.

Such a display of might and wealth would have been
enough to awe Sasimi and Ewunnu; it was the presence of the Adept that brought deep bows. He was
plainly dressed, in the mottled coat of a hunter; unarmed, save for a flint knife at his belt. The blood of
the First People was stronger in him than was common, showing in the dark skin and flat, high-cheeked
face. Laugh lines crinkled beside his eyes as he gravely
returned their salutes; he could sense their unease,
that a sage should be in the company of armed violence, New Way radicals though they were. Silently,
he motioned their attention back to the mail-clad figure. That one smiled, and touched the symbol of the
New Way on his chest; it was graven on his followers'
armor as well, a circle opened at the top with silver
flame leaping through the gap: change and rebirth.

"Come in; rest, eat, and let us give each other our
names," he said in friendly Minztan wise. "My name
is Narritanni." As was the custom of the New Way,
he had taken a use-name: Narritanni, in the Minztan
tongue "Man of Stone."

Later, bathed, fed, soft clean clothes on their backs
and horn cups of hot mead in their hands, the questions began, quiet and friendly, but very thorough.
Narritanni and his detachment had been given the
guest-hall traditionally attached to the chapel and had
moved in maps and racks to make one chamber his
office.

"Like this?" he asked, showing them a page in a book. It bore the likeness of a fanged skull impaled on an upright sword.

"*Doa*," Sasimi replied. "All of them had that on their chests, on the armor."

"Stonefort," the commander mused. "No worse a nest of robbers than any other, but rich. They could field two thousand lances ... How many horses did you see?"

Sasimi shrugged and tapped his kinmate on the shoulder. "Ewunnu had a better chance to count," he said.

She blushed at being singled out in such august company. "Well, enlightened one," she began. She was unsure of the title, but the term for a sage was the only honorific apart from "elder" that her people possessed. "There might have been as many as two hundred mounts, or even more. Apart from the ones the scouts were riding, of course."

"So," he mused, running a hand over close-cropped fair hair. What that meant would depend on any number of factors.

"Many sleds, you said?" he continued.

"Yes, twenty at least. It looked as if they were loading grain from the Newstead storehouse. Why would they steal grain, when their land is so much richer for crops?"

"For the horses," Narritanni answered absently. His mind churned. *So!*

That would explain how they managed the raid in this season. The Seeker had used some of the wealth of the New Way to buy her aides a comprehensive military education. Narritanni's lakelander teachers had never tired of saying that any reasonably intelligent human being could master strategy and tactics; it was logistics and supply that took real talent. On the steppe, Kommanz lancers liked to keep at least four remounts at hand. That way they could cover up to a hundred kaelm a day, changing mounts every half hour or so. The limiting factor here was fodder. Even if they went more slowly on the return journey, the horses would still have to eat, not as much as when they were being pressed for speed but nearly as much. And there would be the problem of feeding the captives as well ... He leaned back and sipped at the hot, sweet mead.

"Fine," he said to the two hunters. "Go and rest now: you'll need strength soon." He took it for granted that they would join the rescue party; they had kinmates in enemy hands, and that was the strongest of ties.

Worry was on their faces. "You ... you can do something for our folk?" Ewunnu asked softly.

"Of course." Narritanni was crisp and decisive; another legacy of his training, never to show doubt or hesitation even if he felt uncertain. That was essential for morale, but sometimes he wondered how alien such thinking made him to the ways of his folk, whether he would ever again be able to live among them wholesouled.

When the Newsteaders had left he sighed and turned to his second. "At least a hundred of them," he said. "Four Banners, and I doubt they took many casualties storming Newstead, since the fools left the wall unfinished. Maybe a hundred and sixty of them, maybe more."

"Not fools," the Adept said. Narritanni started; he had never grown used to the way the man could make you forget he was there. It was not even a Wreaking, merely a serenity so deep that it left nothing for the attention to touch on unless the Adept willed it. The sage had taken little part in the interrogation, but the Minztan commander knew his calming presence had been an aid.

"Unused to war, perhaps," the man continued. Like most of his kind he had abandoned his human name; such was unnecessary to one who simply *was*, without consciousness of self as separate from the world.

"Even so, they should have had warning-from the Inner Eye, if nothing else. I fear . . . the plainsdwellers have brought an Eater into the forest with them."

The Minztans shuddered. The sage went on: "I am not a man of war. Or even of politics; but this is more. The Land and the Otherworld are menaced too, and they will fight for you, in such wise as is permitted."

Narritanni grimaced. "It will be welcome; we have twenty of the Fellowship here, and let's not lie among ourselves, none of us is a match for the average steppe killer in a stand-up fight."

The second-in-command stroked her swordhilt. "Well, yes," she said, glancing sidelong at the Adept. He had said that they could call him Leafturn if a name was needed, but somehow it was difficult to think of him as anything but *himself*, purely. "But we don't have to stand and fight their type of battle; we'll have volunteers, not well trained, but they can ski and shoot. And . . ."

She hesitated; what she had to say touched on forbidden matters. "Wasn't there an Initiate in Newstead?"

"Maihu Jonnah's-kin," Leafturn said. "An Initiate, and one who might have been more, if she desired it." He paused, closed his eyes. "The Snowbrother is a strong friend," he continued at last. "To those it knows; I have not walked these woods in winter. Some things I could do, but not that. Maihu could."

"If she's still alive," Narritanni said. "If she has access to the instruments, and if she thinks of it at all."

He sighed again, frustrated. This was not at all like the staff wizards his instructors had told him of. "We can't count on . . . it."

He was not a reverent man, but he still hesitated to shape that word.

"What I can do, I will do," Leafturn said with un-ruffled calm. Then he smiled, with a hint of a child's impishness, and touched a ball of rock crystal that hung on a leather thong around his neck, no larger than a bird's head. "For instance, if there were to be heavy snow . . ."

Narritanni swore eagerly. "Exactly! What we need most is to slow them down. All they have to do to win is get back to the steppe; a guerrilla can harry them out, but that won't rescue our folk. But if we slow them, perhaps . . . And if the New Way can't offer protection, why should the folk make sacrifices for it?"

"Truth," the Adept said. "And best I make my prep-arations." He rose gracefully and left with a swiftness that was somehow unhurried; the soldier noticed a faint, wild smell of leather and pine as he passed.

Narritanni closed his mouth and laughed ruefully. "I was going to ask him to help us with the elders," he said. "But . . ." He gestured helplessly.

The other soldier grinned and began packing a pipe with Maishgun tobacco, a habit picked up from the lakelander mercenaries she had studied with.

"I know how you feel," she said. "Try to ask him something he doesn't want to do . . . Well, it just doesn't happen, somehow." She flicked the flint of her ceramic firestarter and puffed. "If he keeps the Eater off us, that will be enough."

Narritanni's mouth twisted. "Don't remind me." He ruffled a sheaf of papers. Organization did not come easily to his folk; if the stories were true, escaping it was one of the reasons his ancestors had come to these woods, even before the Fire and the Dark. Still, he forced briskness. "Let's get the elders in, and see how many volunteers we can bugle up."

They walked through the door: the heads of kinfasts, those respected for wealth or wit or holiness, the closest thing a Minztan settlement had to a government. Not very close: they had no authority to compel, save in small matters such as cleanliness, or to levy tax in labor or kind. The forest people had many customs but few laws; mutual helpfulness sufficed, enforced by the shunning of evildoers in the rare cases where serious offense was given. It needed many hands working together to live in this land, a fact anyone could see. Narritanni considered them. Most were middle-aged or older, dressed in the embroidered jackets reserved for festival or serious occasions. And they regarded him with grim attention; at least there would be none of the blank incomprehension he had met in the central regions, where outlanders were seldom seen. Still, those not of the New Way would tend to be more fanatical about the nonviolence canons for all that.

Best come to the point, he thought. "Dwellers-in-the-Circle, Newstead has been raided and taken."

There was a collective sigh, mingling sorrow and horror with the relaxation that comes when the long-suspected worst is known.

"We of the Fellowship are going to attempt a rescue, but there are too few of us to have any chance of success alone. We need help, to travel and to fight. Will you counsel your kinmates, and give of your substance?"

A sharp-faced oldster leaned forward, gnarled hands gripping the arms of a chair, wood carved into the likeness of paws.

"You mean, you wish our help to make war!" she said.

He answered gently. "No, to help defend our folk. Your own blood has been spilled at Newstead—"

"More death will not help the dead," the elder said stubbornly. "But it can harm us, not only what is done to those who go but what they do to themselves by going."

"Defense has *always* been within custom," Narritanni replied heatedly, then forced himself to calm. "So has aid to our kindred. That is *enjoined* on us by the Way. And not everyone in Newstead has returned to the Circle; there are live prisoners. Would you let them be slaves? Blinded and chained to millstones, or sold to the Valley merchants?"

The elder subsided, silent but unconvinced. Well, he had not expected to make conversions. Missionary work *was* for others. "Those of you who feel you cannot do this thing, at least do not hinder us." Perhaps a third of those present left. By custom, they would not actively oppose the majority. The leavetaking seemed as much a spiritual as a physical act.

"Well, at least most of you are going to be sensible," he said. "How many will come? It should be a goodly number, this being winter." In the warm season many would have been faring about, or doing farmwork that could not be delayed.

"Perhaps eighty, I think," said one. "Not all are of our way of thinking, and of those some will be ill, or too old, or pregnant . . ."

Narritanni pulled thoughtfully at his snub nose, set in a typical wide, flat Minztan face. He could count on perhaps twice that from smaller settlements within reach, but the timing would be more difficult.

"You've wealth to spare, though?" They should have, with Garnetseat's trade and craftsfolk. They nodded. "Then offer rewards for the reluctant."

That brought a gasp of shock. He might have been

suggesting eating the dead or setting a forest fire or killing animals for sport.

Patiently, he began: "You've no objection to fighting in self-defense?"

"No, but—"

"You don't think it's wrong to go help the dwellers in Newstead who've been attacked?"

"Of course not, but—"

He let a hint of irritation creep into his voice. "Then why is it wrong to help others to do what is lawful? This will take time, and some of us are going to return to the Circle rather than our homes: our kinfasts will suffer more than grief, they'll lose those hands and skills. Perhaps some will hold back for fear their kinmates and children will suffer. Why shouldn't we reassure them?"

"Yes, but fighting for *pay!*"

In the end, they agreed. There was little poverty in a Minztan village: no one need go hungry or cold except in famines when all suffered. But there were those who had little more than was necessary to face another year of labor, even some who lacked the dowry most kinfasts demanded before allowing marriage-in. And the numbers of such had been increasing in recent decades, as population built up and foreign trade became more important. Few would seek battle merely for goods, but there would be waverers for whom furs and food and tools would tip the balance. That was another lesson he had learned, that to desire the end was to desire the means to achieve it. If you were not willing to do what you must, then you had never really wanted it at all.

Morning dawned gray with low clouds, the cold less bitter but carrying a hint of damp, an omen of snow to experienced eyes. Narritanni looked to where Leafturn stood, leaning negligently on his ski poles, and met calm, unreadable friendliness.

Nearly a hundred villagers had gathered to join the rescue party, stoutly dressed in their winter-travel gear, long skis on their feet and hunting weapons in their hands; on his instruction every one had a tree-felling axe thrust through their packroll. Breath misted from them, but less noise and talk than might have been anticipated; a few came shyly to the Adept to have their weapons touched, cleansing the steel. The commander could feel their mood, compounded of fear and excitement and determination; he weighed it, found it good. These were tough, hardy men and women, used to long journeys and living out in rough country; and they were all good shots. It was the lack of weapons and harness and skill in close-quarter combat that worried him, and the lack, as well, of discipline. They were willing enough, but simply not used to a swift unquestioning obedience that was outside their day-to-day experience.

"Hear me," he called out. A few at a time, they fell silent. "We go on a sacred mission." The word actually meant something more complex, implying naturalness, an active intervention to restore the rightful and accustomed Harmony of the world. It was the term used to describe cutting diseased timber, or culling a deer herd that grew too quickly, or appeasing angry spirits that brought bad weather.

"The land will fight for us, against despoilers who know nothing of the Harmony. We can move faster here. We know the ways of the woods. But fighting is an art and calling which I've studied. Think of it as raising the roof beams of a building: if we pull together, in unison, to the chant of the work leader, everything will come together, strong and joined."

He linked his fingers and held them up, twisting

and tugging. "If we act at cross purposes, the timbers can break free and crush us." It was a little daunting to have to repeat such basics. But his people had traditionally fought skulking in twos and threes when they fought at all, striking and harassing with techniques adopted from their hunting methods.

"So listen when those of us who follow the Seeker speak. Even if what we say seems to make no sense at the time, don't stop to argue or ask the reasons." That might save lives, if they could learn to do it. Some might, but he would still have to explain any plan carefully before ordering them into action. Which meant he would have to keep it simple.

"And now let us ask that our actions be taken into the great Harmony, in the fullness of the Circle."

They bowed their heads, falling into meditation and reaching out to touch their neighbors. Narritanni strove to empty his mind of plans and numbers and contingencies, to feel himself one with the land and folk: it was well to remember the purpose of the fighting and striving. Then he hooked the curved toes of his boots into the ski straps and pushed off across the silent white expanse. The first soft flakes drifted down as the others followed.

6

Ting-ting-ting! The sound of a smith's hammer echoed through Newstead, iron on hot metal.

Shkai'ra heard the belling from the enclosure of leather ropes where the remount herd milled. She had been spending the late-afternoon hours with her horses: currying, checking hooves, braiding their manes. That was needful not only to keep them in good condition, but to cement the deep bond between rider and horse that was life and death in war. Besides that, it was one of the few times a Kommanza could afford to love without reservation or distrust.

With a happy chuckle, she pushed aside a soft muzzle that nuzzled at her face and strolled idly through the lanes of the village. Two days had taken the edge off its strangeness, but that lent an extra interest as eyes saw through the alien patterns to focus on detail. Roofs were wood shingle, high and steep-pitched, with jutting beams shaped into flowers and branches laden with berries and the heads of doves with eyes of colored stone. The houses themselves rose three stories, the upper levels often joined by enclosed walkways.

There were many windows of real glass. She wondered at the display of wealth; Stonefort itself had only two such.

Construction was stone to knee height, then massive logs cut flat on their upper and lower sides and left gently curved on the outer: some of the timbers were carved in low relief with swirling abstract patterns picked out in paint, and she supposed there would have been more, if the settlement had lasted. For all the massiveness the overran effect had an airy lightness, compact yet uncrowded; it was obviously incomplete, but you could sense how the finished village would have been, not just a collection of buildings but an artifact in itself. Less than two years old, Newstead seemed to have grown like a tree from the soil that bore it. The thought of the labor that had gone into the project was daunting.

She ran fingers over the join between two balks of wood—almost seamless, and held in place by the huge weight of the building as well as by pegs. Minztans had an almost instinctive affinity for wood; cut, shaped, laminated, rendered down for tar and synthetics, it was the substance of their lives. Musing, she drew her flute and began to play, a wild slow skirling. Her first reaction to Newstead had been that it was simply an easy target: poorly sited for defense, and badly built. Her own people would never have erected something so small, or easy to burn.

It's like . . . a tune, she thought. *But of no music we know.*

The concept was satisfying. Her own reactions had been puzzling her, and the Kommanz were not an introspective folk. The simile made her less uncomfortable. Still, she would be glad to be back on the grass sea. Even the fangs of a midwinter wind blowing three thousand treeless *kylickz* from the Westwall mountains to Stonefort would be welcome. Her eyes ached from staring at distances that were not there; it was not natural for the horizon to be so *close*. And the ever-present forest made her feel as if something were always about to pounce, a continuous low-level crawling between the shoulderblades.

It was then that she realized what she had been playing: the Song Against Witches. That brought minor irritation. The Mek Kermak's-kin were descended from the Mighty Ones. Even if she was not fasted into the kin, not fully adult, she had been born to it. The Ztrateke ahkomman would guard their own blood, and the Sun their home looked down on the forest as well as the plains.

The smithy was a long, low building detached from the rest. Minztans did not worry as much as her people about fire arrows, but sparks were sparks. A wide stone chimney jutted up through roof overtopped with stone slabs. Before the door were two pillars: on the left a half-human beaver holding a rose in one paw and a sickle in the other; on the right a woman with the head of an owl and wings wrapped around a child that held trustingly to one feathered pinion. Above the door itself was a symbol Shkai'ra had noticed again and again: a circle cut into halves by an S-shaped curve; one half was black, the other golden, and each half had a spot of the other's color in it.

A bored guard nodded as she entered. Even so, Shkai'ra touched the lucksprite at her belt as she walked into the smithy. Metalwork was powerful magic, involving the sacredness of weapons, and you could never be sure if ill luck was going to burst free of the mysteries and spirits chained in the metal. Even shamans felt it; Shkai'ra had long noticed the care they took to avoid cold iron.

Inside was a floor of gravel, and walls hung with a

variety of incomprehensible tools. A treadle-powered leather-and-wood bellows took up most of one side; the forge and anvils were in the center, and workbenches holding vises and a hand-powered lathe filled the other walls. The skylight let in ample light for work, but the glowing charcoal still gave the room a reddish, smoky cast. It was hot, with a smell of scorched metal, glowing stone, and heated wood, oil from the quenching bath and the dusty scent of dry gritty rock beneath her feet.

Maihu stood by the anvil, pounding on a hot iron shape. Sparks spattered on the long leather apron she wore. Holding up the piece of steel, she decided the final quenching could wait. It was just too difficult to get the temperature right without expert help. Her lips tightened. Those hands lay dead, or penned like cattle in a barn. Mostly, she had wheedled permission to come here to get away from those accusing eyes, working on some of the multifarious repairs they needed, that any large group would generate. It had not done any great harm to tell what she had told; the Kommanza would have torn it out with iron and twine from someone soon enough. And it was necessary to make her captor relax wariness enough for her to do what she planned.

Bitterly, she wondered how much that was a self-lie, to soothe her own spirit. Her plan was a forlorn hope, at best. Still, trader hardheadedness told her it would do scant good to get herself pushed back into the prisoner herd, or to excite enough suspicion to start the westerners working on her with knotted cords and heated metal. Pure luck, perhaps, that no one among the captives had let drop enough to arouse their captors' superstitious fury.

Or perhaps not. The plainsfolk did not know enough about her people to know what questions to ask, and under their ingrained suspiciousness they had less pure curiosity than Minztans. They made little idle chatter, and few of them understood enough of the forest tongue to follow whispers or grasp subtleties.

She laid aside the workpiece, turned, bowed. Shkai'ra perched cross-legged on a bench, hands on her knees and braids hanging to her waist. The great hood of her tigerskin coat jerked and a head popped out; black-furred, prick-eared, and yellow-eyed, the cat flowed out over her shoulder and down to her lap. He sat with his tail curled neatly around his feet and watched the Minztan unwinkingly.

"Come here," the Kommanza said. "You'd better get to know *Dh'ingun-Zhaukut-Morkratuk.*" Black-night-Demon-Stealthkiller, the name meant: a tom, leanly huge and scarred and sleek. Maihu extended a hand, halted at a warning hiss between bared teeth and laid-back ears.

"Friend, Dh'ingun," Shkai'ra said sharply in her own tongue, catching the beginnings of a lunge with a hand around the animal's neck. His temper was always uncertain, and not improved by a week in saddlebags or a sled. "Friend!" Reluctantly, the animal submitted to a quick, nervous pat. "He doesn't seem to like me, Chiefkin," Maihu said. She was surprised that the Kommanz chieftain had brought a pet along on a raid; the steppe-dwellers were not much given to sentimental gestures. Of course, she reminded herself, there was as much individual variation among them as among any other race.

"Cats are more honest than humans," Shkai'ra said. "You don't smell right to him, I think." Reaching out, she slicked fingers down Maihu's neck, then licked them. "Your sweat tastes different from a Kommanza's. And Dh'ingun must have been one of us in another life, he's so eager for battle and slaying and blood."

She gave a fond smile and scratched the beast under its chin. Dh'ingun slitted his eyes in pleasure and purred.

"Have . . . you any commands for me, Chiefkin?" Maihu asked uneasily.

Shkai'ra shrugged. "No." Wryly: "This expedition is over-officered: good Bannerleaders, and a clutch of experienced staff types. So far, nothing has befallen that needs my care. I saw to the horses, checked the wounded, and sent out scouts—or watched my officers do it. For the rest, all I can do is wander around looking fearless and noble as a Mek Kermak should."

She studied the smith. The Minztan was centimeters shorter than she; her head would barely reach Shkai'ra's chin. In build she was halfway between stocky and wiry, typical of her folk, taut and well muscled from her work and much running, hunting, and traveling. That prompted a thought.

"Squeeze my wrist," she said. "Harder. Hard as you can. Ahi-a, pounding iron's given you a good grip."

She produced a ball of imported rubber and began tossing it from hand to hand, squeezing hard: a habit from childhood. After a few minutes she continued: "But I'd still have thought some of these tools too heavy for you."

"My kinmate Dennai helped me with the heavier tasks, Chiefkin. He was a good smith, even if he lacked the finer touch. He was the one you killed when you captured me and Taimi."

"Pity about that," Shkai'ra said casually, regretting the loss of a skilled servant. Her folk made little of death in battle, that being the commonest and most honorable ending. "But he would try to match fighting skills with me. 'Don't try to outrun the horse or bite the tiger,' as we say."

Glancing around, she picked up a piece of work. It

was a ceramic plaque, a circle a little wider than her
fingers could span. The base was softly iridescent in
blue and green, and over it had been laid an intricate
pattern in silver and gold wire, soldered, with the intervening spaces filled with turquoise. The pattern reminded her of ... what? A snowflake? Stars? Or
sunlight through a raindrop?

She traced the lines with a finger, and wondered at
the pleasure it gave her. It was well and skillfully
wrought, to be sure, but it was useless and not in the
prairie style.

"This is ..." She hesitated, searching for the word.
In her own language she could have called it well-
made, or pleasing, but that was not what she was trying to say. And Kommanzanu had no word for beauty
in the abstract. "What is the word ... pretty?"

"Thank you, Chiefkin," Maihu replied. Anxiously,
she watched the ornament. It was one of her favorites
and had taken half a year to fashion. "You don't want
to break it up for the metal, do you?"

"Hmmmm? Oh, no, I'll keep it. No, you hang on
to it. Does the pattern mean anything?"

Maihu stared at her blankly. *How could a* Pattern
not mean something?

"Of course. Ah, of course, Chiefkin, everything has
meaning—otherwise it would break the Harmony of
the Circle."

Shkai'ra frowned and made the sign against magic,
but leaned forward with interest. "What *does* it signify,
then?"

"Why a vision-dream. One of us asked the Indweller
of the forest, and this came to him as he slept in the
woods. It shows how the Otherworld looks around here,
the lacing of the patterns making up the whole ..."

Shkai'ra struggled to follow the explanation, almost
meaningless in her people's terms. The words the

other woman was using were not familiar in the simplified trade-pidgin she spoke herself; that had a specialized vocabulary that did not include much in the way of religious or philosophical terms. And she had begun to suspect that her understanding of the words she did know was often twisted in some subtle way, that in a manner she could not quite grasp simple terms like "time" and "death" carried a different significance when she spoke them in this tongue. It was a disturbing thought and a new one.

"So . . ." she said at length. "Is that a dream of the spirits you worship, or a picture of the dreaming the spirits make?"

"Well . . . both and neither, Chiefkin," Maihu said in a baffled tone. The difficulty of explaining was a welcome distraction, but she did not want to arouse the murderously unstable Kommanz temper with suspicion that she was evading. Shkai'ra was silent for some minutes, stroking her cat.

Then she rose to prowl the confines of the smithy, occasionally stopping to touch some unfamiliar shape.

"Maihu," she said, producing some dried fruit from a pouch and tossing a piece to the Minztan before herself chewing on a tough sweet section of apple, "I'll be glad to see the last of this place."

Not as glad as we would be to see you go, the Minztan thought silently. She bent her attention on the Kommanza. The conversation disturbed her. There was an enforced intimacy to it that made her skin creep, and she sensed a probing intelligence more menacing than the straightforward brutality of most of the raiders.

Musing, Shkai'ra half-chanted in her own tongue, not suspecting the other could understand:

"Endless spaces under sky/Sea of Grass where falcons fly/Horse between thighs/And banners snap/Smell of the sod crushed/Under the hooves—

"Not," she continued, "that this hasn't been a profitable raid. Not much glory, but plenty of loot for small loss. *Mek'ame!* That is war the way I like it! But this land weighs on the soul."

"It is our land, and the spirits do not welcome you, Chiefkin," Maihu said, greatly daring.

Shkai'ra shrugged and touched her lucksprite; it was a little six-armed joss of Glitch, godlet of uncertainties, grinning under a half-coyote face and a red roach of hair.

"Don't seem to be able to *do* much about it. Our gods are stronger." Grinning, she added, "Another legend of ours: when Eh'mex the Godhammer struck down the cities of Darkness and ended the Before, the Ztrateke ahkomman left the earth to live in the Sun. And they left the earth for a legacy to us of the Zekz Kommanz their children. 'To you,' they said, 'we leave the world of humankind, and all that is in it— but only so much as you have the strength to *take*.' Or so run the Sayings of the Ancestors."

Maihu could not hide a wince of distaste. "Not to your liking?" Shkai'ra asked. "But your ways are strange to us.

"We've never gotten along well, your breed and mine. Apart from your being so tempting to attack, I mean. There's something about you that puts us on edge."

The phrase she used translated literally as "puts an itch in our saber hands."

"More than your being so witchy. I don't quite understand what it is."

"Perhaps envy, Chiefkin," Maihu said, surprising a giggle out of the Kommanza.

"There, see what I mean? It's as if we lived in different worlds. That didn't matter so much years ago, when there was less contact. Most of my folk don't care, they think things will just go on as they always have.

"I don't. I've listened to the old songs and stories and thought much about them. Why, a few generations ago the nearest Minztan steading was twice this distance from the grasslands. And very far back, when the Sky Blue Wolves of the High Steppe"—she paused to spit into the forge at the mention of the hereditary enemies of her people—"drove us eastward off the shortgrass plains, there weren't any Minztans within reach of the Red River country. A few came as traders after a month's journey."

She pulled the Minztan closer and caressed her absently, as she might have stroked a dog.

"The world is changing, and not for the better: more people, more trafficking between them. The cityfolk merchants come to us, and our cousins southward in Ihway; it seems that brings us wealth, but always we feel poorer."

Her eyes grew hooded. "The southrons press on us, and we bicker among ourselves; they say that in the far south the Wolves push into the desert country, burning the steadings of Mehk, and there are wars in the Great Valley . . . Things will change in the dealings between the forest and the steppe, within my lifetime. I'll be a high one in Stonefort before too long, and Stonefort stands high in the Komman of Grantor. To steer well, I'll need real knowledge of your folk.

"Maihu, that's why you're worth more to me than the wealth your work will bring, or the pleasure of a tumble now and then. By knowing *you*, I'll be better able to deal with your landsfolk, to understand how they think, how they're likely to react to what I do. For example, if more of you come to dwell in the near borderlands, it might be worthwhile to force regular tribute in goods and slaves, instead of raiding. We're not so many we can afford to fight on two fronts every year. And why shoot the cow if you can milk it?"

She felt the Minztan stiffen. "I wish you *could* understand us, Chiefkin," she said quietly. "It would change you."

"Or maybe the other way around," Shkai'ra answered, releasing her. "But think on this also: if I gain advantage, and become a mighty one, a favorite of mine could gain also . . . Perhaps as my agent among Minztans, although that would be years in the future. Then you'd have a place after the strength to work is gone, instead of being thrown out for the wolves. And there would be reason to keep your living kin around. Perhaps you could even earn your way back to a measure of freedom, in time. Think on it. I can tell you're a deep one, and used to foreseeing years ahead."

She squeezed the other's thigh, just short of painfully. "Don't tire yourself too much here. We're holding a feast tomorrow night, and you'll be serving there after the Sacrifice."

She called to the cat. It streaked to her and swarmed up her coat like a black shadowstreak, settling down in the hood with alert yellow eyes showing over the rim. Eh'rik waited for her outside, and so did Walks-with-Demons. That one was more still than was his habit, and he made no challenge, waiting silently. Dh'ingun stuck his head out of the hood and considered the shaman unwinkingly, then turned and hissed at the warmaster, producing a grunt of annoyance.

"Why do you keep that beast, Chiefkin? If it can't do something useful like catching rats, it could at least make a pair of gloves."

Shkai'ra reached backward to ruffle its ears. "Dh'ingun is a kinsoul of mine," she said. "Any more trouble?"

"Not since we chased off those two forest rats."

"Only two?"

"From the tracks, or so those who've hunted in the woods tell me. Probably just returning hunters or trappers, but I'd be more glad had we caught them."

"Ahi-a, as we thought; not likely that we could catch every fugitive when they've more woodslore than we. As it is, we lost the warhounds for no good purpose."

Eh'rik glanced uneasily at the carved pillars of the smithy. "The troopers swear the woods rats must have had spirit help to get away so clean."

"Sheepshit, they have more skill in running and hiding. Well, scant good that'll do them, being as unready as they are." She cocked an eyebrow at the shaman.

He shrugged, and skipped his fingers across the drum. "No great magic, yes, that's true," he said. "I would have felt that, from the World Beyond the World. But a small working wouldn't have caused much . . . rippling. Not Minztan witchcraft, it's sneaky and sly, hard to catch."

He wrapped his arms around himself and glanced sidelong. "Better to leave as soon as we may; the earth spirits are hostile here. Hungry, and strange."

Shkai'ra hawked and spat into the soot-tinged snow. "Aren't they always?" Kommanza believed themselves children of the Sun; their gods were sky powers, spirits of storm and fire, ever at war with the old dark ones of the soil. Her hand made the gesture against ill luck.

"If the westernmost steading of theirs proves this easy to pluck, we should be clear out on the grasslands before any great host comes up. And even a Minztan isn't crazy enough to come out onto the plains after us."

She put her hands in the small of her back and stretched, yawning. There were a few small clouds in the sky above, which otherwise was the pale blue of good steel. She sniffed at the air.

"Weather could turn," she mused. "Clear enough, but the air smells wet. Tricky." That brought thoughts of other matters. "Is the Sacrifice ready?"

"Ahi-a, yes," Eh'rik said. "One of the ponies we captured; the shaman says that's lucky enough."

The shaman nodded. "Goods taken in war are always pleasing. Though a charger might be better, or a human." His eyes flicked toward the metalworker's shed.

"No sense wasting a good war-horse," Shkai'ra said. Slightly shocked, Eh'rik turned his head.

"You'd not grudge the Mighty Ones their share!"

"No, no . . . particularly since many of our doughty, fearless warriors tremble at the thought of ghosts eating their souls while they sleep! But we've no need to make a Great Calling; this should be enough. Victory shows the gods favor us. Would they like us to come whining to them for help every time some zh'ulda sees a shadow?"

She bared her teeth at the shaman, who returned the smile with the same bright hatred.

"My part of the ceremony will be ready," he said.

"So will mine," she answered. "The Mek Kermak's-kin know the Mighty Ones, and their wants, spellsinger." Her palm caressed the eagle-head hilt of her saber. "We're alike; we also don't care to be angered . . ."

He gave the salute with the faintest trace of mockery as she and the warmaster moved off, their boots squeaking on the packed snow.

Inside the smithy Maihu clutched her hammer in a sudden dizziness of hope. It could only be Sasimi and Ewunnu; the Seeker's people would know, and follow. And if she could slow the Kommanza down, weaken them . . . For a moment she scarcely heard the crunching of gravel as the Eater slunk into her work-room. She darted erect and retreated toward the forge, frank terror on her face. Nor was it feigned. Bracing herself against the anvil, she faced her enemy.

He was clothed, this day, in sheepskin coat and cap, only the scars and drum marking him. At ten paces she could smell him, the cold stink heavy in the forge-warmed air, blue eyes hooded.

"Don't piddle yourself, Minztana," he said dryly, bending to examine her tools. Maihu swallowed, forced herself erect and her mind calm. Odd, how careful he was not to touch the iron; Adepts were like that too . . .

"I'm . . . under the Chiefkin's ward," she said. She used the Kommanzanu word; it actually meant that she was the commander's exclusive prey. "You can't touch me, wizard."

"Oh, I know, yes, well pleased she is with you. And I know her thoughts, and her plans, better than she thinks. A deep one, that Mek Kermak, with strange knowledge. But she doesn't . . . know all."

He looked her over, carefully. "Witchborn, you are. But not mage-strong; I could tell if you had the knowl-edge. Power is not gained without pain and trial, even the devil power your forest witches have."

"Then why do you want me dead?" she said. She could sense the Eater's killing-lust, more than his usual malevolence.

"You're alive, are you not so?" He laughed, and her spine crawled with a feeling that had little to do with her own peril. He sobered quickly, mercurial, the light of madness on his face. "I *smell* . . . a wind blows out of your future. You are a branching. I scent . . ." His eyes closed, and he muttered in his own language. "Curse the demon-dung tree-fog! If only I could see more clearly!"

He snapped back to alertness; suddenly he was close to her, his hands making grasping motions without conscious volition.

"I sense a fate in you, and no good one. Know this: one hint of witchcraft, and the Chiefkin's shield drops away. She commands, but I smell out witches. One slip, and you"—his face thrust forward—"are *mine*."

Maihu stared back, with a loathing so strong that it cast out fear. For long moments they stood, regarding each other, before the plains wizard turned and strode from the room. Shuddering, she relaxed.

It would have to be done carefully, very carefully.

7

The wheelbow spoke, hum of string, rattle of pulleys. The flat smack of steel driving into flesh sounded across the frozen river.

The Kommanza cursed. He had been riding with a shaft on the string, normal on a scouting mission like this. The deer had been a flash in the corner of his eye and his reaction instinctive. But there was thick undergrowth, reed and thicket, along the banks of the river he had been following. Beyond the forest was no longer pure stand of pine; there were groves of birch and the occasional aspen or ash or maple showing bare and skeletal against the snow-flecked green of the conifers. Cautiously, he examined the ice along the edge of the westward-flowing stream he had been tracing. Even when the deep water was frozen solid the edges might be rotten, laced with weakening stems. He tied his remount's string to an overhanging branch and led his mount up the low bank, shoving frozen bush aside and taking care not to risk his horse's feet.

There! he thought. Fresh blood on the snow, gouts of it, and a thick blood trail leading off. He had been certain that the arrow stuck just forward of the hind-quarter, and there were a couple of big arteries there. The arrowhead had been a narrow pile-shaped armor piercer, not the broad three-bladed hunting head designed to slice an animal's insides open, but even so the beast ought to bleed out fairly soon. The more so as it was running heedlessly, judging from the crushed bush: the fear-driven heart would quickly pump it dry. There would be little delay in his task—and he was supposed to comb the woodlands as well as the direct route to the west. Some fresh venison would be a welcome relief from jerky and hardtack. . . .

Scraping up some of the snow, he tasted a little of the blood, sweet and salt and still faintly warm. Decision was swift, and he swung back into the saddle. To follow the blood trail was no great matter. The scout came from a village near the forest edge and had often hunted the fringe of the woodlands: game for food and fur, Minztans for sport. At the thought he grinned with hatred. Witches, traffickers with the Zoweitz of the Dark, worshipers of Illah, the loathsome, cowardly and sly. Nothing was more pleasing to gods or humans than killing a woods rat. Still, campaigning against them on their own ground called for real skill. They could hide under cover you'd swear wouldn't conceal a rabbit, and they would track a ghost over naked rock.

He touched his scalp belt. In the end, though, to fight you they had to come out and *fight*.

All the while his eyes moved endlessly in well-trained wariness, scanning back and forth across the dusky avenues of the forest. Even the bright sunlight of midmorning cast little illumination here; scant fugitive gleams slanting down into a pale green gloom, crisp white snow crunching and creaking under hooves, ceaseless soft murmur of wind through branches. The scout relied on a lifetime's experience to alert him to the subliminal consciousness of movement, disturbance, the minute disruptions of the pattern that give a few seconds' warning of danger. The air lay on his skin like liquid, too cold to carry scent; sounds were muffled by the weight of helmet, padded lining, and coif.

He relied more on his horse for those senses. It needed little guidance from the reins looped over the high horn of the saddle: knees, voice, and balance were enough, a union of bodies born of years in the saddle, the art of a people who rode from the time they could walk. It was the mount's snort and forward flick of ears that alerted him to expect his quarry. The deer had halted in a small open glade, trapped by snow too deep for its weakened legs. The flight feathers of the arrow were sunk flush with the fawn-colored hide a handspan below the spine and just in front of the hind leg. He was amazed the beast had managed to run half a *kylick*. Blood still flowed, not spurting but in a steady trickle down the flank to the snow.

It was not worth risking damage to the delicate feathering of another arrow. He swung to the ground and began floundering forward through the drifts; the snow was deep but light, less packed here than under the forest canopy where little of the last fall had penetrated. The deer awaited him with the curious fatalism that wild things show before the predator, knowing their own deaths and accepting them. He was wary still, for deer had been known to deal shrewd hurts with hoof and antler, especially a young two-year male like this. But weakened by pain and bleeding, it stood passive. He twisted the head aside and cut its throat, catching the blood in his helmet and drinking it hot and delicious. That done, he made haste to drag the body back to the trees. It was important to gut it before it froze stiff, and that would not be long in this weather; also, the smell of blood might bring predators, timber wolves or perhaps even a tiger. In cold season hunger-rage wolves were a real menace even to an armed human, and a snowtiger was nothing for a single man to meet at any time. Working quickly, he ran a rope through the slit tendons of the hind legs, hoisted that over a convenient branch, and made the first stroke from throat through paunch to anus. The work was messy and foul-smelling but familiar and soon finished. He tied up the quartered carcass into a bundle in the hide, slung it over the saddle, and began to lead his mount back along the broken trail to the river.

And all the while, he was watched. By eyes that missed little, by nose and ears keener than any humanity had bred, by senses more subtle, by an awareness that knew itself. That mind did not think as a human might: it used no words, different images, and dwelt in a timeless Now that had only shadow-knowledge of the past and faint concept of a future. Yet it was no beast and could reason in its fashion, limited only by lack of a vocabulary to conceive abstraction. And it had a oneness with the land that no human could match. The smell of blood agitated it; only the instinct of stealth prevented moans of unease from breaking forth. There should be no killing, not here, not now. That was not the way memory said things should be. And the smell of the human was wrong. Where were the food and warmth? Where were its friends, where the feathers and dancing, music and gifts of sweet meat and fire? Strangeness plucked at its mind; to this one there was no barrier between the physical and the Otherworld, all were a single rush of sensation. Mixed drives of flight and aggression fought in intolerable confusion. Curiosity won out, and it followed after the man, drawing concealment around itself until it drifted as undetectable as a ghost.

The scout would not have noticed the tracks on horseback. Indeed, he had overrun them on the way in. On foot, chewing with relish on a slice of warm, raw liver, he had a different perspective. From the ground even slight irregularities threw betraying shadows, and also his horse was nervous. Not nervous enough to make him fear immediate danger, but enough to justify extra vigilance. What caught his attention was a row of depressions in the snow at right angles to his passage, very faint, for last night's snowfall had overlain them. He halted and stared, frowning. There was not enough detail to make out what sort of creature had made the tracks, and a trial showed that there was too little of a barrier between the layers of snow to brush off the top covering and find more data.

Yet it was not the trail of a game animal. His mind calculated angles and distances, added in the outline and size of the tracks. He ended with puzzlement. Not the right size for a human even on snowshoes, nor for aught that went on four feet. It would be well to seek further into this; the safety of this trail was his to say yea or nay, and he would not care to face the Chiefkin if he proved wrong. That meant following this trail, which meant dumping the meat for a space. Cursing again and calling on Glitch, godlet of fuckups, he lashed the venison into a tree beyond the reach of most scavengers and set out down the line of tracks.

He made only scant distance before suspecting that he was on a worn trace. Not a well-traveled one; the signs were faint and hard to detect in winter. But the marks were there to see on bark and bush, in the branches and the feel of the land; a path had been here, might still be in use, and the . . . whatever he was following had walked down it not two days past. He kept his bow ready, pausing first to scrub the blood from his short blond beard with a handful of snow.

Two *kylickz* brought him to the clearing. It was not large, perhaps half a bowshot around. Neither was it natural: a perfectly regular circle amid the sort of tall timber that showed rich soil by Minztan standards.

It was noon now, and the vertical light poured down pale yellow on the building that stood in the center. It was not small; three single-story cabins joined to make a U around a central court in the manner of the forest people. No smoke came from the chimney, and the windows were shuttered. The decoration on the walls was lavish even by woodland standards, but much was hidden where the snow had drifted up to the eaves. The drifts lay heavy against the door. That meant the clearing had not been visited lately, perhaps not since the first snowfall. Not in the last month for sure, he thought. It ought to be safe to approach.

Despite that thought, he made a wary circuit of the cabins before trying the entrance. What he saw added to the mystery. This was too elaborate for a hunter's shack, too small for a permanent dwelling even if anyone could have lived thus alone in unpeopled wilderness. And it was *old*, well built and well maintained but decades older than the new-founded village the Kommanz had sacked. Well, Minztans had hunted and traded over these borderlands for generations beyond number, more so than the steppe people this far from the open lands. But why had they gone to the trouble of rearing such a garth?

Wading through snow, he used his shield to dig a passageway to the door. The last part of it was difficult, needing a cutting deeper than his head, and the labor left him sweating and in no good humor when he reached the portals. Those were intricately carved, with flower symbols picked out in inlay work. The beauty was lost on him, but the stout panels' refusal to yield to the hooves of his horse when he reared the animal against them awoke rage. He unlimbered an ax from his saddlebow and went to work. The steady *thock-thock* echoed from the walls of the forest, and presently white splinters began to show. That gave him a vicious satisfaction, as if the wood were an enemy he could punish for the delay and trouble these accursed-of-Zaik tracks had forced on him. Soon he could reach within and use his knife to pull the bar out of its brackets. He entered with shield up and ax ready.

His shadow waited within the sheltering forest. So much meat within easy reach had tempted it to stay where the Kommanza had left the carcass of his kill, but it had satisfied itself with the discarded entrails and forced its steps on down the well-marked trail. It watched in growing distress as the man beat in the door. Sacredness was not a concept it could entertain, but seeing this place despoiled awoke revulsion. A thought was born, that there were two types of human: the ones to which it was accustomed, and this new breed, who smelled *wrong* and did things that were worse, were not what years of unchanging sameness had taught it.

The inside of the building was reassuringly musty; from the smell, he judged there had been few visitors, and none in the last month. Yet all was in order, furniture and bunk beds for a dozen, leather bedrolls, even the makings of a fire ready in the stove. The second room brought a yelp of delight: rat-proof bins full of grain, salt meat and nuts, dried fruit. A trapdoor revealed a cellar full of still more provisions. Whatever their reason, the Minztans had done the Stonefort warband a great service by leaving so much provender right on the path of their retreat. It would be a powerful aid, enough to swing the decision around to taking this route. To have supplies waiting here without taking up space on the sleds would leave that much more room for loot.

The third room also held boxes and chests. Confidently, he threw open a lid. What he saw within sent him back with a groan of dismay, clutching at his amulets. Carved wands, masks and feathered headdresses, rune-graven stools . . .

"Witchcraft, witchcraft," he moaned.

The sweat burst out on his face despite the cold; he could feel it trickling down his flanks. Breath pumped, pupils went wide, almost he turned and ran from the gruesome sight.

Slowly, a measure of calm returned. No blasting spell withered him, and strength returned to his shaking limbs. Carefully he used his ax to close the lid of the chest and backed into the first chamber, calling on the Mighty Ones by the secret names the shaman had told him at his adulthood ordeal. He had always made the sacrifices the law prescribed and never broken discipline or turned his back in a fight. Surely the gods would protect him.

In fact . . . yes, merest chance had brought him here, sheer luck, and there was often the will of a god or spirit in luck. Perhaps he was chosen to find this spot of foul spell-wreaking so that it might be cleansed. Should he set the fire himself? No, it would be better to let the Chiefkin decide. The Mek Kermaks were descended of the gods themselves and knew how deal with such matters.

Of course, there could be no question of remaining here for the night as he had planned. That thought set him shuddering anew. Best to head back at once. He had gone far enough west to know where the river emerged into territory he had hunted over before, and there would be no difficulty in guiding the main party through to the steppe. Pushing his remounts, he could be back in the village in a few days, and in the meantime his hide sleeping bag under the clean stars would do.

Swinging back into the saddle, he held to a steady pace as he rode down his backtrail. He sternly suppressed an impulse to gallop, but the sense of menace was so strong that he made no check on his cache of venison; the wolves could have it for all he cared, so long as he put distance between himself and the spellhut. Once back on the pack snow of the river he heeled his mount into a canter.

The haste saved his life. The watcher trailed back from the cabin, uncertainty growing into rage. Yet this was the hungry season and the venison was tempting; when the man passed under the cache the thought of its passing beyond the watcher's reach almost triggered attack. When he left and returned to the river it was enough like withdrawal to damp the sense of territory violation and take the edge off killing anger. The smell of meat was rank and sweet, irresistible. It settled down to feed.

Snow was falling, soft and thick and straight. Huge puffy flakes spilled down out of the darkening sky, batting at faces like kitten paws; sound was muffled, until the hiss of ski and crunch of poles spiking down into the deeper layers sounded hushed and remote through the cold dampness of the air. None of the Minztans minded much; shadows flitting between the trees, they stroked tirelessly onward with the smooth sustaining rhythmic stride of hunters. There was a comfort to the silent closeness of the snow, and a peace.

The man the others called Leafturn speeded his pace, until he drew level with Narritanni.

"Old Bone Place ahead," he said, matching breath to movement.

The commander nodded, and signaled. Soon the first travelers broke through a narrow screen of underbrush into a clearing perhaps a thousand meters broad, traced with lines of mound and wall too regular to be natural. Normally they would have avoided the ancient buildings, but there was need and they had an Enlightened One with them. Besides, these ruins had been sparingly mined for some time; their folk had fewer taboos about such workings than most, since there had been little of the lingering death hereabouts. That was natural enough. These woods had had no targets worth a missile, and most of the real fighting had been beyond the atmosphere. Still, the dwellers here had found some way to die; it had been easy, that year when nine-tenths of humanity had fallen. It might have been hunger, in a world turned night-black and icy, or the flaying sunlight that followed when the clouds lifted. Or the diseases that had scythed through famine-weakened populations; some of those had been gene-tailored to lie dormant for generations as spores in tainted ground. Or they might have been overrun by starveling refugees from the south, hungry enough to kill for a few cans or the meat on the villagers' bones.

Three millennia had not been enough to soften the memories of terror; the Minztans were uneasy as they settled in to camp, unrolling their sleeping bags and kindling small fires in sheltered corners and nooks. Their own ancestors had suffered less than most; they had been smallholding farmers and craftsfolk by choice, reviving old skills that had stood them in good stead, and remoteness had sheltered them from the worst of the chaos that followed the death of the cities. Even they had been surprised at the degree of their dependence on the urban-industrial civilization they despised, but enough had survived to form the nucleus of a new people, a core for refugees and the last survivors of the tribal folk to form around.

The Adept found a corner that should be sheltered from any wind, dug a clear space, spread a pelt, and watched with calm approval as Narritanni oversaw the band. No fire was kindled where it could be seen from any distance, and careful watch was posted; he was glad to see that his folk were not placing undue reliance on his skills. That would be a dangerous crutch. Narritanni slid up to Leafturn's resting place, kicked his boots out of the ski loops, and braced the skis upright on the poles. One of the volunteers brought them both wooden bowls of oatmeal laced with maple sugar, dried fruit, and nuts. They pulled horn spoons from their belt pouches and ate with the silent intensity of those who had worked long and hard in bitter cold. The Minztan commander threw back the hood of his winter jacket and turned his face to the sky.

"My thanks," he said, with the flakes catching on his cropped yellow beard. "I was surprised you suggested this place; I thought the Old Ones' makings were the death of magic. All the iron."

The Adept scrubbed out his bowl with snow, filled it again, and leaned it near their fire to melt. "The snow's taking care of itself," he said easily. "It just needed a little push. Plenty of wet in the air, wind from the east . . . snow weather for the next week, I should think."

Narritanni drew his sword and considered the edge. It was a double-bladed weapon, as long as his leg from mid-thigh to foot; the guard was a steel strip with a ring welded on. After a moment he decided against honing. It would never do to oversharpen; you could thread the edge or wear past the strip of hard steel welded onto the core. He took out two small flasks and began to coat the blade with a dull-colored liquid from one.

The Adept continued, "As for the iron . . ." He spread his hands and closed his eyes for a moment. "Less trouble than you might think; most of this place was plain brick or wood, not steel-rod-in-stone. It would be a problem if I had to do anything active, but a passive watching is all I need. The Eater, now, he'll be handicapped; anything he does will go against the grain. I doubt he could touch us here."

Narritanni smiled; that was good to know. Also that the Wise Man was intelligent as well. The two talents did not necessarily go together.

Leafturn sensed his thought. "Some of my . . . colleagues make too much of the Mysteries," he said. "We're no more immune to self-importance than most humans." He chuckled. The war leader noticed again how the ageless face seemed younger when it laughed. Odd, because that showed the fine network of lines that grooved it, through the roughened woodsrunner texture of the skin.

"For that matter," the Adept went on, "the worldheart is *made* of iron."

He smiled at the other's surprise. "Not a useful piece of knowledge, but we can . . . feel the influence. It shields the earth from the *things-beyond*, the dwellers in the Dark Between, and it's not strong enough to hamper the Wreaking." He glanced around. "And here, it's the Pattern that hinders."

"I thought Wreaking moved with the Harmony," Narritanni answered. He himself knew little of such matters, less even than the average uninitiate, since he had spent so much time among outlanders. It was rare for an Adept to say so much, and he did not intend to lose the opportunity for knowledge.

"Yes, but ..." The Adept paused, musing. "It's a matter of dispute, whether the world was different then, or the folk." His hands moved in circles. "We perceive the world, and our seeing shapes it. The Old Way was against all magic—they wouldn't have built buildings that were cages of cold iron if it wasn't!—and the ... world-seeing sank into everything they made. I can feel it here, faint, still locked into the patterns of their makings. Crumble the stone, reshape the iron, and the Pattern becomes ours; wind and weather and rain will do it, more slowly. Which shows how alien the Old Ones were to the Harmony of all that lives. ..."

A companionable silence followed, until Narritanni, less comfortable without words, spoke.

"So, what can we await from the Eater, once we're closer?"

"Not much," Leafturn said. "Nor the Kommanza from me, with him there. He's likely to be more skilled in war-wreaking and such vileness, but the Otherworld here will work for me, so—" The Adept's words cut off like a knife.

Alarmed, Narritanni watched his pupils flare, then shrink to pinpoints. In a single smooth movement Leafturn came erect, wheeled to face the west, and stood tree-still. At last he shook himself, strode to the nearest cookfire, and fetched back another bowl of porridge and a mug of sweetened herb tea.

He ate quickly. "I'll not be staying here in camp this night," he said.

"What—what happened?" Narritanni asked. It would be very bad for morale if the Adept began acting strangely ... and even on short acquaintance he was sure that *this* Adept did not start at shadows.

"I don't know," the Adept answered.

Already, the friendly fellow traveler was changing

into something remote, ungraspable. Narritanni felt the Adept's withdrawal from matters physical, like an adult who leaves the games of children when serious business calls.

"Something . . . stirred. Something monstrous, and I was so clever I put myself in the one spot for a month's travel where I could not See clearly. I'll be walking the woods tonight; the body needs fuel, when you push beyond the natural limits. Nothing for nothing." And he was gone.

His second joined Narritanni by the fire. "What's bothering him?" she asked as she settled in by the flickering light. "I saw him going by as if the Bent One was on his trail, then he . . . faded."

He shrugged. "Something about a threat. Circle give thanks I'm a practical man and no more Harmonious than most; it makes for fewer worries. No trouble; we're well outside the line of the Kommanz scout screen, and I doubt he'd be in much danger even if we weren't."

"No change in plan?"

"No. We need more information on their route and strength before we do detailed contingency calculations."

She was silent for a moment. "Thought you might be interested in this," she said.

He took the object she offered: it was a beautifully-made spearhead of glass, pressure-flaked and notched at the base for binding into a spearshaft. The glass itself was unfamiliar, green and very clear. Fragments of binding showed around the notches, a peculiar cord like nothing he had ever seen before, not woven at all. Some Minztans used stone points; they were cheaper than iron and required less care. More of their cousins among the wandering hunting tribes of the north did so. Neither could have made this; they ground and polished stone tools rather than flaking them, and the style was wrong.

"It was in the heart of a dead tree some of the volunteers broke up for firewood," she said. "Stone-maple—an old stump, growing out of the ruins.

"Not of the Old Times," he said; they would have used metal, long since rusted away—or reforged, even if it were of the peculiar steel that did not rust.

"No, but I think that's Ancient glass," she said.

Narritanni shivered slightly, turning it over in his hands. *Plastic*, the bindings must be. Perhaps the spearhead was made by some of the first ancestors of the Minztan folk . . . *How long?* he wondered. Time enough for the Ancients to vanish out of the memories of peoples less past-bound than his; time enough to redevelop the art of flaking stone in a world where metal was scarce, but where Ancient glass and plastic could still be salvaged. Then to be discarded, for a great tree to grow around it, and die, and wait un-counted years to be found. He shivered again, more deeply. How many peoples had washed over this bor-derland? He turned the blade again, firelight catching glints off it. Three tens of centuries . . .

He yawned deliberately and slipped into his bag. "Wake me at third watch."

8

It was after sunset when the Kommanza gathered in the largest kinhall. Most heat and light came from the cunning Minztan stoves and lanterns, but a log-fed blaze crackled and boomed under a center-set smokehood. That fire cast unrestful shadows on the ranked figures around the walls, gleaming off polished silver and fine fabric; tonight they came dressed in the best they had brought along, and the pick of the loot. Even the poorest had a gilt armlet or string of colored beads; the wealthier were gaudy with plaited head-bands, embroidered blouse-tunics, belts and boots of tooled and studded leather, massive necklaces of silver and turquoise. Every Kommanza was there to garner a share of the luck and holiness; only the posted sentries and unfledged youngsters brought along to do squire service were absent.

More silent than was their wont, the Stonefort war-band waited. They were unarmed, not even carrying the belt knives that were as much tool as weapon; to bring iron would displease the Mighty Ones. This was a stark people, who saw their gods in their own image:

quick to anger, implacable in revenge, jealous of privilege. Gods greedy for sacrifice, demanding fear and awe rather than love.

Around the circle of their ranks the shaman danced. He was naked, save for headdress, loincloth, and the rattles strapped to wrists and ankles. Bright paint daubed patterns over his body; the drum tapped patterns under the sound of a bullroarer that he whirled around his head. At the last, he took a bowl from the hands of his unwilling and temporary acolyte and passed it to each of the warriors; the herbs were the jealously guarded secret of his guild, prepared in solitude, tasting harsh and burned. The dregs were thrown on the fire, and a hush of expectation settled over the throng.

Shkai'ra could hear the harsh rustle of their breath as she entered the hall, and the sound of the shaman's rattles and low chanting: *Ahea-hea-he-he-he* . . . Pausing at the gate, she shrugged out of her robe and stood naked save for her headband. A chant started as she paced by, low-toned, in a dialect so archaic that only one trained could have given the true meaning. Behind her came the three closest to her in rank; they led a horse between them. It was a shaggy little forest pony, not one of their tall rawboned steppe-chargers, and its eyes were already glassy with the drugs that ensured no ill-omened struggle would occur. This was no great sacrifice such as folk made on the prairie at the four Year Turnings. Then, each of the gods got the offering most pleasing: sheep for Jaiwun, hounds for Zailo, horses for Baiwun. Zaik Godlord was last and greatest, Begetter of Victories, and for that one only humans were enough. Here the pony would do for all, and they would join in the rites pleasing to the whole kinfast of the Sundwellers.

Across her palms Shkai'ra bore a spear. It was made

to a pattern that had been sacred since memory faded
into legend: a two-meter length of hardwood dark with
age, tipped by a narrow steel head graven with symbols of power. The original of that weapon had been
a bayonet lashed to a pole; lives without number it
had drunk, and through her hands she could feel the
numinous awe of the thing, an aura of blood and fear
and godhood. Now she was priest and Chief in one,
and the Carrying was on her. At the fire's edge she
swept the spear through an intricate pattern and thrust
it upward. The chant rose to a shout and ceased, as
if cut off with a knife, but from somewhere she could
feel the straining tension of her followers' fear and
adoration and hopelessness.

Aloud she shouted, *"Ztrateke ahkomman!"*

The rolling voices of the warband answered: *"Gods
of Sky, of Storm, of War!"*

The ceremony continued in a rhythmic pattern of
statement and response.

"Ward the folk! From the Zoweitz of the Dark, Zaik
Godlord deliver us!"

The first of the praise-names answered: *"You of
Might! Victorious!"*

Zaik, remote and terrible, god of warriors and chief-
tains, overlord of the battlefield and winnower of the
slain. All would go and face that One to be judged
before their next life.

"Baiwun Thunderer! Seek out the foe!"

"You of Terror! Avenger!" That came raggedly. Of
all things, lightning was the most terrible to these
dwellers on the empty plains. The heavenfire sought
out oathbreakers, hated of the Avenger of Honor; likewise the clean flame was a barrier to all evil magic
and creatures of the dark.

"Zailo Unseen!" Shkai'ra's body was sweat-slick and
gleaming in the firelight, eyes dilated and staring sight-

less at a vision beyond the rafters. "From sickness, from drought, from feud and kinstrife protect!"

"*You of Earth! Shield! Protector!*" Not the god most dear to these wild and reckless youngsters, mostly still single, but worthy of respect still.

"Jaiwun Allmate! Send cattle, send grain, send children! Give pleasure, keep holy the kinfast bond!"

"*You of Blood! Fruitful!*"

Every Kommanza brought a booted heel crashing down and clapped clenched fists together. Fear struggled with awe on every face, for by their beliefs now the Mighty Ones *came*. Only freeborn Kommanza of warrior age could witness these rites, and only the god-begotten ofzarz, the Chiefkin, could lead them. All through the Zekz Kommanza, the Six Realms, this ritual held. From distant Kai-Gara under the Westwall range, through Paizrav, Rh'eginz, Maintab, their own Grantor down to southerly Ihway, it was the same, cementing the world of humans with the World Beyond the World.

All watched anxiously. The slightest misstep could signal the worst of luck, enemy attack, drought, sickness, hostile spirits breaking free. But tonight nothing went amiss. Far otherwise. Shkai'ra threw back her head and sought.

You Above, she prayed silently. *Take what I offer. Blood and slaying, cunning and craft and powerhunger, all these are pleasing to You. Sweet incense rising to the Sun. All these I bring to You, whose blood is mine. Give me then what I desire: protection to these my people, to me victory and undying fame!*

Then suddenly PAIN. The pain lasted forever, and less time than she could grasp.

COLD.

There had never been warmth. She was blind in a universe of torment, yet she could perceive as never before, raw data pouring through a nervous system never designed for such overload: *highhigh-earth-curves-energyflowsthroughairiseepastfuturebranching-maybemaynotselfspreadearthdeathskydarkness-sunstarscallingtouchingdownintohazywet* . . .

For a moment she saw herself from an impossible perspective: a long blurred worm of potentials, possibilities, narrowing from the future/past to a single hard definite *now* that was the fixing gaze of the creature humans had called a god. And she felt with emotions too vast and wild for human nerves; amusement, need, pleasure, they were the faintest and most misleading analogues.

She felt decision.

And was herself; boards beneath her feet, smooth wood in her hands, the bent neck of the Sacrifice before her. Impossible memories fled from consciousness more swiftly than the mists of dream.

In a corner Walks-with-Demons stood, mind unshielded, arms and legs making a tau-cross that barred the place of sacredness from spirit presences. Almost, he screamed aloud at the sudden wrenching torment, worse than any he had known in the shattering ordeals of his training. Only that training kept him erect. He knew what this meant, knew from old legend among his kind what this presence was. Without names such as the common ruck used, for names were human, and this . . . Was. He willed unbeing on himself, far from that single Eye.

Across forty kilometers that was no distance at all the Wise Man sprang erect at the tearing of the Veil. The shock ran through world and Otherworld, as a thing alien to both reached downward, vastness narrowing to a point finer than a hair, stretching from a blazing energy that was cold with a coldness that made this winter's night like a crackling fire. Time and possibility twisted, stirred, then settled back as the Presence withdrew. Knowledge faded from his mind, but not wholly. Vaguely, faintly, he could sense the turning of the earthlines, and laughter. A hunger and cruelty vaster than worlds.

"Steel Spirit, Horse Spirit," Shkai'ra chanted. "Bring our offering to the Mighty Ones."

Turning, she leveled the spear and thrust hard and swift, with a *huff!* of expelled air. The helpers turned the sacrifice's neck, and the bright steel went in to withdraw red-black. The shoulders of the blade severed jugular and windpipe as she twisted; the drugged animal gave a single heave before sinking to its knees. Blood spurted into a bowl of soapstone, red and steaming. Ritually she touched the bloody steel to brow, breasts, and loins. Then the horse was butchered: the severed head would be impaled on the spear to preside over the feast to come, the entrails left out for the scavenging beasts that were the Eyes of Zaik, the flesh roasted and eaten.

Handing over the spear, she took the bowl and poured down a long salty-pungent draft. Raising it on high she shouted:

"See the sacrifice! O you who will in the end devour the world, you have given us victory! So shall we put our boots on the necks of all the peoples!"

The carved soapstone vessel passed from hand to hand as each dipped a finger to mark his forehead and touched lips to the cooling redness. With that, the formal part of the ceremony was over. Now they would be glad to show their thankfulness to their gods.

The Stonefort warriors sprawled about as the new slaves came in bearing smoking platters. There was food in plenty, albeit less wheat bread and beef than they would have liked. But there were roast pigs hacked into savory heaps, venison, bear meat, eggs, sausage heavy with garlic and herbs, milk, cheese, blood puddings, onions, broth, great loaves of fresh ryebread, potatoes and turnips and sauerkraut and dried fruit and nuts. And drink-barrels of honey-mead and good Minztan whiskey, a few kegs of southland wine, even some of their own fiery-clear Kommanz lifewater. Joyous, the clamor lifted to the rafters. This was a time to let down the barriers a warrior normally had to maintain, when words could be spoken that otherwise would end in deathfeud. Talk, song, japes were swapped back and forth; here two rose for a friendly wrestle; there half a dozen were playing *bannak*, the knife game, taking turns to see who could stab a blade most rapidly between the spread fingers of one hand. These were youngsters, on their first warfaring in the outlands; they meant to make the most of it.

A would-be songsmith stood before the company could grow too fuddled to listen:

> "Bright as sunlight our banners flew,
> Now black and crusted with battle-dew
> Sun-born Chieftain   Wisely leads us
> The cunning killer   To plunder flies
> Scalps of foefolk   Clatter hard-frozen—"

Propped on one elbow at the head of the hall, Shkai'ra threw a string of gold southland city-made coins to the praise-singer, an extravagance that brought a yen of acclaim from the band. It was well to have a name for being an open-handed giver as well as lucky and skillful; that was expected of a chief. From time to time one warrior or another would stand to praise the deeds of a friend or lover; to each she gave their due, in words and gifts. It was important to gauge the cries that followed; what was for the praised one, and what for the reward. Too little or too much could arouse murderous jealousy, start feuds or leave resentment festering against her. In fact . . . yes, suddenly the importance of getting the band back quickly seemed clearer.

Better to cut cross-country if it was possible at all; that conviction formed clearly in her mind. The fighting had been too easy; there was too much pent-up bloodlust still swirling around.

Maihu watched the sacrifice through a hole in the carvings. The sight was disgusting. Her people made no animal offerings. For a moment, unwillingly, she resonated with the massed emotion that welled out at her, then she turned with a shudder as she felt a touch of rage and hunger that seemed almost inhuman. No spirit within the Circle would accept blood offerings; she supposed that the Kommanz gods must be of the outer realm, the *saaitisfor* beyond the mantle of life that surrounded the earth. Or . . . what had that philosopher in Raddock, in the southland, said? That if horses had gods, they would give them hooves and manes? Either the Ztrateke ahkomman had made their worshipers in their own image, or was it the other way around? Shocked, she put the impiety out of her mind: all the Otherworld was part of the Harmony, even the darker side. Only conscious will could put a creature outside that unity.

She turned to her work. There was an endless line of Minztans swinging through from the kitchen, and she had been put in charge of a section of them. A mark of favor, she thought wryly, and saw the scowls and mutterings many aimed at her. That hurt. *But what can I do?* she thought. Now there was hope for those the Kommanza would leave behind. Surely the hunters had made Garnetseat by now. The rescue party would come, and if only she could leave word for them there would be hope for all her people. She did not expect outright attack on the village while the westerners held it. That would be an invitation to another disastrous defeat.

For a moment, red fantasies of victory and revenge ran through her mind, to be rejected with a shudder. Long ago, her ancestors had been pacifists. They had shed that, along with much other foolishness, those pampered children of machines and cities and crowds, those of them that lived through the terrible years and the thousand years it took the wounded earth to heal. Their descendants were tougher, far less sentimental; in a sense, they had become in truth what their forebears had played at being. But much of the original philosophy survived. Maihu would do what was necessary, but she vowed to herself that even now she would do it with regret and without pleasure. Small victory, to fight and overcome if you became what you battled.

As to what would happen in the woods, that would depend on her, on how much she could lull the suspicions of her captor, and what advantage could be taken of that. She would have to be cautious. The Kommanza was cunning and wary, and came of a people skilled in deception.

The noise within the hall rose as the food was finished and the serious drinking began; dice came out, couples and groups fell to loveplay with each other or the servants, and the weaker heads were rolled into furs and stowed in the corners. Maihu took a deep breath, hefted a tray with a jug, and walked into the room.

Shkai'ra had been drinking lightly. *Just enough,* she thought, sipping at her wooden bowl of juniper-scented beer. *I'd not want to booze myself into a stupor tonight.* Sighing with contentment, she lit a pipe of dreamweed and drew the acrid smoke deep into her lungs. That was better for a night like this; it enhanced the senses instead of dulling them, made her aware of every hair pressing against the body she had not bothered to clothe again, of fire-warmed air moving over her skin, the rustle and mutter of her followers, crackle of hearthfire, smells of smoke and meat, sweat and blood and spilled beer. It was just as well the weed was so expensive, she mused: otherwise folk would spend half their time on it. There wasn't even a hangover.

That struck her as somehow very funny. She was giggling helplessly when Maihu passed by. For a moment she was content to watch the sway of Maihu's body as she dodged grasping hands; tonight she was wearing a long shirt, southland silk worked in Minztan animal patterns.

"Hoi, what've you got there?" Shkai'ra called over the uproar.

"Wine, Chiefkin," Maihu replied, sinking down beside her.

The Kommanza passed her the pipe. Maihu hesitated. Her folk used dreamweed only on holy days, to bring spirit visions. *Better to take it,* she decided. Disobedience would undo her work, and the weed would help her relax and do what was needful. She puffed, and cooled her throat with some of the iced drink: white grape wine, a rare luxury here in the northlands. Soon she felt the floating, detached languor: fear turned into a faintly pleasurable sadness, weariness and disgust became things outside herself.

They lay for a few minutes in silence, passing the drug back and forth. "You've been useful," Shkai'ra said at last, her voice a soft purr. "Your landsfolk seem to take it ill, though. D'you need a guard?"

"Oh, no," Maihu replied dreamily, dropping the

honorific "Chiefkin" unnoticed. "My people would never *hurt* one of their own. They just don't . . . understand."

"Indeed," the other chuckled. "But they understand who's stronger, well enough."

"Chiefkin, what about Taimi?"

"Put aside," Shkai'ra replied absently. "Never say I don't keep an oath, even to a slave. Besides, he'll need some rest before he's ready for me to take again."

She rolled over on her side, and Maihu followed her eyes, to where Eh'rik was struggling with a young Minztan. Thoroughly drunk, he was having trouble about it despite the bear strength that showed in cable-thick muscle running over his shoulders. The forester was a few years short of twenty, lithe and agile and desperate, the harder to grasp since her skin was wet-slick with spilled mead and sweat. Shkai'ra watched with dreamy interest; the villager was putting up a good fight for one untrained. And the warmaster was barely able to focus; he kept losing his grip and falling over. She giggled again at the comic sight. At last he got her bent over a low bench with one huge hand locked on the back of her neck, mounted, entered, and began thrusting heavily. The first sharp cries of pain gave way to sobs trickling harshly through clenched teeth and muffled by furs.

"He'd need even more if I let Eh'rik at him. The warmaster has a rough way about him, and no patience at all."

Maihu sighed and rolled onto her back, floating now. The sight had merely deepened her melancholy. Shkai'ra pulled off the Minztan's shirt and touched a bruise lightly where it lay yellow-brown on her skin.

"Does that hurt?" she asked.

"Yes," Maihu answered, closing her eyes. "Yes, a little."

"Tell me if anything I do hurts too much. I've no wish to give you pain tonight."

Puzzled, Maihu looked up, expecting mockery. She met a gray gaze cool with a predator's innocence in the narrow, hawk-handsome young face. And noticed how, bathed, the westerner smelled of fresh linen, smoke, clean sweat and beer and hard female flesh. With a sigh she closed her eyes again and put her arms around the other's neck. "As you will," she said. Their lips met, and their tongues. Drifting away, she dreamed herself into the past, into a night with a kinmate months ago.

Slowly, the hours passed. Neither was bothered by onlookers: Minztans had little sense of privacy, the Kommanza none at all. Much later, Shkai'ra rolled away.

"Enough, for a while," she said, and lay quietly as her pulse slowed. Then she yawned hugely, stretched, and raised herself on one elbow, looking down on the Minztan with an unreadable expression. The room was darker now, and quieter; most of the celebrants were asleep.

"You did too, that time, didn't you?" she said.

Maihu sighed wordlessly and rolled on her side, curling up and nuzzling her face into the pile of furs. The drug had helped.

"Well," the Kommanza continued, leopard-sleepy and content. "You weren't hurting anyone but yourself by holding back. It's pleasant, but I don't set any great store by it."

She looked over to where the warmaster lay snoring. There was blood on his thighs. "That way you get pleasure for the count of ten, after as much work as roping and branding a calf . . . well enough every now and then, but . . ."

Shkai'ra touched the Minztan on the cheek. "Maihu,

you've striven to make yourself valuable to me. Take advantage of it. You should get used to asking me for things."

Maihu struggled to think. It was difficult, with wine and dreamweed and afterglow surging slowly in her blood, urging her toward sleep. Still, this was the opportunity she had striven for, so . . .

"Well . . . if I could have some of my things, when you take us away?"

"Your tools? They'll go with you in any case."

"No, I mean things of my own . . . like that ornament you said I could keep, yesterday, and my books and . . . well, other things, that could remind me of home." That would sound thin to a Minztan's ears, but she hoped it would pass muster to someone unfamiliar with her people.

"Well enough, as long as you don't take too much weight, or witch-gear; I'll check. See, that wasn't hard, was it? Keep on the better side of me, and your life might be less bad than you await."

She nodded off toward sleep. "Work tomorrow," she said. "The scout should be back from the west. It'll be good if we can cut cross-country. The trade trail winds to keep to the watershed. Yes, best if we can head straight for home, down that frozen river."

Maihu stiffened. It blazed in her: that would be right past the Place of Summoning! Hope, hope beyond calculation; not only the news relayed to Garnetseat far faster than the Kommanza thought, not only the Seeker's band there ready to speed in pursuit, but this promise of aid from the Circle itself. Help that would wipe out the advantage of discipline and warskill that made rescue uncertain. . . .

Even on the edge of sleep, Shkai'ra had noticed. Maihu moved to still the curiosity. The Kommanza laughed as small rough hands stroked insistently down over her breasts and belly and thighs.

"All right," she chuckled sleepily, coming to all fours. "No, roll over . . . legs up under my arms . . ." They were both tired. A half hour later, the Kommanza continued:

" . . . and now tell me the rest of that story, the one about the beavers who adopted the child they found crying by the stream."

Shkai'ra settled warm under the bearskin, falling asleep to the murmur, to dream of kindly unhuman faces and a baby playing unafraid in sparkling sunlit waters. But Maihu lay awake for minutes after, listening to the soft regular breathing in her ear. Her mind was on tales more darksome, of a certain tune learned at her Initiation, and the uses of it.

Narritanni reflected bitterly that there was a great deal of difference between drawing lines on a map and deploying fighters on real ground. The lines looked so solid, so real, that you could forget that they were made up of individuals, each isolated by tens of meters of empty ground. That *they* could not soar like eagles over the terrain. And the lines could interpenetrate. That had been how his advancing ranks had run into the Kommanz screen. Even with the speed they'd made he had not expected the enemy to still be in the village. They must think they had all the time since the Beginning, to be dawdling so! Of course, he reflected, on most previous raids they would have been quite right.

Luckily they had heard the scoutscreen coming long before the riders had a chance to detect them. No mistaking the crashing, clattering passage of an armored steppe warrior through the forest, nor the precisely spaced whistle signals. By the time the Kommanza had ridden into view all six of the Minztans had hidden, the Garnetseat villagers nearby as invisible as his own rangers. And so they might have stayed, slipping through the outer links of the Kommanz mesh, if one of the volunteers had not let eagerness overwhelm a rudimentary sense of discipline. The man had stepped out from cover and shot with a reaction too swift for his companions to check.

The mounted warrior saw the motion from the corner of her eye. A frantic heave threw her down beside her horse on the side away from the attacker, hanging with one heel over the pommel. It was too slow to escape a hit, but the bolt struck glancingly on the curved surface of her shoulder guard. It clanged as the hard surface of the armor shed the iron head, and the bolt skittered away among the trees. But the motion was so violent that the whistle dropped from the rider's mouth.

What followed had a dreamlike slowness that reduced blinding speed to a nightmare crawl in the eyes of the helpless onlookers. In a single wrenching motion the warrior heaved herself back into the saddle. The horse waited only long enough to feel foot touch stirrup before it charged the Minztan archer. The Kommanza did not even bother to strike. The tall steppe charger knocked him down and trampled; Narritanni distinctly heard bones snap, saw blood spurt under the slamming hooves. Distantly, it occurred to him that once again his people had been betrayed by their reflexes: here, not to harm an animal without dire need. The horse was as deadly an opponent as the woman, and together their might was greater than simple addition would make it. But no one had thought to shoot the mount *first*. Not even the leader; he cursed himself bitterly for the lapse.

Two of the volunteer's fellows had risen from the snow to aid him: too late, and now the curved plains sword was out, swinging up and down with dreadful skill, cutting right and left. One of the Minztans dropped her spear and flopped, keening and clutching at a wrist three-quarters severed. Her life poured out on the snow. The other staggered back with a flap of face hanging down his neck and showing a red-and-white grin. The westerner followed, stabbing.

Alone against the three villagers, she would have won in scarce threescore heartbeats. But Narritanni and two of his rangers were there, and they were drilled fighters used to working in groups, skillful enough to help and not hinder each other. Two figures rose out of the bushes, ghostly in their patterned off-white camouflage smocks. One swung a hamstringing blow at the hocks of the war-horse, dodging the kick that might have spattered his brains. The other sent the spur of her billhook under the Kommanza's armpit, braced her feet, heaved. Unbalanced by the movement of her mount, the warrior fell with a jarring thud. The horse shrieked, high and terrible.

But the westerner was still quick and deadly dangerous. Rolling, she avoided the two-handed downsweep of the billhook. Her return stroke with the edge of the shield nearly broke the Minztan's knee. Collapsing, the horse had driven back its slayer. Beyond the crippled ranger at her feet stood Narritanni. The factors flowed through the Kommanza's mind in effortless calculation: she sprang to her feet and charged the man in chainmail.

It was a slim chance, but if she could kill him quickly enough she might distance the two with pole-arms, or perhaps find a spot where she could stand her back against cover and defeat them both. Despite the hero tales, nobody stood a chance in the open against two good opponents. For that, you needed advantage of position.

He shot her at twenty paces. The bolt nailed shield

to arm as she charged at a dead run, the round bull-hide-and-fiberglass protector covering her from neck to thigh. Even then she might have reached him if the weapon had been a conventional one. It was surprise more than pain that made her shout as the second bolt thudded into the center of her breastplate. *This is a terrible weapon*, he thought as she staggered, crumpled, and fell. Blood leaked out of her mouth, first a trickle and then thick gouts pulsing out to soak the ends of her russet braids. Dying, she crawled toward him. Hating blue eyes locked on his. Drowning in her own life, she grunted out the name of her god and with a last convulsive movement slashed her saber into the snow a meter from his feet.

The two soldiers of the New Way came up, one limping badly. That could mean a serious delay.

"Hurt badly?" he snapped.

"No, no, I—" The Minztan put more weight on the leg. "It's not broken, nothing's torn. I can force it if it's bandaged tight."

"Good." He tilted his head back and listened. The trilling came, first the simple recognition symbol and then something more complex and forceful. That message would be traveling back along the net to an officer. More of the steppe-dwellers would be coming, and very soon.

"Quick!" he said. The Garnetseat villager with the face wound had died: a stab through the throat. Grunting with the effort, for she was no light weight, he bore the body across to where he himself had stood to kill the westerner and put a hunting crossbow into stiffening hands. A corpse cooled swiftly in this weather.

"Come on, by the Circle, get the tracks covered up! Let's get out of here! No, leave it"—reflex, to salvage valuable metal, but not here—"leave everything.

Wait." He took the dead woman's spear and thrust it through the threshing horse's neck. That noise ceased. "With luck, they'll think these killed her and then died. Get out on our own backtrack." Skilled woodsrunners knew many tricks to hide a trail, and the Seeker's followers had learned still more. They faded into the forest.

The volunteers were astonished when he ordered them to fall back. Patiently, he explained: "We can't fight them in open country. Even the clearing around Newstead is too large. We *want* them to withdraw, to get out into the forest where we can hit and run, perhaps free our people, harry them without presenting a target for their bows and lances. Now they'll be alerted unless they were fooled into thinking it was Newstead hunters who killed the sentry.

"We'll move forward after they pull out of the village. We should be much faster in the forest anyway, knowing the woods and not having unwilling prisoners to drag along."

The Bannerleader rose from his crouch and surveyed the scene. Then he bent over the body of his trooper and looked again at the position of the crossbow bolts, touching one with a thoughtful finger.

"What happened, honorable?" one of the troopers asked, looking around with a trace of uneasiness. Battle she did not fear, but not being able to see what might be creeping up was unnerving.

"Saaaa ... Th'ruka was riding by. The first shot from this one"—he kicked the corpse of the male Minztan—"hit her in the shoulder, then all three of them jumped out and went for her horse. Then she killed the woman, and the other over there went under the hoofs. Th'ruka was thrown, but she charged this male here, took a bolt through the chest before she died, but killed him while she died."

"Honor to her," the others said.

His gaze rested on the treetops for a long moment. "But this"—his foot nudged the dead Minztan crossbowman—"took two wounds, the cut across the face and a stab through the throat. And the slash was disabling; he couldn't have shot with it. Not a woods rat, they haven't the stamina.

"Th'ruka was one of my best killers, but even she wouldn't have struck twice with a bolt through the lungs. Spitting blood like that, she was lucky to keep on her feet for one deathstroke."

The trackers returned. "Honorable, three sets of ski tracks, but blurred. *Could* have been more, with some following the others single-file, and we can't tell which way they were going."

The Kommanz officer stood stock-still, eyes closed. This was the last sweep before the scoutmesh began moving westward behind the main column. Was it worth signaling for delay and probing the woods farther east?

No, he decided. Even if there were more Minztans than the three corpses here, mission priority was to return home with maximum speed. There were probably a dozen or so hunters and woodsrunners still out who had been on journey when the attack on the village came. Best report the skirmish and get on with the move.

"*Haailzuz*," he said: Move out. "Get Th'ruka over a horse. Get the scalps and gear. And put out over the net: hostiles in vicinity, one casualty, double vigilance." He glanced down into the sightless eyes and spoke, musing. "Either she wasn't such a fierce one after all . . . or I'm missing something."

9

Walks-with-Demons needed little in the way of material things to practice his art; long ago he had gone beyond that stage. Magic worked from the lesser to the greater. The more power, the smaller the cause needed to produce an effect.

In darkness, he crouched in his tent. A Minztan building would have been too full of their *essence*; even the patterning of the land itself to their Way through near a hundred generations was a handicap. Before him was a circle of leather tanned from human skin: within it were teeth of beasts and men, tufts of feathers, objects less nameable. An ember smoldered in a cup of horn. The smoke was invisible among the blackness, but the acrid smell of the herbs overrode scents of leather and rotting blood and rancid mild curd. Quietly, he chanted; fingers danced across his drum, a droning irregular sound, maddeningly always on the verge of rhythm, never achieving it. Gradually, sound and movement slowed, ceased, but the nonpattern went on in more subtle ways.

Layer on layer, the shaman peeled back his awareness. Reason and reflection went first, leaving the *I*

143

floating in a bath of uncensored data. The process continued; long training took effect. His withdrawal from physical sensation began, rerouting sensory input into closed loop circuits that had no exits. At last, there was nothing but the steady murmur of internal sensation; bloodflow, heartbeat, lymphatic pressure, the endless anabolism-catabolism balances that marked the body's long losing fight with entropy. Those too were filtered out; in a fragment of hindbrain, a pseudo-mind construct was created that would monitor the essential functions while the identity itself was elsewhere. The body lived, but barely. Breathing and heartbeat slowed to imperceptible levels, temperature dropped; even the pupils ceased to react, and fire could have been pressed to his skin without evoking response.

Satisfied, the ego disengaged itself. With a nonphysical wrench it flared outward from the horsehide tent into the blizzard.

Detached, the wings of mind rode the storm, perceived it *whole* as a flow of energy-system interaction. Parasenses expanded and probed; reasoning on this level was not verbal, concepts flowed and meshed with an immediacy impossible to ordinary consciousness. The blizzard flowed around him, its stored energy differential interacting with ground and air in patterns so complex as to be almost a living thing.

Ah, yes . . .

He scanned backward along the time element, weighing the broad zones of probability that hedged the *is* of the storm with manifold *might-have-been*. It had been likely, this storm; the great circle of air that massed over the eastern lakes was prone to them. But he suspected—

A sideways leap. The World Beyond the World was easy of access here; he shifted to the plane of Absolute Essence. He experienced the Symbol of the storm;

yes, a slight nudge had been given to the potential/ possibility *here*. It was good work, next to impossible to undo: the difference between starting an avalanche and stopping one. Time existed here, but as a static element; the spellsinger could walk it as if it were distance. Circling, he drifted among the forest-analog, studying the span in its entirety, from inception to the limit where possibility drifted into the entropic fog in which all events were equally likely. Magic was as individual as a fingerprint; he would know this witch-work if he ever scented it again.

He grew aware of a scrutiny. If he had been conscious, his mind might have interpreted the input as a tall man in Minztan furs, with milk-white eyes glowing, beneath the pine boughs. Words were not possible in this place, nor was conflict; for humans to impinge on elemental Symbol required detachment as the first condition.

Communication of sorts was permitted; more akin to an interpenetration of personalities than speech.

you caught me unawares, this time, wood switch, he unsaid.

as always, came the reply. evil blinds itself.

contend with me, then, yes.

no need. you will destroy yourself.

The shaman's reply was emotion rather than information; a rising storm of hatred, fury used like a club as a deliberate instrument of the will. It rent the patterns around them, shattering delicate webs of meaning. Nottrees lashed in the gale, and beyond the Veil men cowered as branch and trunk groaned and splintered more violently than the storm would warrant.

And the Symbol of Walks-with-Demons raised its muzzle and howled through bared fangs.

eat, I will eat, you and all with you!

They whirled, the Wise Man struggling to disengage

before the shock of violence could disorder the world still more. Then they were-not forced-rendered incompatible with that Place.

In the horsehide tent the shaman's chest gave a convulsive leap, then another. Metabolism spiraled upward toward normal; consciousness returned, and with it a bitter pain that was perversely relished. And with awareness, information fell into the patterns imposed by logic and culture and conscious thought. Hissing, he thrust his head through the slit of his tent. Dawn was breaking, but there was little sign of it in the whirling snowshot blackness.

The storm began quietly, in the third watch of the night; a wind that whistled through the pines, flicking ice crystals up and driving them beneath helmet brims. By the last nightwatch it was a howling presence, strong enough to turn dawn to a mere graying of its wailing dark; inside the strong log houses the air was dry and dusty with the fine particles forced out of the timbers by the pressure of the wind.

The Kommanz officers were impressed enough to delay departure by an hour, and to hold the final staff meeting indoors. Shkai'ra watched the scout's final report while dressing; there would be few enough chances to be warm without layers of wool and fur, in the next two weeks. The trousers were sheepskin, soft-tanned, the fleece worn inward and lined with linen, tucked into high boots with quick-release latches. A tight-strapped halter bound her breasts, and over that was a heavy tunic of coarse wool, smelling of sweat even through the cold. A meter of knitted wool wound around her neck, and a knitted cap confined coiled braids. Then came the gambeson, a long-skirted leather coat thickly quilted with padding of felt to give protection from impact and a little warmth.

Over all that went the armor. Corselet first; that was

the foundation. Breast and backplate were four-ply lacquered leather on a web of fiberglass, hinged at the top and laced down her flanks under flaps. She shrugged into the familiar weight, settling it in the least uncomfortable position. Greaves with hinged knee-covers went over her lower legs, and armguards of bullhide flared at the elbow on her forearms. Lobster-tail shoulder protectors extended to the elbow; chaplike skirts of the same pattern fell past her knees; both laced onto the corselet on their undersides. The gorget settled around her throat; she checked the underflap thongs and rolled her head to make sure the fastening was not tight enough to restrict mobility.

Crossed weapon belts linked at a central buckle carried saber, pouches, long slender stabbing dagger, and broader-bladed utility knife. She tucked her gauntlets into the belt while she ducked into her helmet; that was the simplest piece of her equipment, forged from a single sheet of steel except for the riveted noseguard. For most purposes the weight and adhesion of the liner would keep it stable, but she buckled the two chinstraps for caution's sake; she did not intend to die blind in a steel bucket because a blow turned it around. The plume of scarlet ostrich feathers that rose in a Y from the nasal was no ornament, but a practical way of marking rank in a fight.

Shkai'ra had worn war harness most days of her life since she braided her hair; before that, it had been double-weight practice armor. Nobody could suit up unaided, but she leaned, turned, and bent to let the unblooded youth assigned to her get at the laces without conscious thought. All her mind was fixed on the forerider where he crouched and drew on the floorboards with a burnt stick. The heavy-boned, freckled peasant face was intent, the words flowing with quick, concise accuracy:

". . . with open snow, here and here," he continued. "Then this river—must be the source of the Grey-cut—frozen hard down to two meters, then a lake, then maybe four-five *kylickz* to ground I've hunted over before."

Shkai'ra remembered he came from a village near the forest border.

"Mounted, with grain, pushing the horses, five days to open country. On foot . . ." He shrugged.

For the first time he became uncertain, glanced around at the hard, blank faces of the commanders, paused looking sidelong at the shaman.

"Here," he indicated, "is where I found the . . . spirit-house." No flicker of expression crossed their faces, but several made the warding sign against ill-luck.

"How much in the way of supplies, there?" Shkai'ra asked.

"Enough to feed one hundred for five days," he replied shakily. He summoned courage. "But, Chiefkin . . ."

"*Ia?*" She glanced up sharply.

"I wouldn't eat it. Or feed *my* mounts on it. Of your pardon, Chiefkin, honorables."

The shaman nodded. "I've heard of such places, yes, indeed," he said. Producing a set of carved bones, he rattled them in one hand. "Minztan witches summon woods demons, feed them in return for power. Always out in lonely spots. Much magic to make the food clean; much time." He glanced up slyly at the commander. "Maybe I should throw the bones, see if too much ill luck lurks there?"

"*Nia!*" Shkai'ra said. She smiled at the scout. "You won't have to eat it, *zh'ulda*," she said. "We'll feed it to the Minztans. Who are only our mounts at night."

That brought a ripple of appreciation from the officers; it would simplify their problems, and nobody would have to fear cursed provender.

"Ah, yes, the spawn of the Mighty Ones fears no magic!" the one called Walks-with-Demons said. In Kommanzanu that was a very subtle insult; there was a fine line between courage, which was admired, and reckless stupidity, which was despised.

"Not while I have so wise a spellsinger with me," Shkai'ra drawled. She turned to the scout.

"Forerider," she continued, "how many Minztans have you killed?"

"Why . . ." He hesitated, and counted on his fingers. "About six, Chiefkin, not counting those that got away with my arrows in 'em."

"Any of them stop you with a spell?" she asked.

"*Zaik-uz,* no!" he replied enthusiastically.

"Then let the ofzarz and the *dhaik'tz* worry about magic," she said dryly. "Now let's consider the alternatives on their merits. Horsewarden?"

A gaunt, scarfaced woman scowled at the scout. "Forage?" she snapped. A Kommanz war-horse took a good deal of feeding in these grassless deserts; each warrior had at least two remounts; with the looted grain . . . Her eyes glazed over with calculation as she weighed loads and distances.

"Not much, honorable," the scout replied. "Horse-warden, I couldn't have fed my own *remakka* on that trail without grainbags, much less a remount herd of three hundred, and sled beasts. And what there is, you have to dig for."

One of the Bannerleaders spoke. "Hmmm, not too much the way we came, either . . . and now we've better intelligence and no need for stealth. Better to make time by cutting directly, *ahi-a?*"

The horsewarden nodded. "*Ia,* and not just less distance: on ice covered with pack snow we'll make better speed per *kylickz.* Less strain on the beasts pulling loads, too."

"Warmaster?" Shkai'ra said.

"Campsites?" he grunted.

"Plenty, honorable," the scout said. "Lots of good deadwood for fires, too."

"Caravanmaster?" Shkai'ra continued around the circle.

"We'd need that," he said. Years spent herding trade trains and supply columns across the prairie had gone into the tally sticks he produced. "Seize, it's like carrying water in a leaky bag." Frowning, he dipped a cup into the bowl of hot milk they had been sharing. He would have preferred *naizburk*, or even heated mead, but of course no one would fuddle his wits at a staff conference.

"The faster we force the pace," he continued, "the more slaves will die each day . . . but there'll be fewer days overall. Even with the captured sleds, we won't have as much food as I'd like, and cold kills the hungry. Worse with new-caught Minztans; they just give up and die, sometimes: stubborn beasts. Even the ones who don't sicken and pine won't have the sort of will that endures hardship. The more they feel frozen and hollow-bellied, the more we'll lose."

He imitated the action of a balance with his hands. "Too fast and they die of exhaustion; too slow, of hunger and despair. Best to save any time, distance, or strain we can safely avoid."

All turned to Shkai'ra. She crouched and studied the map. The forerider might be illiterate; so was she, nearly. But that map would be accurate: good judgment for distance and terrain was a survival skill among their people.

"*Ahi-a*," she sighed. "Fourteen days?"

The Caravanmaster nodded confirmation. The horsewarden added: "Chiefkin, don't expect the mounts to be battleworthy at the end of it. Not after riding scoutmesh through wooded country on either side of the track for the whole two weeks."

She rocked back on her heels, eyes closed, considering. Better to take the track the scout had found. The trace they had followed coming in was the summer trade route, and it wound about to follow high, dry ground; that was needful to avoid swamps that were hard-frozen in the cold season. The slaves were more than half the value of the plunder; if many died, it would reflect on her leadership, the more so as there had been scant glory in this ambush of witless barkeaters. She was aware of the shaman's unwinking glare; *he* had his flanks guarded. If she took the slow, safe way her Name would be diminished; if she struck cross-country against his advice and ill luck resulted, that would be even worse.

She was aware of his hatred, of course, and undisturbed by it. Most people hated each other, that was the way of things. As the sayings of the Ancestors went, "Let them hate, as long as they *fear*." But there was more in this than the normal ill-wishing. There were only two candidates among the Mek-Kermak's-kin who could be considered for the High Seniorship, in her generation, and the *dhaik'tz* would much prefer her kinsib Zh'tev.

Strong as an ox and twice as witless, she thought. No, that was unjust; he was a good fighter, and clever in an utterly conventional way. Just the type the shamans loved to manipulate. Leave that for later, she mused; the High Senior was far from dead. Her skin crawled slightly at the memory of her kinmother, who was one of the few human beings she regarded with frank terror.

Her fingers dropped to the chiseled brass eagle-head pommel of her sword. The eagle was the symbol of Zaik Godlord, fierce and all-seeing. For a moment a half-remembered coldness crawled at the back of her brain, then faded instantly, leaving decision.

"Throw the bones," she said to the spellsinger. His pupils narrowed in calculation; she shot out a hand and gripped his. He whitened at the pressure; Shkai'ra had the wrists of one who had swung saber or practice blade every day of her life. They flowed almost smoothly from forearm into hand; a little of that strength made his bones creak.

"Throw for my luck, and the will of the god in this," she said. Walks-with-Demons would not directly falsify, but there were ways and ways of asking.

There was a muted gasp around the circle of officers; their craning forward was more a tension than a physical movement. The shaman swayed, yelped, threw the human fingerbones graven with runes into the air with a practiced flick. They tumbled rattling among the riding boots of the warband's commanders; sweat stood out on their faces as they forced themselves not to move or flinch. Walks-with-Demons traced patterns, muttering.

"The warrior, upright," he said. Danger and accomplishment, no surprise there. But . . . the hand of the god, claw of the demon: the herosword. Branching of the ways; a mighty fate, or the beginning of it. He rocked back, then gathered the future-reading bones and dropped them back into the pouch. "As you will, Chiefkin," he said. This was more than he bargained for . . . yes, only a fool let the pleasure of an internal squabble benefit outlanders.

"We take the direct route," she said firmly. "It'll bring us out on the steppe farther from home, but we can pick up remounts and supplies and make up the time, and more. We'll have plenty of extra space on the sleds by then." She looked around the circle at her Bannerleaders. "Standard double-diamond scoutmesh. Warn your riders to keep it close—distances are tricky among these accursed-of-Zaik trees, and they'll tend to spread. Have them keep their remounts with the main herd; no sense in tiring them out in unpacked snow. Assign details to bring them out at intervals. Any questions?"

"Game?" someone asked.

"Only if you don't have to stop. Hardtack and jerky will keep us going: at need, we can tap blood from the horses." That was standard emergency procedure.

"Or from the slaves," one officer said, grinning. Everyone snickered.

"Enemy action?"

Shkai'ra flicked her hand at Eh'rik, who brought both palms up in a curled-finger gesture.

"Not enough to bother your killers. Ski is faster than horse, here, *ia*. But we had complete surprise: even with the warning of those skulkers who escaped us, you know Minztans. They'll sit around buggering trees and talking to ghosts until it's too late. At most a few will come join the outrunners and try to hang on our flanks, like those who chopped at the edge of our scoutmesh. We'll be ready for that."

A ring of carnivore smiles ran among the Kommanz leaders.

"Enough," Shkai'ra said, slapping her breastplate. The fanged-skull emblem of Stonefort grinned redly under her fingers. "Brief your squadleaders and be ready to move at—" Her hand pointed accurately to where the sun would have shown in two hours, if the sky had been clear. "Standard hostile-country whistle-code. Zailo shield you."

"Zaik lead you, Chiefkin," they chorused in reply.

Maihu and Taimi worked steadily at loading the travel sled, she thoughtful and abstracted, he with increasing sullenness. Pine oil was loaded, several clay bottles of wine, a small cask of the best-quality mead; fresh provisions were secured around the exterior to freeze ready for use, and a bin at the rear held charcoal for warmth. And there were delicacies, toasted nuts, spice sticks, cane-sugar candy . . .

Around them seethed an ordered chaos, the last minute preparations that could not have been done the day before. Wind and snow hurled savagely between the houses; vision faded into swirling whiteness half a bowshot away, and hearing to less than that. The Kommanza used whistle calls among themselves; gestures, lancebutts, cuffs, and kicks for their captives. Minztans would not have stirred in such weather unless driven by dire need, but nothing stopped a Kommanz warband when its leaders ordered a march. Indeed, this would be easier than a blizzard on the steppe; the trees did not let the wind build up the killing force it could generate on open prairie. The warriors wound scarves around their faces, bent into the wind, and cursed as they continued about their work.

Coffles were forming up, lines of a dozen Minztans linked neck-and-neck by tethers of wood and iron-hard leather shrunken on. Maihu had been surprised to see the slaves allowed their own winter-travel gear; on reflection, that was merely sense. Valuable livestock would not be allowed to perish from the cold: the Kommanz were cruel but not stupid. The villagers were even being served a last generous hot breakfast of porridge with cheese and honey and dried berries from their own kitchens. After all, she thought mordantly, the Kommanz were stockbreeders, and knew the importance of good feeding. Concentrated foods, high-energy fodder for a drive in cold weather.

Whips cracked; there was an occasional muffled yelp out of the snow curtain as a boot thudded home, but little deliberate brutality. This was business, not sport. Even the villagers judged unsalable were being treated as promised. They had been herded into one building and tied; the raiders would toss in a broken bottle when they left, so that they could free themselves before they froze. And the village itself remained, with enough scraps to keep them barely alive on their trek back to the long-established villages to the east. Maihu had had to bear that word to them, and keep herself shielded from the Inner Eye. Silence had greeted her, and stares that were more sheer bewilderment than accusation, twisting like a knife.

But of course, she thought to herself, *I feel no guilt. I could scarcely tell them outright what I plan.* Nor let them sense it, not with the Eater so close. She looked up into the gray sky. There was something about the storm . . . She shrugged, returning her mind to more practical matters. With a detached wonder, it came to her that a Kommanza could scarcely have carried on a masquerade such as she had, this past week. Their deepest dread was to be shamed before the folk and the gods: they were less concerned than her folk with inward terrors, and more with appearances. It was strange to think that there could be so much difference in the souls of human folk.

A sharp crack brought her back to the present. The youth assigned to drive their sled was two years younger than Taimi, still bearing the shaven skull with a scalplock that was the sign of a preadult among the Kommanz. She had watched them silently; no Kommanza would labor for another if there was an outlander to hand. Now Taimi's slowness had finally brought action. She had sprung down from her seat, kicked his legs from under him, and begun slashing at him with her whip. He was rolling, trying to escape; perhaps worst to see was the total lack of expression on the young Kommanza's face. That blankness became expected after a while on the warriors, but it was still chilling on a visage not yet past puberty. And what emotion leaked past her shields was more disturbing still.

There was nothing else to be done. The youngling spoke no Minztan, and Maihu was not ready to give up the advantage her own supposed ignorance of Kommanza rendered. Instead, she threw herself forward over Taimi. Her face ground through the fresh snowfall to the dirty, granular layer beneath. She could smell the mealy scent of it, hear Taimi's shuddering inhalations. And feel that it was pure rage that drove him, as he quivered with the effort it took not to fling himself at the plainsdweller. He tried to throw her off, but she pinned him, clenching her teeth against the impact of the thin braided leather. The first stroke was not too bad; the heavy winter trousers blocked most of it. *He must control himself, he* must *or he'll die,* she thought in a cold rage of her own. Shkai'ra did not mind—she preferred the boy to fight when she used him, which was their only contact—but defiance anywhere else would leave him bleeding out his life.

The second whipstroke never fell. A lance descended in front of the girl with the whip. She looked up in surprise, hand raised for another stroke, then bowed and stepped back up to the seat. "Honored eldersib," she said, in the form of address prescribed for speaking to a full adult. "The gakkaz were given under my care. The shoat will not work, and the ewe came between us."

The warrior nodded dryly, his voice coming muffled from behind the windings that covered his face to the eyes. "Of your wisdom, hairless one. But that is the Chiefkin's *pet* gakk. If they can't bounce around enough to please, and tell the Mek Kermak why, who do you think will smart for it?"

The unblooded youngster was speechless with indignation. To think that a *gakk*, a slave, not even born in the Keep, could have a freeborn put in trouble!

The warrior saw her expression, too faint for any

but one of their people to detect. The butt of his lance struck out, catching the girl just under the breastbone. She folded off the seat with an *uff* of amazement. That was the last sound she made as the lance descended, the hard ceramic knob smacking down with nicely judged force on sensitive spots.

He stopped, and she glared up at him with silent hatred. That was good. There was a Saying of the Ancestors, that hatred put fire in a warrior's belly. The true killer should hate everything that lived, himself not least.

"Hairless, you were expecting it to be *fair*, weren't you?" he asked genially.

"I admit the fault, honored eldersib," she said through gritted teeth. That was a piece of stupidity she should not have been guilty of, at her age. Not if she expected to survive long enough to grow warrior braids. "My thanks to the eldersib. Of your wisdom, enlighten me."

"Nothing is fair, and only the weak seek justice. Grow strong, and *take*," he recited. "Lesson over."

She bowed. An unblooded was under perpetual instruction, not only from the warmasters but from any adult who cared to offer it. And she dared not antagonize any of them; soon her half-year would come, when she was turned out to wander and return an adult. Or not to return at all, for no law or custom protected the inbetween. This had been a lesson of value.

The warrior turned to the Minztans and spoke slowly in their language. "Work. Must *work*. Or whip. Understand?"

Maihu bowed deeply, rendering Kommanz titles into her own tongue. "This slave thanks the Great Killer. Of your forbearance, master, I will instruct my kinchild. He will work. May I now report to the Chiefkin, as ordered?"

He nodded distantly, returning his lance to its rest;

his lips moved slowly as he rendered the words into Kommanza and translated them to the youthful guard.

Meanwhile Maihu seized her kinchild by the scruff of his neck, thrust him into the sled's interior, shook him, and hissed at him.

"Fool of a boy!" she cried with exasperation, and forced herself to lower her voice. "What in the name of every turning of the Circle do you think you're trying to *do*?"

He stared at her. It had been brave to try to shield him, but . . . "Why should I work?" he asked. "So *she* can be nice and comfortable in here? So she can have lots of fun when she decides to have us, like, like last night? Kinmother, how could—"

"Don't you realize where we're *going*? Or that I'm an Initiate?"

He began to speak, then stopped as his mouth flew open in a comical O of surprise. "Right past the Place of Summon—"

She laid a palm across his mouth. "Yes." A nervous glance at the entry slit of the sled. "But I must have . . . what is needful. If I have to act, with her, then I'll do it. To do that well enough to fool her, I have to deceive parts of myself as well. And so will you; for your kinparents, and the whole village, and the New Way. I didn't tell you before because I didn't think you could keep the secret well enough, but you forced me. *Remember the Eater!* If he even *suspects* . . . !

"Can you do it? Can you act as if you had no hope at all, except to please them?" Her voice had turned gentle.

He nodded breathlessly. "I'll . . . try," he said. The shining of his eyes made her heart lurch with fear.

The shaman lingered after the other officers had departed. For long moments they squatted in silence, the

spellsinger fingering his pouch while Shkai'ra ran knotted tally cords through her hands. At last, he spoke.

"Chiefkin, this storm. Witchstorm, yes."

"More bogies?" she replied impatiently.

"No . . . Chiefkin, of your forbearance, please—for
the Folk. The bones—the fall was . . . strange. Why
such mighty signs, for a raid of no importance?"

Shkai'ra's lips tightened. "You've come late to being
helpful," she said. "If this is a spell-raised blizzard . . ."
She paused, considering. "The more reason for haste;
if the forestfolk have brought up a band from the east,
and a wizard with it, best we get away. No point in
taking losses thrashing about in the woods. As for
magic—why are you here, then? Or can't you deal
with it?"

That stiffened his back with pride. "Yes, indeed; but
little help can I be, if the witch and I must duel along
the trail, in the World Beyond the World."

She nodded impatiently. "Then do it, and leave the
blade and the bow to us."

With the dawn, the wind eased a little, coming in
brief savage gusts rather than blowing continuously,
but the flakes fell more thickly, and there was a smell
of damp in the air. The leaders looked up with foreboding; the cold was less bitter, but dampness was a
worse enemy than chill in this season, and the snow
would slow them. The warriors finished striking camp
with swift efficiency under the pawky-critical gaze of
the squadleaders; they were in full war gear now, but
experienced officers could sense the infinitesimal signs
of slacking tension. The battle was over and they had
rich plunder for scant loss. Now they were thinking
of home, winter evenings spent in boasting and squan-
drous gift-giving around the kinhearths. Of the orna-
ments they would buy, the war gear and horses, and

dowries that would see them fasted to the kin of their choice for those still single.

The commanders saw, cursed, and drove them harder; only time would grind home the lesson that lack of vigilance ended only with death. And even in the afterlife it paid to keep up your guard.

Shkai'ra spent a few minutes looking over the remount herd; like anything to do with horses, that was accounted among the most important and honorable of tasks. She was looking forward to the trip back, with two personal servants and a Minztan travel sled. She brought her attention back to the horses; they were restive, and left to themselves would have waited out the storm with their tails to the wind. This being winter in forest country, each warrior had brought only two remounts, but those were of the finest: hand-reared from colthood, drilled to respond to voice, knees, balance as well as reins. They were trained to fight snowtiger, human, and the giant steppe wolf, as much a part of their units as their riders. The Kommanz considered their war-horses to be younger siblings, souls on their path to the exalted destiny of Kommanz birth; as such they were treated far more gently than children, who were considered strong enough to take rough handling.

Shkai'ra ducked through the milling, snorting throng, wishing the seeing was good enough to look them all over at a glance; with training, you could detect the first hints of sickness or injury. There was a touch of nervousness about them, only to be expected with all this fuss; horses were creatures of habit, after all. Still . . .

She cupped hands around her mouth and called: *"Thunder-Wind-on-Spring-Grass!"*

Out among the dark shapes moving through the dancing white vagueness, a tall horse threw up its head, whickered, trotted over; it was a big roan gelding seventeen hands high, shaggy, rawboned, with long sturdy legs, deep chest, compact withers, and a large squarish head. The Kommanz bred well, for the qualities they valued; this breed might not have the beauty of the fabled Kaina bluegrass stock, but they could take weather and treatment that would leave others windbroken or dead.

Shkai'ra laughed and buried her face in the long coarse mane as the animal nuzzled at her, lipping her neck and investigating the pouches at her belt. *Thunder-Wind-on-Spring-Grass*—that was a single word, in Kommanzanu. The steppe tongue had over two hundred terms for describing grass, depending on weather and season; there were nearly as many for horses. It also had over thirty-two separate and distinct forms of the verb "to kill." Of course, it was less specialized in other areas. The nearest a speaker of Kommanzanu could come to saying "sea" was "big salty lake too broad to see across"; "humanitarian altruist" came through roughly as "insane traitor"; "freedom" as "ability to accomplish." And there was no word for "mercy" at all.

"*Ahi'a*, greedy beast, plunderer, apple-looter," she murmured, feeding it a handful of dried fruit and planting a wet kiss on its nose. The air steamed with its breath, full of the sweet scent of horse. An attendant brought her gear, and Dh'ingun riding on the high cantle of her saddle. From there he sprang to the withers of the horse, spitting in annoyance when she brushed him off.

"*Bh'utut!*" she said: Get off! "I don't keep Thunderwind to warm your furry toes."

Unconvinced, the cat sulked as it circled in the snow, flakes dusting its glossy black fur. She saw to the saddling herself, only natural when her life would depend on it. First came the woolen blanket, then a fleecy sheepskin, then the war-saddle itself, with its long stirrups and deep U-shaped seat. Finally she strapped on the overfleece, buckled the breastband with its chest protector, and started to do up the padded girth. Without warning, she whipped a knee straight up into the charger's stomach. Startled, it pigjumped a handspan into the air with a "whush" of expelled breath. She tightened the girth—before it had a chance to inflate its belly again. Reproachfully, it stared at her over its shoulder as she fastened weapons and saddlebags.

"Rrrr-up, Dh'ingun!" The cat leaped up, scrambled into a bag, and curled up out of sight in its accustomed refuge, safe from the detested snow. She put a hand in and felt the sharp bite on her gauntlet.

"Hoi, that horse must have been a southland trader in its last life, to know so many tricks," Eh'rik hailed her. "I'd not have noticed the swell-belly."

"*Ia*," she replied. "And wound up riding arse-to-sky the first time you put weight on a stirrup . . . What do you want, Maihu?"

The Minztan glanced down. She was dressed in Minztan outdoor gear—brightly colored embroidered deerskin jacket lined with cloth, knitted blue cap, boots; only the hunting knife was missing.

"Of your pleasure, Chiefkin: you said that I should show you those things of mine I wanted to take along . . . just a few things; my flute, which I thought you might like to hear me play, and some books."

She stood smiling wistfully, a short, wiry, blue-eyed woman with the round face and snub nose of her folk, snow hanging thick in her eyelashes and black hair. Tucking a curl back into her cap, she lowered her gaze to the ground once more.

Shkai'ra nodded indulgently and jerked a thumb at a nearby trooper. "Hoi, Ih'kren, go with her—let her gather what she wants, as long as it isn't weapons. I'll be along later to look it over."

"Chiefkin . . ."

"Something else?"

"Could I say farewell to my kinmate who's being left here? It would only take an instant, and we're not likely to meet again."

"Hmmmm. They didn't seem too friendly when I sent you there with a message. Oh, all right: Ih'kren, let her go where the culls are penned—not more than a few words."

Eh'rik watched them leave with a scowl. "That's a sly one," he said. "Too tame, too soon. Kill her. Belike she's plotting to do you an injury."

"Her and half Stonefort," Shkai'ra said with a shrug. "Why waste a good slave? I have plans for that one, and she's already trying to curry favor. You're just jealous I won the throw." She grinned and slowly licked her lips. "You should be; not just a fine blacksmith, but a good lay. Ask again when I want her bred and I might let you fill that womb. The boy's not bad either; sullen, but interestingly so."

"I still say she's dangerous. Don't underestimate them; that one is deep."

"Ahi-a, that's a 'sheep-bitten wolf.' Minztans pine away, or run, but how often do they kill? Most can hardly bring themselves to it while you're coming at them with a saber. We've plenty of them at home; meek enough, with an occasional drubbing. The boy now, he's the type who broods—were he four years older and a quarter heavier, I'd have to tie him before I could mount. The kind who might risk a long week's dying to knife me: I'll watch him."

"The dam is more cunning."

"Ia. A Minztan cunning; patient, and not fierce. Look you, she doesn't like me. Belike if she had a hope of escape, she could plot my death easily enough. But she hasn't a means, and without that she'll keep waiting, and hoping for a chance to escape—which will never come. Once we're out on the steppe and she has only me to look to, I'll hand-break her to the bridle. In a brace of years, I'll be able to fly her from the wrist like a hunting bird; she'll become what she pretends to be, without even noticing it. And that will be more useful to me than a smith or bedmate: plenty of those. You'd have me starve and beat out all the qualities that will be of use. And a dead slave's dead meat; beef is much cheaper. Poor thrift, that."

"Well enough," he grumbled. "You've told me of your schemes. But these Minztan leaders, they're all witches and sprite-kin. What if she puts an ill-wishing on you? Fucking puts anyone close enough, as often as you do with her. Maybe the shaman was right; I don't carry a lance for the spellsinger, but it *is* his craft. There are others for your use."

For a moment Shkai'ra was daunted; she made the warding sign and touched her lucksprite. Then she rallied. Still, it was well that Eh'rik worried. Partly it was concern for her; that was rare among their people, and she valued it. Not that it had made him easier on her when she was in training; he had been even more merciless than the law demanded, out of determination to drive her to her limits. And he wanted her in the high seat someday. Surprising, since he was as conventional as her kinsib Zh'tev, but he said to her once that it was for the warmasters to know the rules, and the Chiefkin to know when to break them.

"*Nia,*" she said, slapping him affectionately on the back of the neck. "The land-sprites here can't be too strong. They didn't stop us from winning, could they? And the battle's what counts—what good is a spirit that can't aid you in war? The Mek-Kermak's-kin are godsborn; a little lousy woodsmagic is nothing to us. Besides, it may not matter to you prongers whether it's a knothole, a woman or an ewe—different for us."

He shrugged, forbearing to point out that she was merely born to the Mek-Kermaks, not yet fasted to it. "The Chiefkin wishes," he said formally.

"*Ia*. Now, let's go on with the trek."

Sadhi looked at Maihu with dull indifference as she slipped into the cowbarn. Lame, he was no use to the Kommanz on a journey that would stretch the endurance of even the healthy. She went down on one knee and began whispering in his ear.

" . . . and don't act differently!" she finished, as he began to straighten, hope coiling up into the dead pools of his eyes.

"What do you want me to do?" he asked, turning his face aside into the straw to hide eagerness.

"Don't tell *anybody* until the raiders are gone. Then, yes, let them have the hope. The Seeker's people will be here soon, as soon as the Kommanza pull out. Tell them—tell the commander—not to count on *It* too much. They probably won't have an Initiate among them. I can't exert too much control over it alone, and from a distance. Tell them they'll have to use *It*, make plans. That's what the Seeker had them trained for, to improvise. But you know how superstitious the horsefolk are. *It* will frighten them as nothing else could. I'll try to alert some of the prisoners; they all know the ordinary rituals and chants at least. That will be a help."

Her calm broke. "Tell the Seeker's people to help us!"

The corridors had a curious, deserted air as Shkai'ra walked them for the last time. Her breath puffed white in rooms left unheated, but more warmth remained than she would have expected. Logs made good insulation, she thought; a pity wood was too scarce on the prairie for such use. And too vulnerable to fire arrows, of course. Her folk built in stone or rammed earth and roofed their buildings with sod or slate. For a moment she was sharply homesick for the crowded brawling winter life of the Keep, and somehow at the same time for the huge emptiness of the snowbound steppe. Whiteness stretching out of sight under a sky that was a bowl, stars hard and clear and bright beyond counting. Leafless aspen thickets, the weight of the hunting bow in her hands, the coughing grunt of snowtiger in the moment before it charged. And the great hearth of Stonefort, folk curled on the floor wrapped against the drafts that fluttered crude bright hangings. . . . Yes, it would be good to be home.

The room where the Minztan awaited her was small, little more than a cupboard; there were chairs, a table, a rack of books on the wall. Maihu worked silently at strapping together her bundle.

Shkai'ra took down one of the volumes. It was bound in tooled leather dyed crimson, the title inlaid in gilt in an alphabet strange to her. Not that she had much fluency even in her own, only enough to read a trader's letter if not too complicated. Reading was for shamans, the *dhaik'tz*, keepers of legends and healers of the sick, technicians and magicians, half feared and half despised by the ruling warriors. Most Kommanza would not touch a book. Shkai'ra thought that fearful, and so unworthy. True, there was great magic in writing—but so there was in childbirth, or forging steel, and one dealt with those often enough. With reasonable precautions there was much use and power in books.

"I heard how you dealt with the unblooded," she said. "That was cunning." The term was Kommanzanu: it implied prudent wariness. The steppe-dwellers valued courage, but thought berserker fury wasteful except in the last extremity. "If you'd tried to strike her, I'd have had to beat you bloody for form's sake."

"Taimi is young and reckless, Chiefkin," she said in a subdued voice. "He'll learn."

"Or die," Shkai'ra said. "It's hard for him to remember to be afraid." She smiled thinly. "Maybe he'd learn faster bent bare-arse over Eh'rik's saddle ..." Her gesture dismissed the matter as unimportant. "Don't worry; teaching fear is a talent we have." She glanced around. "Why so many books? All for one village, and there must be at least twenty here!"

Maihu blinked, then remembered that literacy was uncommon outside the Haamryls-an-Minztannis; even in the southlands most peasants were unlettered, and the Kommanz hardly had a written language at all. Of course, her people had the advantage of having neither a government nor a standing army to support; folk were free to use the enforced leisure of winter as they pleased. Most practiced a craft, writing among others.

"We ... find them useful for storing knowledge, Chiefkin," she said.

The Kommanza looked at her suspiciously. "Witch-knowledge?" she asked warily.

Maihu replied in haste, fearful the westerner would order the books burned if night terrors were aroused. "Oh, no; we never *write* our rituals."

"What's in them, then?"

"Well ... this one is from Raddock. See the script they use?" Shkai'ra nodded recognition; she had beheld that writing before, when the southron traders came to Stonefort. "It tells of a new type of kiln, and how to select the clays to make better ceramics. It also says the knowledge came to Raddock from farther

south and east—many tools and weapons are made so
there, to save metal."

She had been helping with experiments along those
lines herself. It was infernally difficult to duplicate the
results described by the southlander earthsmith; much
had been left out. Minztans had never been able to
get the strengthening matrix of glassfiber to set right
in the ceramic. Perhaps the foreigners used a Wreaking
to get it right. A forest Adept would not use her powers so, of course.

"Ahi-a," Shkai'ra mused. "A pity so many of us feel
books harbor evil magic; we might gain much, if we
used them more. The dhaik'tz wouldn't like it, of
course." She slipped through the volume in her hands,
admiring the heavy solid feel of the paper and the
brightly colored illustrations. "But how do these letters
come to look all alike?"

Maihu tried to explain printing, a difficult task, since
she knew only the general principle herself. Minztans
had never lost that knowledge, but it was only in recent generations that population and demand had
grown enough for it to be really useful. These books
had come in trade.

"Saaaaaaaaaa, like a brand on stock," Shkai'ra said
after a brief mental struggle. Maihu was astonished
that the concept had been grasped so quickly. "You
Minztans are full of clever ways, more than Kh'oytl
the Trickster itself. What does this made-by-machine
book tell of?"

"It's a book of tales, Chiefkin, the sort you've had
me tell you these past evenings. Old stories. Some of
our—" there was a pause while she tried to convey
what "scholar" meant—"hunters-of-knowledge col-
lected them. I was told that many of them come from
the Before, from the Cities of Folly. There's something about sounds that we don't use anymore; I didn't
really understand it myself."

"You forest runners have arts we lack." A hard amusement. "It makes you useful slaves. . . . What song-story is this?"

"Ah . . . *Prince Andrei and the Firebird*, Chiefkin."

"So." She handed the book back to the other woman. "Bring it. I like to hear such things; the winter nights get long." She winked and patted Maihu's crotch, before looking over the rest of the bundle. "Fine. Now report to the sled."

The column had formed up nicely, curling snakelike through village and fields, ready to uncoil into the woods and toward the distant steppe. The snow had settled to a thick steady curtain, gashed by occasional savage gusts of stormwind; visibility was down to twenty meters or less. But the whistle code knit the warband into a smoothly integrated whole, a knot of order in the wild chaos of the woods. Shkai'ra silently acknowledged that she was glad to be riding with the main column. Out on the plains you could be more alone than anywhere on earth, emptiness stretching white and windswept to the blue bowl of the sky; but it was never as sheerly desolate a feeling as the woods could give you. She squinted through stinging whiteness toward the forest; scarf and coif and helmet muffled sound, but through it all she could hear the moaning of the wind through the branches. She spat and brought her horse to a canter with an infinitesimal shift of balance.

The train flowed past. A full Banner led the way, then the baggage sleds, the slave coffles, more sleds, the remount herd, and last of all the few small ponies and scrub cattle this steading had kept. Those were not many, scrawny and undersized by plains standards, but it would never have occurred to the steppe-dwellers to sack a holding and not lift the stock; the notion would be blasphemous. Also, they could be eaten along the way as they weakened—food that carried itself.

Bellows and whickers ran under the whistling of the wind; shouts and clatter of harness, cracks and oaths, gray light on lanceheads and helmets and the harsh vivid enamelings on armor. Herding the Minztans was the most challenging task; they were being grouped in double coffles, each file of twelve bound by the wrists to a neighbor, and the couple-links to a central pole. That gave them enough freedom of movement to carry burdens and move without being able to free themselves with any speed or stealth. The work was hindered less by opposition than by sheer clumsiness of folk unused to moving in large groups. The Minztans cried out to their kinmates and children left behind, weeping with shameless openness.

Shkai'ra noted the spectacle with disgust as she trotted by. *If they can't find the courage to end their lives*, she thought, *at least they might try not to abase themselves so totally as to weep before enemies*. Truly, the stuff of slaves. The sight made her queasy.

The forward position was the least dangerous in a faring like this; it went to the junior Bannerleader. Still, that one was some years older than Shkai'ra, which fact she kept in mind as she rode up the column of twos. The troopers sat their mounts quietly, shoulders hunched against the wind, eyes slitted in the narrow space between helm and scarf. The horses shifted and stamped in a creak and rattle of harness; the Banner was in good order, almost like a parade exercise. Shield on back, lances in scabbards at the right rear of the saddle, elbow through the lance sling and hand gripping the reins.

"Bannerleader Mh'arutka," she said conversationally. "Snow looks like letting up." Then she leaned closer and spoke quietly. The blond woman shifted her helmet to the crook of her arm and glanced inquiry. "Your Banner is ready for a patrol on the open steppe."

The officer flushed deeply. Shkai'ra continued: "Those lances are nearly three meters long, Bannerleader. Add another meter and three-quarters for the height to the saddle. How high are the lowest branches on the trees? It's five *kylickz* to the open river."

"The Chiefkin wishes," the Bannerleader ground out, anger directed at herself rather than the commander, who had at least tried to save her face in front of the troops. Village chieftain, trained officer, and she had to fuck up like this, she thought. As if she was barely old enough to grow braids, and not a blooded warrior with children of her own old enough to walk. She decided to offer a sheep to Glitch as soon as she got back to the homestead; this was the sort of thing he inflicted on you for neglecting him. Also, it was a bad sign that none of the squadleaders had thought to remind her. Unpopular officers were like weak ones, unlikely to live long lives.

"It does at that," Mh'arutka said gravely, glancing up in turn.

Shkai'ra kept her own face expressionless, until she had turned and heard the Bannerleader's voice lift behind her: "Turn those lances in to the baggage train, on the double! Then bows out and eyes on the woods. Don't sit there like lumps of nomad shit on a hot day, *move!*"

At that, Shkai'ra permitted herself a slight flicker of laughter, less an expression than a light behind the cold gray eyes. The troopers peeled off and trotted back toward the sleds, stolidly indifferent. That was war for you: bust your ass to do something, then hurry up and change it back the way it was in the first place, rest five minutes and do it all over again. Well, a warfaring was one thing and home another; they'd all have a jape to tell, once they were back among the fields and herds, and Mh'arukta could chew her braids if she didn't like what she heard.

Shkai'ra swept back down along the lines, reins loose, lifting a hand in salute now and then. Yes, there were Maihu and Taimi, sitting at the rear of the travel sled, shackled to the frame. Eh'rik rode up and handed her the horn. It was as long as her forearm, glossy surface carved with skulls and devil-faces, tipped with walrus ivory. She paused for a final check, found all in readiness, raised it to her lips.

The sound lifted through wind and clamor, a deep wolf baying: *Arrrrrrrrrhhhhhaaaooool* through the tossing trees. The command whistles spoke, a great complex trilling that wove together, wove the band into a single huge organism, thousand-fanged, a delicate tool responsive to her will. Pride swelled in her as the column wound under the great pines.

That evening, after Shkai'ra slept, Maihu played her flute. Wild, yet with an icy precision, the notes skirled through the warm dark interior of the sled, and outward, through the neat rows of Kommanz campfires on frames above the river ice, on and on into the woods. The last of the storm was fading; the branches tossed and soughed gently under a starless sky. The sound of the flute wove through bone and wood; her body played on, though her eyes were more sightless than mere lack of light could explain. At the last, the notes rilled through the Veil, and her tranced mind tuned them into the fabric of forest and Otherworld. It was an ancient song; it spoke of wholeness, balance, health; of the endless fight of life and death. Of those who were kindred to the Woodspeople, and those who knew not the Harmony.

Next morning, a scout was missing.

10

The Minztan warparty slid their skis cautiously into Newstead, a few scant hours after the rear guard of the raiders pulled out. Narritanni ordered the woods thereabouts scouted carefully before allowing his motley followers into the steading itself. Silent, they poked about among doors scarred by rams; there was a curious feeling of abandonment, as if this were a ruin long untenanted.

The leader and Leafturn walked together through the shattered doors of the Jonnah's-kin hall. The inlaid tables had been hacked with careless dagger slashes, and hangings drooped greasy and tattered along the walls. At the head of the great room was a wall of fine woods, carved in the ancient divided-circle emblem of their people's faith. A double thunderbolt clenched in an eagle's claw had been smashed across it, by a battle-ax from the look of it: the sigil of Zaik Godlord, Begetter of Victories, Mother of Death. Below in a corner was a blackened hand kicked out of the way and left to lie.

Narritanni stood for long moments contemplating

the hackmarks, lost in certain memories of his own. Then he sought the captives.

The first storm of tears and babbling had died down; the freed prisoners were oddly quiet. Some wandered back to their shattered homes; he saw them standing hesitant, perhaps lifting and shifting refuse and fragments in a futile parody of repair. He noticed a grizzled Garnetseat hunter trying to get a girl of about ten to drink. She sat rocking herself, ignoring him and all the world with her wide-eyed sightless stare. She made no sound except a low crooning that went on and on, quiet and steady and ceaseless. Leafturn walked behind her and laid a hand on her head. She stiffened, then slumped bonelessly.

"Sleep," he murmured.

Narritanni shivered as he looked at the other children. His life and beliefs had made him less squeamish than most of his folk, but such things went beyond cruelty. Obscurely, he felt they must be the sign of some deep primeval wounding in the souls of those who wrought the deeds. A confused grief for all human kind overwhelmed him.

One of his rangers stumbled out the door and was noisily sick. He turned to his second-in-command, who stood steadfast but pale.

"Make sure everybody gets a look in here," he said. "And at the other prisoners as well."

"You don't think it will daunt them?" she said.

"No," he said softly. "Not for long." More briskly: "Now, you screen the survivors, then we'll see what information we can get out of those who kept their wits during the sack."

With a sigh, he sank down to crouch against the wall. Only a few vagrant flakes were falling, although wind whipped icespray from the thick white sheathing on roofs. The cold seemed to have seeped into his bones; he should get up, go seek warmth, get on with the work of the day. He rested his hands on the cross-guard of his sword and bowed his forehead against the hide wrapping of the hilt.

Leafturn sank down on his haunches before him. For moments he kept silence, then reached out and touched the commander between the eyes with a fore-finger. It was . . . cooling? No, for suddenly the cold seemed to lie outside his skin once more, instead of in his marrow. Refreshing, that was the term. He smiled crookedly. "My thanks, but don't overspend your energy," he said.

The mage laid his head on one side. "No lifestuff of mine was needed," he said. "You were wasting your own in inner conflict and unwarranted guilt. Do what you can. Then, what must happen, will happen."

He regarded the other shrewdly. "You're not so hard a man as you think, so don't trouble yourself about it. Come."

They rose together. "You're right, Enlightened One," Narritanni said. "So many times, I've seen it. So much work and effort and pain, and still . . ."

He waved a hand at the village around them. The soot-blackened, smashed windows looked obscenely incongruous against the white purity of the snow; the smell of old smoke and the slow decay of dead meat in winter was there, faint but inescapable.

"Anger is a wrong turning; but the New Way needs it. The southrons take our land—our best, and it's been part of Minztannis from time out of mind—and clear-cut it and kill any who object, breaking treaty after treaty; the lakelander merchants cheat us without any shame and steal forest for their tree-farms. And the westerners hunt us for sport. So I . . . use it, as a tool to make the fighters' spirits strong."

Leafturn shrugged. "Don't take so much on yourself. First, the People would see this and be angry whether you showed them or not—even the Seeker couldn't stop that, and you're only one of her officers. Anger has its rightful place. Second, only the totally Harmonious—which neither of us is!—can fight evil without being stained by it."

His eyes sought the clouds. "Evil is a human problem. And good, which can be as poisonous, in its way. The natural world is neither. Or both." Shivering: "Something outside nature happened here."

"The Eater?" Narritanni said, alarmed.

Leafturn shook his head. "No ... that I was expecting. But there was a ritual held here; I can feel it lingering. And an answer, not of World or Otherworld."

The freed captives turned out to be a maddeningly scanty source of information. Untrained in the military arts, they did not know what to look for, or how to describe what they did see. Yet piece by piece, Narritanni and his officers were fitting the picture together. Then the lame man came.

He was tall, sallow, limping badly on his right foot. Narritanni guessed that the expression of melancholy was long-settled habit rather than acquired recently. The villager bowed his head awkwardly.

"No need for that," Narritanni said with restrained impatience. "I am just a traveler along the Way, like you. Has your hurt been tended?"

"Enlightened One? Oh, this." He looked down at his leg. "No, that's old. A tree I was felling broke the wrong way and landed on my foot. I've come to tell you about the raiders."

"Good! Now perhaps I can make some progress. How many? What were their numbers and losses here?"

He knitted his brows. "About a hundred and fifty of the warriors," he said. "Maybe two hundred, no more. And twenty youngsters, who drove the sleds and helped with the horses."

That fell in with the information he already had, but it was bad to hear it just the same.

"We lost thirty-five dead," the Newsteader was saying. "And . . . well, they took ten dead and twice as many wounded. Some of the wounded were still able to ride and fight."

Narritanni winced. It was humiliating, even with the further death that his troops had inflicted.

"They carried off more than sevenscore of our folk; all the strong adults, and most of the children past their First Change. And all our goods and most of what food we had stored for the winter."

That was bad, but not irreparable. The neighboring villages to the east would take in the fugitives and help them with tools and seed to make a new start. Of course, many would never succeed in putting together the shattered pieces of their lives again, undone by grief, unable to fast enough new members to keep their kins alive. The children able to forget would be the luckiest, adopted into new families without much trouble; Minztans had less attachment to any one parent than folk with less flexible family systems.

Newstead itself would have to be abandoned for the present, and that was a harsh blow to the New Way. This steading had been long planned as a barrier to protect the more thickly settled lands to the east, and perhaps to encourage peaceful commerce once the raiders found their sport growing too expensive. Narritanni had always thought that too visionary, believing Kommanza would never make peaceful merchants, but such was policy. Now all that could be salvaged would be a few recruits for the full-time service of the Seeker. There would be little hope of persuading new settlers to move in unless most of the captives were rescued. And that, he thought unhappily, was unlikely. He had barely twice the enemy's numbers, and most of his force was composed of peaceful farmers and artisans with little combat experience and no training. They could use their forestcraft and harry the outriders, free a few of their folk if they were very lucky, but to release all the captives would mean a stand-up fight against an opponent stronger in arms, skill, and weapons.

Hopeless, he concluded. I will not court more losses trying to abide with a failed plan. Still, they would have to chivy the Kommanz out of Minztan lands. Leaving aside revenge, which he was still Minztan enough to feel wary of, it would help teach them that the forest folk were not deer for their hunting.

He noticed that the lame man was still there, patiently awaiting the ending of his thoughts. Their people had a great respect for meditation, and would not interrupt it without pressing need.

"Enlightened One," the villager said, "my name is Sadhi Jonnah's-kin. I am nothing, just a smith and farmer, but my kinmate Maihu was—is—an Initiate."

That brought him up. It had been beyond hope for the Initiate to survive and have an opportunity to use that power. It was rare even for such matters to be spoken of; at the word, others around them began to move away. That was less a conscious reflex than instinctive reverence.

"Better we should speak of *that* under six eyes," he said, drawing the man aside. Leafturn drifted after them; the man seemed reassured to see him there, inconspicuous as a tree, and as comforting.

"I'm . . . nothing special," the Newsteader repeated. "Not even as good a smith as Maihu, except for heavy work. And, well, I make the offerings, try to feel the Harmony and travel within the Circle, but my kinmate, she's traveled really far along the Way.

"She learned . . . I mean, the leader of the western-ers kept Maihu with her some nights, and she talked. The Kommanz aren't going back the way they came. They're heading straight west through the woods, then down the ice on the Sunfall River. Right past the Place of Summoning."

Narritanni shaped a silent whistle. "Marvelous," he said with quiet happiness. "The Circle has turned fate for us—"

"And she said to tell the leader of the Seeker's folk that Snowbrother will aid us, but we'll have to do most of the . . . work ourselves. And she said that Fear would fight for us too."

Narritanni conferred with his second, Leafturn, and one of the volunteers; not a leader, but one whose words would be listened to with more than usual respect.

"This is great good fortune," he said. "The different route, that wouldn't help us of itself. The opposite. It was a good move for the Kommanz: less distance, and more clear space. But with . . . *It*"—they all drew the sign of the Circle over their chests—"we can have some chance of cutting through the net of scouts and striking without warning. And it will sap their strength, to know the land fights for us."

That was how a Minztan would see it. The Kom-manz, he knew, would fear black sorcery and soul-eating witchcraft. But the result would be the same.

"With this stroke of luck, we have a fighting chance to rescue most or all of our folk, perhaps even destroy the war band completely."

The volunteer tugged at a wisp of her hair, dis-turbing one of the ribbons braided there. "Do we need to fight at all, then?" she said doubtfully. "Not that I shrink from it—my kinfast's traplines and hunt-ing grounds run near the border, and we've had trou-ble with the plainsfolk attacking us before."

She chuckled. "And now and then some of their stock has, hmmmmm, let's say, strayed into those of us who just happened to be out at the edge of the grasslands. But nobody in his right mind will fight a Kommanza unless necessity drives. If the Circle turns for us—" She looked at the Adept.

He spread his hands. "I'm not a warrior," he said. "It's surprising to me that one who is"—he nodded at Narritanni—"puts as much hope in this as he does." Pausing, he pondered over what to say. This touched on Mystery; not forbidden, exactly, "restricted to protect the ignorant" would be a better way of putting it.

"The Snowbrothers can be fierce, yes. That was one reason that we made our Pact with them, back in the days right after the Death, to prevent clashes. They have their place in the Harmony, too. And they're very hard to see, if they want to be hidden; partly natural talent, and their intelligence, but also because Wreaking is part of their very being, not a learned skill as it is with humans. So it was they managed to live when humans overran the land and grabbed at every creature's living space. After we became a rare animal again, they flourished. But even if Maihu can tunetalk the Snowbrother, I don't see how it could destroy all the raiders."

Narritanni had been studying the patterns made on the floor by light filtering through the broken panes of a window. It was a calming exercise; he forced his mind back from overconfidence. His lieutenant muttered a foreign oath she had picked up in the eastern cities and forced reasonableness with an obvious effort. She addressed the volunteer with a sigh.

"Look, fellow . . . I mean, Fellow Traveler on the Way . . . the Wise Man is right; one of *them* isn't enough to kill four, five Banners, more than a hundred good fighters. And *they* won't question orders, or find an excuse to slink off at the first—"

"Fine words you've got for those murdering—"

"Peace." Leafturn's word was soft, but both found themselves suddenly calmed. They subsided sheepishly, like children who realize that the adults are laughing at their quarrel.

He inclined his head to Narritanni.

The commander smiled. "Maihu Jonnah's-kin had the right of it," he said. "We can't overfall the steppe-dwellers ourselves, and the Snowbrother can't do it for us. And the Initiate couldn't tunetalk it without our Enlightened One here to distract the Eater. But together"—He spread his palms.—"we have a chance. Fear *will* fight for us, and make the raiders vulnerable. Let's not quarrel, let's make plans. We may not be able to communicate with it, but it won't be hostile to us as it would be to outlanders. That will be the basis of our *strategy.*"

He used the lakelander term perforce; there was no word for the concept in their tongue. He began to draw a map on the floor. "Here . . ."

The Kommanz scout was tired, but not enough to dull her senses. Fatigue was one of the first things the warmasters taught you to conquer; easier than fear or pain, and a good foundation. Often enough before she had shaved her scalplock she had stood for a score of hours balanced on unsteady rocks, brain foggy with the need for sleep, fielding questions and solving tactical riddles with the ever-present thought of the quirt behind her to keep her on the bounce. Or she'd lain out at night with the herds, waiting for the wolves to make up their minds and determined not to let them find her asleep over the watchfire.

The weather had cleared, and the cold was fierce on her face despite the tallow and the extra scarf she had wound around her face under the helmet. Above, the stars were painfully brilliant through the overhanging boughs; it was nearing the end of her watch, she judged from their position. Hers was the third of the four watches which made up the hours of darkness. Clucking quietly, she moved her horse along at a slow walk, just enough to keep it from stiffening, the snow creaking under the weight of hooves. Utter silence, save for hoofbeats and the occasional branch cracking in the cold. Moonlight filtered through pine needles, through air dead still, every trace of moisture frozen out of it.

Anxiously, she flexed her bow. Cold this severe could lock the bearings in the pulleys if you let them sit, or even damage the laminations in the stave. Longingly she thought of her skinbag by the fire and a bowl of warm milk. Tomorrow she would be riding in the column and could sleep in the saddle.

It was the horse that warned her, snorting and dancing sideways, ears up and nostrils spread wide. She trilled out the whistle relay signal as it came by on routine check and looked around more closely. Even well-trained eyes could detect nothing, but her mount was growing more and more restless. Wolf, cougar, tiger, hostile humans: nothing should have made it this skittish. It was a war-horse, trained to fight in team with its rider.

"*Ahi-a*, saaaa, saaaa," she soothed it. "What's wrong, Macefoot-Harrow-Heart? Good kinsib."

The mount began to buck. "Hold still, bastard kinless offspring of a nomad sheepswine!"

Normally no amount of horse-temper would have unseated her; she had ridden since the age of three. But this was totally unexpected. She had to keep a grip on her bow, and war-saddles were not designed for unbroken horses. A huge convulsive twisting leap sent her flying into a low snowbank with a squawk of surprise and a clatter of armor. By the time she had bounced back to her feet the horse was only a fading pounding of hooves, receding at full gallop, reckless of the uncertain footing. That meant it was frightened enough to run in blind panic, risking its legs on roots and hidden bushes.

Quietly, she cursed the whole pantheon and the equine race with the Horse Spirit thrown in. How was she going to explain this to her squadleader? Being *thrown*, of all things! He'd say for sure that she had been sleeping in the saddle. She winced. Punishment detail for the rest of the trip, and a public shaming when the war band split up and returned to the villages. And that meant the rest of the winter doing more than her share of the roughest chores, no hunting, having to shun the feasts or be ridiculed before everybody. The only solution was to find whatever had spooked her mount and prove that it could not have been helped.

All the time she had been scanning the area, her back to a thick trunk. It suddenly occurred to her that whatever had frightened her horse might find *her*. And she had only one shaft; the quiver was clipped to her saddlebow. Her mouth turned dry, and her heart beat loud in her ears; the moonlit forest turned alien and hostile, the haunt of Zoweitz-creatures, perhaps even the dreaded demon *mhaigz*. Fear awoke anger. She started out on a cautious search, without calling for help over the whistle-code net. It was a few minutes until her next call-in when a report in detail would be needful. There was no warning but a deep heavy creaking, as if a great weight were pressing down on the snow, and when she whirled there was nothing there. A flash of movement; she snap-shot, and the shaft went *crack* into a tree, a centimeter deep in the iron-hard frozen wood.

Then it let itself be seen, and the bow dropped from her fingers. A hand fumbled at swordhilt, but it was strengthless, Distantly, she was aware of how her sphincter loosened and fouled her. A dim mewing came from her lips. Then there was nothing.

Maihu woke early and eased herself out from under Shkai'ra's arm. It was hours before the tardy winter dawn; snow hissed at the covering of the sled, driven by winds strong enough to set it swaying on its springs of horn and wood. But she recalled what the Kommanza had told her of the rule for commanders: last to bed and first to rise. The travel sled was her own, as long and broad-bodied as a three-horse hitch could draw; trade and travel went more briskly in winter, when the crops were in and snow made smooth roads of tracks that would be bone-breaking ruts and bottomless mud in the warm season. The roof was leather stretched across wooden hoops, thickly padded to keep out the cold and lined with bright rugs. The floor held blankets, pillows, and furs; heat came from a tiny ceramic stove, light from an alcohol lantern hung from the center hoop; the ends were laced tight against the chill. It was an oasis of warmth and light in the vast white-black emptiness around them; Shkai'ra had been quite taken with it, for her people had no such luxury.

The stove could cook as well as heat. She crawled over to it and fed in more charcoal, fuming up the air intake. Water and milled grain had been heating slowly on top overnight; she added maple syrup and nuts to the wheat porridge as it bubbled. She sliced strips of bacon off a slab and set them to grill, then split a small, only slightly stale loaf of bread and hung it above to toast. The smells began to fill the sled. Work done, she sank back against the curved wall of the sled and watched Shkai'ra as she slept. As usual, the Kommanza lay on her face; the fur had slipped back to her waist, and Dh'ingun was curled up on the small of her back, just above the smooth hard curve of the buttocks. Sleeping, her face lost the trace of cold wariness that never left it waking, even at the height of pleasure. The relaxation took years off her age; her mouth had opened slightly, and she nuzzled her cheek into the long soft wool of the blanket.

Gray eyes flickered open; Maihu felt Shkai'ra's mind spiraling up from the long slow rhythms of sleep. Even with shields clamped down, to one who had the Inner Eye there was a spillover, when you spent so much time in a person's company. Shkai'ra reached out to touch the hilt of her saber, then pushed the cat off her back. They both yawned and stretched, so much alike that Maihu was surprised into a laugh. Shkai'ra looked, saw the resemblance, and let warmth trickle into her eyes. She stretched, arching her back and curling fingers and toes with pleasure.

The cat stalked over and rumbled, patting at Maihu's knee for emphasis. The Minztan poured him a cup of the milk; he crouched, sniffed dubiously, and began to lap, purring absentmindedly as she scratched behind the nightblack ears.

"We *are* alike, Dh'ingun and I," Shkai'ra said, stretching out a long arm for a bowl of the same milk. She sipped, then looked up in surprise. "What did you put in this stuff?" she asked.

"Sugar, vanilla, a little cinnamon."

"Not bad," Shkai'ra said, tossing off the rest of the heated drink. She propped her shoulders against the side of the sled. "Glitch! I could've sworn we were settling in for a stretch of clear cold when I turned in . . ."

She looked sidelong at the Minztan. "Shaman says your folk are dogging our track, that they've got a weatherworker with them, bringing the snow down on us."

"The porridge is ready, Chiefkin," Maihu said, tensing.

She spooned out a bowl, then flipped the backbacon onto the buttered bread, added some pickled tomatoes, and closed it to make a sandwich. Shkai'ra ate with noisy relish, belched, wiped her mouth on the back of her hand and her hands on the blanket.

"Nia," she said easily. "That wizard, she'll learn it takes more than a little bad weather to stop a Granfor warband on its way home."

Maihu relaxed, and winced at the grease stains on the wool. This would all be easier, she thought, if only they weren't so *filthy*.

"Feed yourself when I've gone," the Kommanza said. "It'll be another hour before we break trail, and I wouldn't want you to go into a decline for want of eating, not when it turns out you can *cook* along with everything else."

She braced the soles of her feet together, pressed the knees down on the furs, and touched her chin to her heels.

"That's easier than it would have been if I'd been under the stars in a skinbag," she said, beginning a series of exercises. Dh'ingun flopped down beside her, waiting patiently for her to finish before rolling onto his back. She began rubbing him absently.

"Cat's the only creature under sky that can look dignified while having its stomach scratched," she said, and sighed. "It's a pity I'll have to give this up once we're back home; it makes a winter journey a real pleasure. But the killers would think me soft and useless did I keep it. Perhaps one of the Valley traders will give a price for it, and then a bag in the open will have to content me."

"Well, I hadn't noticed it made me less hardy, Chiefkin," Maihu said. "And I slept out often enough on hunting trips without feeling weakened."

"Yes, but who owns who?" Shkai'ra replied, beginning to pull on her clothes.

"Why do you Kommanza cultivate hardship, though?" the Minztan asked with genuine curiosity. She doubted that they did it to improve their souls by ordeal, as some Enlightened Ones of her own people did.

Shkai'ra opened her mouth to answer, thought, frowned, and paused. "Saaaaa . . . I don't really know," she answered at length. "It's the custom." That would have been enough for most of her folk; still she continued: "The Sayings of the Ancestors tell that it makes us brave and fearless, but"—she licked her fingers clean—"slaves and nomads live even rougher, and I don't notice it helps *them*. I think it's . . . indirect. We haven't the skills of hand and eye that you forest-dwellers do, but we'd have to waste time better spent on training for war to gain them; better to do without."

Now that, Maihu thought, is almost perceptive in a perverse sort of way. Concentrate on war, so you can take what you cannot make, because you concentrate on war, so you can . . . A stubborn sense of justice made her add: but they do need to fight more often than we, with the other enemies they have. Or is it just that they make enemies of anyone they can reach?

Shkai'ra pulled her tunic on, and mused through the wool: "It just seized me that learning about the way your folk think gives me a new way to look at my own people."

She frowned: the thought was not altogether welcome. Knowledge was power, and power was always good. The Words of the Gods and the Ancestors were clear on that. But something gave her a feeling of vague disquiet, as if the ground were moving under her feet. "Come, give me a hand with the armor. You've a better touch than that cowhanded stripling."

A little later: "No, that lacing has to be *tight*. Use both hands and brace yourself with your feet. Good, smithing's given you a fine set of arm muscles."

Smearing fresh protective grease over her face, she loosened the lacings on the front flap and looked out. A blast of icy wind swirling with granular crystalline snow flooded in.

"Black as Glitch's arse," she muttered. "Zoweitz take it, how're we going to make speed through this?" She glanced back. Maihu had wrapped herself, in a blanket patterned in blue and yellow, against the cold. Suddenly, Shkai'ra put an arm around her neck, pulled her close, and kissed her on the mouth; it was firm and possessive but without desire.

For a moment their faces were close. "Now, I wonder why I did that?" Shkai'ra muttered in Kommanzanu. She pulled away and shook her head in puzzlement as she rolled out of the sled to join the waiting officers.

Maihu closed the flap and knelt for a moment in silence. *I wonder too,* she thought.

11

The commanders crouched in the lee of the sled, helmets almost touching and voices loud to carry over the wind. In the dim light, Shkai'ra looked around the circle of faces and felt an interior chill that had nothing to do with the gusts driving fingers of cold through the joints of her armor. There was no open show of emotion; that would take a disaster of monumental proportions. There was merely an additional coldness, a remote, detached withdrawal from the moment, more ominous than shouts or tears might have been among other folk.

"Zaik with you," she said. "Report. What's wrong? Enemy action?"

"Yes, Chiefkin. That is, one of my scouts disappeared from the mesh last night." The officer glanced aside, flakes driving in to lie almost invisible against the ash blond of his brows before they melted slowly. False dawn was making the eastern sky a blur against the darkness. "About two hours ago, just before this accursed-of-Zaik storm started up again."

"Disappeared?" Shkai'ra said, her voice soft and

dangerous. "How does a scout 'disappear' from the middle of a mesh?"

"Chiefkin," the Bannerleader began helplessly, "she—I got a short-signal that there was a gap in the relay, then cross-connected through the inner link and called for a close-in. We swept—"

He offered a helmet. The straps had burst, and the noseguard was hanging loose by one rivet. It had been ripped away, and the padding inside was slick with hard-frozen blood.

"This was all we found. No body. The horse had bolted. Just this and her bow and one arrow in a tree."

Shkai'ra glanced up from beneath lowered brows.

"No tracks?" she asked.

"Just the mount. It threw her and then ran. Fast and far, from the trace. No human tracks around the blood, except the scout's."

"*Animal* tracks, then?"

The officer let his eyes slide away from his commander's once more. "Yes . . . it might have been bear, Chiefkin, but—"

Shkai'ra held up the helmet. "A *bear* did this?" she said. Her voice was normal, even easy, but the Bannerleader went rigid. "And at this time of year?"

The shaman stirred. Shkai'ra quelled him with a single savage jerk of her head that sent him back to his patient crouch. She leaned across to the officer and spread her fingers at eye level, then drew them down into a fist.

"Your Ancestors are ashamed!" she said coldly.

The officer went chalk-pale, then bowed his head and grunted: "The Chiefkin wishes." It was a deadly insult, but there was no excuse for failure. And a commander was always responsible for subordinates.

"Your Banner does double duty from now on, watch-and-watch, until I say otherwise. Perhaps they can learn to be more alert. Dismissed! Zailo shield you," she added formally.

"Zaik lead you, Chiefkin," came the reply.

"Not you, Warmaster. Stay. You too, spook-pusher."

Turning, she spent a full minute staring out over the camp, into swirling blackness that lifted now and then as gusts blew spaces in the storm. And she saw it clearly, with the eyes of the mind. They had halted out on the ice in the middle of the river, to put the most distance between them and the threatening forest. A circle of sleds marked the center, with the slaves penned within. Around it were grouped the off-duty Banners, their fires in neat rows on log frameworks that kept them clear of the ice; each squad had its own, marked by a wigwam of stacked lances. The troopers slept around their fires, feet to the flames and weapons to hand. Most slept in their armor; it was warmer, and they could jackknife their way out of the bags ready to fight in an instant. Their favorite horses were staked out nearby, without the saddles that served the riders as pillows, but with their saddleblankets on.

The fires showed as dim red glows through the snow. She could imagine them moving about; they would be waking now, the squadleaders would see to that. Rolling their gear and heaving saddles onto their mounts' backs, gulping a quick breakfast. The air was very cold, and smelled of pine and smoke, of dung, and of blood sausage grilling over the fires. Shouts and stampings were growing louder through the long surging roar of the wind in the branches. The remount herd milled about, the Minztan cattle lowed for their feed and barns, the slaves were rousing to kicks and curses and blows from the buckle ends of belts. Everything was normal. Shkai'ra felt the creeping-spine sensation of worry, a tension she knew would stay and grow. A gloss of unreality covered the homelike scene.

"No bear did this," she said, tapping the helmet.

The nasal bar was a broad strip of steel, ridged below, and flat where it swept down flush with the surface of the helm from crest to rim, serrated like a saw-edge on the sides. Four rivets held it in place, hammered home red-hot and then plunged in cold water to shrink on and hold the metal almost as strongly as a weld. From the state of the padding and the chinstraps she would have thought that . . . *something* had gripped the noseguard in its . . . hand and torn the helmet loose. Most of the luckless warrior's face and scalp had come with it. She would have thought that, if it had been possible. A tiger or bear would have enough strength, but they had no *hands*.

"No human *wh'uaitzin* one of our killers that fast, without wounding, then got away so quickly. And carrying the body, Chiefkin," Eh'rik said.

"*Ahi-a*, the woodsrats are good at skulking."

"Chiefkin, *nothing* is that good. Nothing natural." He shivered.

"*Zaik-uz*, don't talk like that!" she snapped.

He was the steadiest of them. This was going to wreak havoc with morale. *Zoweitzhum, it's affecting my morale already!* She watched the youths harnessing the sled teams, and having trouble with them as the drafthorses backed and snorted at having their muzzles faced into the snow-laden sting of the wind.

She turned to the spellsinger and bared her teeth. "You're supposed to guard us from witchy peril." The fingers of her gauntlet scraped clotted snow from her scarf. "And you can't even stop the woods wizard from dumping this shit on us!"

Walks-with-Demon's palm thumped down on the head of his drum, a flat banging sound. "There was going to be a storm soon again anyway," he snarled.

"Isn't your magic as strong as his?"

"Not stronger than the weather!" he yelled, then pulled himself back to calmness. "If a man sits on a cliff over me and rolls boulders down, am I weaker than he because I can't throw them back? No human has the power to *cause* a blizzard—the force of it has to *come* from somewhere."

"Great wisdom; what use is it?"

He lurched erect. "This. The tree-fucker is better at weather-magic here, because"—his arm waved up—"the seasons are with him, a pile of energy standing over our heads waiting to be called down. And the land is ... fitted to his hand, here. But war-magic, that I can best him in." His face writhed, mirroring the obsession within. *"And I will eat his heart."* That was a scream.

Shkai'ra's foot nudged the twisted helmet. "Words," she rasped.

"Two can strive at that contest," he said. "Wait for the night. I will teach them to fear the dark."

He stalked away, stiff-legged. She turned to Eh'rik again.

"Something may come of that, or not," she said. At length: "We're on clear ground, now. We can make good speed even in this weather." Another pause. "As far as the band is concerned, the scout was careless and got chopped by a stray gang of Minztans. This"— she tapped the helmet—"was done with a warhammer." Which weapon the Minztans did not use, she thought but did not say.

Eh'rik shrugged and saluted. "The Chiefkin wishes," he said evenly. The warmaster was not an excitable person, even by Kommanz standards. He had lived longer than was common among his folk, and done enough deeds that he felt confident of a good rebirth, perhaps even into a chiefly kinfast next time. The shadow of a smile touched his gaunt, bony features;

after a lifetime of worship, it would be interesting to meet the gods face to face and see what was truth and what poet's lies. A pity if Shkai'ra did not make it back, he thought. She was the best potential leader Stonefort had produced in many a year.

"Is there anything else you wish done, Chiefkin?" he asked.

Shkai'ra tucked the helmet into a bag slung beside her sled. "Nothing, old wolf," she said. "What is there to do? Except pray."

The conversation outside the sled had been low-voiced, muffled by the wind, filtered out by the thick padding that itself hummed under the storm's lash. Maihu laid her head against the leather and used a certain skill to force ears and nerves beyond their natural limits. Not the Inner Eye, that would be too dangerous with the Eater near; this was passive, an enhancement of sensitivity rather than a projection. And it was at the limits of her skill.

At last, she could sink down the curved surface of the inner wall, weak with backlash and relief. The felt was scratchy against her skin; eyes and mouth watered as she fought nausea, and cold needles twisted in her ears. Sound levels faded back, but it came to her that hearing would never be quite as keen as before: there were reasons for the normal limits on the senses, and a price for overstepping them. Well, a person could only do as she might, then suffer what she must.

"Praise the Circle's Harmony," she said, drawing the sign over her chest. "All that is, is part of it."

No time for food, she thought, then made herself scoop up a little of the cold porridge. The Eater's suspicions were locked on the Adept now, but it would take very little to reawaken them. Who should she try first? Yes . . .

Outside the sled she stooped to speak to Taimi where he lay between the runners in his sleeping bag. He was awake, his attention locked on something beyond.

She followed his eyes, puzzled. Half-visible, one of the Kommanz warriors sat his horse in the blowing snow; its knees were hidden in the groundwash, and the outlines of the rider were blurred. He was performing the endless practice drill that kept skills sharp; drawing his bow, first with the left hand, then with the right; then freeing his lance and twirling the long wooden shaft as lightly as a broomstick, striking at imaginary foes with head and butt, then flicking it up to stab overarm to his left. The horse moved and caracoled patiently, even in the weather that crusted mane and tail and coat with a layer of white that darkened as body heat melted it.

She frowned; the intensity of Taimi's gaze was disturbing somehow. She laid a hand on his shoulder. A hiss brought silence.

"Get the sled in order, kinchild. I have business." She forced a smile to lighten his somberness, and patted his cheek. "Don't fuss, now!"

Hurrying along to the slave herd, she flourished an empty sack at the guards who stopped her. "Chiefkin send," she said in broken Kommanzanu. "Chiefkin order." It was enough; she was well known as the commander's personal servant by now. Luckily, she would not be expected to pick up more than a few words of her captor's language this quickly. Kommanzanu and Minztan stemmed from the same root, but three millennia of isolation had changed them beyond recognition, and given the plains tongue a fiendishly complex syntax that was both rigidly positional and intricately inflected.

The captives were up, tying their blankets and spare

clothes into bundles. No hope there; the guards would
certainly not let her near the files of prisoners, and it
was forbidden for them to talk to each other anyway.
From the look of them they had taken the night hard,
especially the children. Minztans were used to traveling rough, but not through heavy snow without skis or
snowshoes, and the Kommanz were forcing the pace
ruthlessly. And despair made for poor endurance.

Maihu bent her head into the keening wind, forced
herself to ignore the shivering misery she saw, and
felt, a little, with the Inner Eye. One captive had been
freed from every coffle to carry bowls of mush to the
others. That was dished out from great kettles slung
over fires, and those had been built near the sleds
carrying the grain. Even through her excitement she
admired the efficiency of the arrangement; the slaves
were fed with the least possible waste of time, and
the smallest possible number of them unbound. The
Kommanza certainly knew how to manage large numbers of people, she thought. Of course, her mind
added sardonically, between war and slaving they got
plenty of practice.

She edged nearer to the supply sled. This would
have to be handled very delicately, even with the
storm masking sight and hearing. There were two
guards nearby, one pacing beside the line of captives
as they carried loads of parched grain to the cauldrons,
the other on top of the sled, his bow in his hands. The
woman carried a quirt with the lash wound around her
glove, making a weighted club of the butt; Maihu
could feel her readiness to use it. The archer stood
easily, eyes scanning restlessly across the Minztans.
She was close enough to see detail, the rigid carved
block of hardwood that made up the centerpiece of
the wheelbow, the centerline cutout for the arrow, the
massive laminated arms of the bow glued and pinned

to the grip. A snapshooter's rack clipped to one side of the bow held four shafts, hunting broadheads that would slash open wounds as broad as paired thumbs. The weapon had a sight and rangefinder as well, but Maihu had learned enough to recognize the sniper's sigil lacquered onto his shoulder armor; that meant he could put twelve shafts a minute through a nine-inch circle a hundred meters away, from the back of a galloping horse.

"*Ik'da yoim, gakk?*" he called: What did she want?

"*Ofzara a-moi naikgutz,*" she replied in Kommanzanu: The Chiefkin ordered fodder.

The Kommanza made no move, simply stared; after a moment she realized that was as much permission as she could expect. Swaggering to the head of the line, she elbowed the Minztan there out of his place. He staggered in surprise, straightened, his face tightening in scorn. It was Frussi, which was a stroke of luck; he was one of the few who had been near to being Initiate.

"Very energetic, after sleeping warm and comfortable," he spat. "You learn their manners quickly."

Turning, she dealt him a clout across the side of the face: mostly show, but hard enough to sting. In a loud voice she called out a few choice Kommanzanu insults; it was the first thing a slave would pick up. Grabbing him by the jacket, she swung him around against the supply sled, pretending to slam him repeatedly against the wood. Above there was a creak and click as the Kommanza eased the draw of his wheelbow back from his ear and relaxed once more. Maihu felt the skin between her shoulderblades crawl; seventy pounds at full draw, the bow would generate a hundred and forty with the pulley effect of the offset cams. Enough to send a shaft right through a horse and kill a man on the other side.

"Act up, you idiot!" she hissed. "Snowbrother!"

The guards were laughing, showing no sign of intervening. She had a few seconds, until their amusement was overcome by the need to keep the lines flowing smoothly. Greatly daring, she let her forehead touch the man's and *bespoke* him, less information-dense than speech, but there could be no doubting her soul-to-soul.

Frussi's face changed, through bewilderment to recognition and back to a poor imitation of his first hostility. Keeping her body between him and the Kommanza, she pulled an engraved flute case briefly from her jacket.

the Great Guardian of the Winter Woods, she bespoke, *but only at night. don't tell anyone you can't trust! for the rest, you're singing to keep up your spirits.*

"The Eater?" he asked in voice-speech.

"Distracted," she replied. "The Seeker's people, and an Adept with them."

He nodded without speaking and touched her wrists by way of acceptance.

"Zteafakan!" she yelled, then whispered: "Down, and yell as if it hurt."

She swept him off his feet and mimed a hefty kick to the groin. His scream was satisfying enough to bring a wider smile to the guards' faces. The man on the sled stepped out into space and touched down lightly, almost weightlessly, the bow still ready in his hands. She approached the two warriors, smiling, blinking against the snow blowing into her eyes, and bobbed her head.

"Oats?" she said brightly. "Chiefkin want, also, oats?"

The guard with the quirt half turned and whipped the butt across the small of Frussi's back hard enough to stagger him.

"Back to work, you," she snarled. "Or the next one will have you pissing red and tasty."

The man peered at her. "Did she say oats?" he asked. "Glitch, not three wits among the woodsrats, all the way from the steppe to the lakes."

"Oats over *there*," he said, struggling through in Minztan almost as bad as the Kommanzanu she had been pretending to speak.

His partner looked the Minztan over. "Well, wits aren't what the commander's bedding her for," she said judiciously. "Not bad hocks, but a little old for my taste. That shoat of hers, he's nicely toothsome. Plenty of room and comfort in that sled, too: a sleeping bag's no good, not even if it was Jaiwun Allmate, much less a sullen woodsrat. Easier for prongers like you, kinless sheep-raper."

Maihu stood, gritting her teeth behind the smile and face of blank incomprehension.

The man giggled. "Oh, it's nice to have space and light. Like to look into their eyes, then sometimes use a knife at the last moment."

"Extravagant tastes you've got, Dh'vik," the woman said with a smile. "Hoi, you'd better help her, she's lost."

For a moment, Maihu met the archer's eyes. This close, her perception still extended from her contact with Frussi, she touched the surface of his consciousness. And recoiled, shivering; she had been lucky.

Forcing her back to straighten, she walked off into the muffling snow. *Death fanatics*, she thought. Time would tell how they measured against the quieter resilience of her folk. She wondered how amused they would have been if they knew her true Wreaking here.

Narritanni had kept the pursuit slow, drifting along behind the rear screen of Kommanz scouts. Still, the

pace they managed to force out of their motley caravan astonished him: a first estimate of twenty-five days
to the steppe boundary was modified to sixteen, if they
could keep the pace. He decided that without the
slave train to slow the Kommanz troops most of *his*
force would have had difficulty in keeping up at all.
But two weeks or so left plenty of time to plan and
to build up the information he needed.

The horse gave them the first inkling. They came
across it at first light, standing head down and shuddering with exhaustion in a clump of bushes. The first
Minztan to see it was a Garnetseat villager with little
experience of steppe chargers. He tried to walk up
and take the bridle. The animal raised its foam-lath-
ered head and watched him, rolling its eyes. His scent
was wrong, and that was enough. It made no move
until his hand touched the reins; then the long neck
shot out snakelike and great yellow slab-teeth sank
into his shoulder. Much of what they gripped was
tough leather and wool jacket; it raised the man high
and shook him. Through his screaming, those watching could hear the sickening crunch of bone parting.
Released, he flew through the air to land against a
tree with shattering force, slide downward, and lie
still.

A horrified onlooker raised her crossbow. That was
a mistake; the horse had been taught what to do about
missile weapons, and charged with a shrill bugling
neigh. The bolt thudded home at the angle of throat
and chest, a serious wound but not enough to stop
seventeen hands of enraged equine avalanche. The
Minztan was trapped by her skis and went down under
the hooves. The bolt had raked the animal to the point
of madness, and it stayed plunging and chopping over
her corpse while the survivors shot it a dozen times.

Narritanni arrived while they were disentangling the

bodies; very little was left of the woman but a bundle of sopping-red rags with ends of pinkish bone and gray loops of gut showing here and there. The Adept knelt by the man who lay slumped beside a tree. At Narritanni's glance he removed his fingers from where they rested against the villager's throat and shook his head. Narritanni sighed.

They paused for only the briefest of services over the bodies of the slain. There was no need for burial; to the forest people there was no better way to dispose of the bodies than to give them back to the land. Scavengers were part of the Harmony, flesh as well as spirit distilled to return transformed in the great sweeping cycles of the Circle. As he stood in meditation with his hands hiding his face, Narritanni pondered the matter of the horse. Full gear, except for lance and bow, and the quiver held the regulation thirty shafts. When the prayer-silence was completed, he knelt by the animal's head and scraped off some of the clotted foam that spattered its neck and shoulders. This horse had run, far and fast, and from the scratches all over its forequarters, without much regard for what was in its path.

They found the first piece of armor an hour later, dangerously close to the left rear edge of the Kommanz guardmesh. It was a gauntlet and arm guard. For a few moments, the Minztans didn't realize that the hand and forearm were still in it. Next came a boot and greave, with the leg to the knee; after that it was as if whatever had carried off the body had realized that the covering could be detached. Not that the method was overly subtle; the pieces were simply ripped off by main strength, the thick hard surfaces twisted and torn like cloth. The torso, what was left of it, they found wedged into the branches of a maple.

"I hadn't heard *they* were so aggressive," one of the rangers said.

Narritanni nodded. "They aren't, usually. But they don't like strangers who don't use the proper rites. They feel sensitive about trespassers. And the Summoning is past due, from what the Garnetseat Initiate and the Enlightened One have told me. It is probably very hungry. This sort of thing is what the rituals were set up to prevent."

"There's only one?"

Narritanni looked at the Adept.

He nodded. "They have large ranges, in winter. As you'd expect, they live in Harmony." Which meant a territory broad enough to support that much body mass without undue pressure. Only humans fouled their nests.

Narritanni glanced aside at the Adept. "The Kommanza will be sweating," he said. "Has the Eater tried anything?"

The Enlightened One's gaze rested on the westerner's body, compassionate but utterly serene. "Yes, he tried to break my grip on the weather. Quite a good try, but I had a better position on the energy gradient. Always, it is easier to move with the Circle than to cut across it." He directed Narritanni's gaze to the shattered corpse. "He'll think this is my doing, and be working on something nasty to counterstrike. I cannot be certain of anticipating him."

Narritanni glanced around the circle of New Way troopers and volunteers. A few were looking pale. The body was not a pleasing sight, and the manner of death touched on the sacred—although in a way the extreme mutilation was reassuring. It made the corpse look more like a predator kill, and all of them were familiar enough with that; it bothered them less than the sight of a sword wound.

"Gather the band," he said.

His second looked up. She had been standing with

her arm around one of the younger troopers, comforting him; Narritanni remembered vaguely that they were lovers.

"What for?" his assistant said. "Won't that slow us?"

"Not enough to matter, now that we're up with them. More snow coming"—he glanced aside at the Adept, who nodded—"and they can't force the captives to march as fast as skiers can travel. Besides, we have plans to make. This will be tricky, even with the Wise Man to help; *It* will be nervous, and we don't have a local Initiate." His smile was wolfish. "The Kommanza do, but I doubt it will do them much good."

"What're you planning on doing?"

"Doing?" he said with an unpleasant chuckle. "Why, singing."

Turning his face aside, Taimi met the lambent green eyes of Dh'ingun, glowing in the darkened sled. The cat was lying less than an arm's length away, paws folded under its breast, watching the act with detached feline curiosity. Mounted astride Taimi, Shkai'ra moved steadily, her hands pinning his shoulders and her braids brushing across his chest. Her face was relaxed, softened by enjoyment, almost drowsy in its introspective concentration on the flood of sensation. The eyes . . . the eyes were cool, considering, lazily tracing the play of emotion across his face. The smell of her sweat and musk was sharp in his nostrils, mingling with panting and the creaking of the sled bottom and the small wet sounds their bodies made moving on the blankets.

He had tried meditation, childhood memories, anything that might relax and distract him enough to thwart her, but the steady pulsing grip was . . . too real.

Well then, he thought, *there is another way*. He

willed himself to let go, moved as much as the confining weight of her body would allow. A few moments later he arched and cried out involuntarily, a muffled sound.

Shkai'ra made a strangled spitting cry of frustration as she felt him wilt. Vindictively, she clamped her thighs and clenched him with her internal muscles, hard enough to bring a wince of pain to sensitive postcoital flesh.

"Jaiwun geld you," she cursed. "I told you to wait until I was ready!"

He glared at her, then dropped frightened eyes. "I couldn't, Chiefkin. You moved too fast, and I couldn't help it."

His satisfaction was obvious under the thin pretense of docility. "You defied me," she said, almost as much amazement as anger in her tone. "You deliberately tried to spoil my pleasure, you little Minztan bark-eater!"

Raising her hips, she freed him and then squatted back on her heels. Now, what was it he had flinched from before? Ah, yessss . . .

She gripped his head and forced it down. "Not there—farther back."

"I won't!" he said.

"*What?*" She froze.

"I . . . you don't wash there after you . . . I *won't!*" His voice edged toward hysteria.

Suddenly he turned his head and tried to sink his teeth into the inside of her thigh. The pain was nothing to her—he found himself trying to bite into what felt like hard, living rubber—but the surprise and her awkward position were enough to put her off balance, and a desperate heave threw her off. He tumbled to the rear of the sled, barely avoiding the red-hot surface of the stove. He did not avoid Dh'ingun, who responded to a sudden weight on his tail with a yowl and a taloned swipe that left bloody stripes down one buttock.

The sight was comical enough to leach out much of Shkai'ra's rage. But disobedience could never be tolerated. She sprang, ignoring his clumsy attempts at defense, got his wrists together in her left hand, and began slapping him across the face with her right. Wide, openhanded blows rocked his head back and forth, cracking loud as gunshots in the narrow confines of the sled. She stopped and released him when she sensed that his resistance had broken.

"Are you going to obey?" she asked, in a normal, even tone. One hand was lifted to strike.

He nodded through tears and hatred. "Yes, Chiefkin," he said and began to fumble his way forward. She pushed him aside.

"If you ever balk at anything I tell you again, that will *seem* like a lovetap. Now get out."

Maihu saw Taimi stumble out of the sled half-dressed, crying, and even in the faint light that spilled past the lacings and from watchfires she could see the redness and swellings on his face. Concerned, she helped him with the buckles, gently moving his trembling hands aside and fastening the clasps.

"Here," she said, wrapping some snow in a cloth and handing it to him as she tucked him into his sleeping bag underneath the sled. "I heard a little. Did she use the whip?"

"No, hit me with her open hand," he mumbled.

"Why? Did you anger her again?"

"She was . . . forcing me, and I wouldn't do what she wanted, so she hit me and threw me out." He was sobbing, not the easy tears of a child but the harsh, racking heaving an adult makes. Maihu's people did not think it a disgrace to weep, but this was wrenching to listen to.

"Taimi, you *must* try, you *must*," she said with quiet urgency. It was not what he needed to hear, she told herself with bitter self-accusation, but what could she say? Despair could make him desperate enough to do . . . anything.

Shkai'ra had been more and more tense these past two days. There had been nothing overt to cause it, nothing that she could grasp at, but the Kommanza's manner reminded Maihu of caged peregrines she had seen, traded down from the arctic, destined for the mews of the lords of the south. *Circle turn with us*, she thought. *She mustn't begin to suspect anything. And they're so suspicious anyway.*

"Taimi," she forced herself to continue, "you've got to keep her from thinking about things. You know what I mean. You've got to act as if you had no hope at all."

"I want to kill her," came the dry whisper. "I want to see her die. I want to hear her bones break and her blood flow out on the snow. I—"

"Stop!" she said sharply. "You must not let them turn you from the Way."

He looked at her in silence for a moment and then turned away, pulling the hood of the sleeping bag over his head. She put out a hand to touch his shoulder. He lay stiff and unresponsive.

"I'll try to distract her," she said. "Taimi, kinchild, will you do what you can?"

"I'll try, kinmother," he said distantly. She sighed. Her own emotions surprised her. Compassion, yes, but also . . . irritation? After all, what had he to face that she did not?

I cannot think straight, she reflected. Who could, under this stress? *Best to get inside before she calls for me.*

* * *

Lacing the flap of his tent, Walks-with-Demons gave a slight smirk. Now that night had fallen, he could begin serious preparations; soon the woodsrat spell-singer would learn who was master. And the Chiefkin, too. All would cringe before him.

He turned to the Minztan youth. She was tied spread-eagled within a circle burned into the leather floor of the tent at its making; the bonds that lashed wrist and ankle were part of the tent itself. The girl's whimpering annoyed him; he touched her throat and it ceased. Eyes full of sick fright watched him as he carefully began painting the rune-symbols on her body from the feet upward. His touch was completely impersonal, since at fourteen she was older than those his tastes ran to.

That done, he lit the horn censer and sat inhaling the aromatic smoke, considering the thing he meant to do. The Symbol was the thing it named, that was the important principle. The physical parts of a spell were mostly important as a declaration of intent and a manipulation of the symbols. His mind groped, swelled, finally encompassed the totality of the working and traced its origins and implications on all the planes.

Next he slipped the wolfskin over his head and took the piece of dried wolfmeat between his teeth. Sightless, his eyes stared. Fingers thumped on his belt-drum, senses broke down, scanned the paired helixes of information, held it ready.

Knowledge, intent, preparation: now the impelling energy. Pushing something the way it wanted to go was easy, like a throwhold in unarmed combat. This was more complex. He began withdrawing his mind, fixing his purpose and direction below the conscious level even as his hand picked up the little glass knife. His first stroke opened the Minztan from just below the breastbone to the top of the pubic triangle down the line of strokes he had painted; neatly, he folded back the layers of skin, carefully avoiding the major arteries and touching a finger briefly to points of bleeding to shock them into clenching tight. The girl's body jerked against the bonds, but they were tight; her throat bulged and her face darkened with the need to scream. As a refinement, the shaman had carefully propped up her head to keep the whole process visible.

He had not cut any of the loops of gut, moving with more than natural sureness in the dim ruddy light, so the smell was mainly the heavy salt of blood, mingled with the musky sweat of fear and agony beyond common conception. At last the whole of the abdominal cavity was open, the flaps pinned back with bone needles; stray trickles of blood ran down quivering flanks to join older stains. At the last, his hand slid carefully in to grip the beating heart.

Good. Now to step *aside* . . . through the Veil, yes . . . He moved in a peculiar and wholly nonphysical way that left the Essence of the scene closer to his sight. His own Symbol stood clear: that of the girl, a human destroyed; the network of the spell binding them together. The alternative reality he had constructed was there, potential, but still vanishingly unlikely. Still, *anything* was possible; knowing that was one of the keys of this art. Perception could alter probability. He sent a single signal down the neural pathways to where his body waited. His hand clenched.

The girl's body arched in a final spasm; lungs convulsed and drove a hoarse grunt past the blockage in her throat. Dying seemed endless, and there was no end; Walks-with-Demons did not allow her to die, not yet. The shadow-pattern of his working blazed into Sight, overlaying the Essence of the real. He pushed his mind into it, directed the energies; most of all, he *believed* completely, in a place and on a plane where beliefs had tangible existence. The wrenching that followed was terrible. Quite possibly the pain was greater than that the sacrifice knew, but the shaman had long since learned how to redirect the pain input to the pleasure centers; had become dependent on that. Existence blurred and shifted; the tent and its contents became both *there* and *not there.* Energy flowed through the structure of the spell, guided by the stored data the shaman held, flowed back into the tissues of his body, down to the molecular level. He screamed, and the sound echoed through the camp, bearing over- and under-resonances that shivered in teeth, set hair crawling with atavistic fear, and made horses plunge and whicker on the picket lines. The screaming became a howl.

At last, he nosed his way out into the night. Eyes could not see him now, not until he chose to let them. Scents flowed down the cold crisp air, paws whispered through the snow of yesterday's fall. In this form he could smell tomorrow's blizzard, and the unnatural vibrations of it; fangs bared in a snarl. He was not thinking as a human thought, not in words, but purpose remained in him, and hatred. He slipped through the Kommanz scoutnet effortlessly, and cast about for his enemies. Magic alone could not have found them, not under the woodswizard's concealment, but he had other senses. He slunk from tree to tree, and found the first of the forest warriors barely two *kylickz* from the steppe camp.

He positioned fangs, then twisted himself into the villager's perception. That gave him reality enough for contact; ivory spikes as long as a man's smallest finger sank in. Prickling surface tension of skin, soft firm muscle fibers, crisp parting of cartilage and larynx, the intoxicating savory tang of blood overwhelmed him, with the delightful overtones of dying fear and pain as the Minztan's mind spiraled down into oblivion. He drank. For a moment too long: the victim's companion had time enough to strike, and the thing that had been the shaman felt the iron of the spearhead sliding through fur and hide and ribs.

His head whipped aside, and jaws closed splinteringly on the shaft. He wrenched the iron free, cast it aside, and . . . adjusted the pattern of his pseudo-body back to wholeness. Then he reached out, took the terror-stricken Minztan's wrists in his mouth, waited a long malicious second before bearing down with shearing force that could have severed the thighbone of a bull plains bison. He left the man staring incredulously at the spouting stumps and faded back into the silver-black emptiness of the moonlit forest.

Smiling to himself, he cast about. There had been enough of pleasure; now he must search out the thing that had been preying on his folk. Quartering through the woods he felt the life around him, dim and muted in this winter season: deer, wolverine, the sleepy grumble of a hibernating bear. Borrowed instincts urged him to turn aside and dig for the fieldmice he could sense running through their tunnels under the snow. Wiser than humans in their way, the things of nature scuttled and scurried to avoid the Presence they felt as a twisting wrongness in the night. And . . . yes, something strange. This body had less power of vision than a man—sight was colorless and shallow— but its nose was incomparably keen. Molecules drifted on the air, and wet black nostrils expanded to snuff them down. Like a man, the scent, yet unlike, as tiger was unlike puma. And a tone of strangeness that shuffled along his nerves. . . . He turned aside to investigate.

The Wise Man stepped out from behind a tree. His staff was in his hands, carved with runes of power; also, he held it with one hand in the middle and another a quarter from the end, an expert's grip. His eyes rested unerringly on the shaman, full of interest.

That one crouched back. The shape he had taken was no breed of these woods; tall as a man's chest at the shoulder, long of leg, with a massive skull to provide anchorage for muscles strong enough to power jaws whose fangs overlapped the black lips even when they were not pulled back in a rictus of killing-lust. The steppe wolves were giants compared to their forest kin; five hundred generations of merciless selection had made them the terror of the northern grasslands as the lion was of the warm deserts, bred to hunt the huge grazers of the prairies. In winter, even snowtigers turned aside from their packs.

He snarled. Drool ran from his jaws, to mix with blood on fur where tufts of white hair marked the scars. Yet he remained cautious; this form was immensely strong, yet fragile. In a sense it did not exist at all. Knowledge and skill and stolen energy had forced it on an unwilling universe; it was a part of the primeval chaos that underlay the seeming order of the world. It could exist only as long as the sacrifice in his tent hung suspended between life and death, and one who knew how could break the linkages with a lucky blow. That would dismiss the form he rode back to the halfworld of unrealized probability, make it never have been. And his tent would hold only a mindless husk clutching a corpse.

The Adept stood, blocking the shaman from a trail that might have shown him too much. The staff twirled in his hands, a blurring circle marked with energies for those with the eyes to see.

"Shall we dance?" he said, pleasantly.

12

Maihu rolled into the sled. Shkai'ra was sitting on her heels, redoing one of her braids. Her long fingers gave the end a final tug, then she took the leather thong from her mouth and began tying it off, leaving a tuft of loose red-blond hair beneath a plait fifty centimeters long. The pale yellow light of the lantern glistened on her skin, showing the smooth ripple of muscle as she shifted position or raised her arms; white droplets clung in the thick reddish curls between her legs. The Minztan waited tactfully for several minutes, busying herself with fluffing pillows and tending the stove. At last she ventured: "Did Taimi trouble you?"

"He was insolent," Shkai'ra snapped. "Tell him there are other things he might be set to that wouldn't need a pleasing manner. Turning a millstone, for example. For that he wouldn't need his *eyes*, either; or his stones."

Maihu froze, suddenly realizing that she had grown dangerously complacent. The tiger might purr, but it was not tame. "I'm ... I'm sure he will learn better behavior," she stuttered. "He's already given you much pleasure, Chiefkin."

Shkai'ra looked up in annoyance. "The whelp is never going to make a satisfactory slave. He just doesn't have it in him. *Ahi-a*, don't worry, I won't blind him . . . That was just a thought. Unless he does something serious. I've no complaint against you, and you seem foolish-fond of the little idiot."

"Well, he's my eldest wombchild."

Shkai'ra grunted again. Of course, Minztans were usually closer to their children than the Kommanz, who turned them over to the warmasters almost as soon as they could walk and regarded them as nonhuman until they reached adulthood.

"He's almost more trouble than he's worth. Sheepshit, it's been a jackalbitch of a day, this raid is fuming into a hellride, and then he starts giving me trouble . . . Maybe I won't have you bred after all, if that's the type of foal you throw."

Maihu swallowed a bubble of rage. "Chiefkin," she said, to change the subject, "you said you wanted to learn more of our customs?"

The Kommanza nodded, interested. "Have you ever had a sponge bath, Chiefkin?" Maihu continued.

"No," the westerner said. "What's a sponge?"

Maihu tapped a bowl of hot water from the jacket that surrounded part of the stove. She dipped the sponge into it and stroked it down Shkai'ra's cheek.

"It comes from the Middle Sea, Chiefkin. Expensive, but very useful. We use them instead of rags for moonblood, very absorbent. And for padding, and for washing. Please, try it. It's quite pleasurable."

And it will make my work easier if you're a little cleaner, she thought. *A fine body, I might have enjoyed lying with you if we'd met otherwise, but Circle, how you smell!* She was not looking forward to the Kommanza's bleeding-time, either.

Shkai'ra squinted at her doubtfully, then laid herself down and accepted the gentle touch of the hot sponge. *Pleasant*, she thought, and wondered whether it was weakening to have hot water on her skin so often. On the other hand, the shamans made you clean your wounds with boiled water, and that did seem to make them heal faster. Women had to wash before childbirth, and after.

Hmmmmm, yes. Her skin did feel lighter, almost as if there had been a layer between her and the warm air of the travel sled. There was a glow, as well. The Minztan rubbed her with a heated cloth.

"This makes it easier to keep the fleas at bay," she continued.

Shkai'ra stretched, yawned, utterly unselfconscious in her enjoyment of the strange sensation. "Nonsense, only sick people lose their fleas," she murmured drowsily. "But they can be as bad as nomads in long grass, in the winter with everyone crammed together. The dhaik'tz do say they can carry ill luck."

She wrinkled her nose at the memory of the fumigants the shamans used—sulfur-based, noxious stuff.

Maihu shrugged out of her clothes at Shkai'ra's nod.

"Wait, Chiefkin," she said, as the plainswoman reached for her. She poured pine oil from a pebbly green glass bottle into her palms. The sharp tangy scent filled the air. The small strong hands began massaging the oil into the Kommanza's skin, starting at the neck and kneading expertly at the tense muscles. Eyes closed, the warrior arched her back and purred at the skilled, almost impersonal touch working its way down her spine. She had been more knotted up than she suspected, and the Kommanz breathing exercises were designed to produce strength and flexibility rather than relaxation. Her joints crackled as they were stretched and twisted; palms and hand edges drummed

along her deltoids and loosened the powerful long
muscles at the back of her thighs.

Maihu finished by probing the pressure points: nape
of the neck, behind the ears, under the shoulderblades, small of the back, upper thigh, behind the
knees, and the sole of the foot. She knelt, digging her
thumbs into the arch and rotating the ankles.

"How do you feel, Chiefkin?" she asked at last.

"*Ahi-a*, boneless," Shkai'ra replied dreamily.

"You have a fine body, Chiefkin," she said. It was
true; long and sleek and tight, the skin smooth and
fine-grained where it was not scarred or marked with
the continual rubbing of the armor's chafe points.

"So do you," the Kommanza said, stroking her with
a foot. "A little chunky, but well-kept. No extra flesh."

Maihu hesitated. It was inevitable, so why not? She
reached up and turned down the lantern, then touched
the other's breasts: the nipples were tight, and there
were a few faint freckles on the milk-white skin.

"You know we Minztans have arts your folk don't."

Shkai'ra closed her eyes and smiled through parted
lips. Her face had a reddish cast in the subdued light.
"Yes," she murmured.

"Shall I show you some of them?" Her fingers
moved in small circles.

Shkai'ra laughed, not the usual shrill giggle of her
people, but an almost silent husky sound. "Lead on,"
she said.

Much later, she lay with her head on the Kommanza's stomach, one hand cupped over her mound, feeling the pulse leap and slow. Her own body felt relaxed
and restless at the same time, as if her skin were too
tight, prickling. Spillover, but . . .

Shkai'ra bent and kissed her. "What would you
like?" she whispered.

"Does that matter?" Maihu said, looking up at her.
"Sometimes. Tonight."

They lay tangled together. The sled smelled pleasantly, of warm fur and pine oil and sex; through the
thick covering the wind sounded cold and distant. It
was easy to imagine yourself outside, Shkai'ra thought,
out in an unpeopled immensity lightless under stars,
endless, traveled by wolf and tiger and demon. Easy
and pleasant lying here in the comfortable afterglow;
her body felt weightless, ready for sleep yet alert.

Best I've ever had, she thought drowsily.

She turned to the Minztan and ran her index finger
over the other's closed eyelids.

"Odd," she murmured. "I ought to despise you. I
did, at first, but somehow, I can't help liking you, even
docile as you are." She ruffled Maihu's hair. "Perhaps
it's because I don't have to be anxious with you, the
way I would with a Kommanza smart enough to understand my thoughts."

Maihu touched the barely perceptible marks on
Shkai'ra's stomach. "You have a child, Chiefkin?" she
asked idly.

"Hmmmm? Ah, yes. An accident. Last harvest but
one, I was too drunk at the festival to remember the
precautions." A smile at the pleasant memory. "But
not too drunk to lie on my back. Then, with the lazy
season coming on and no war, I decided to bring it
to term." Not that she had seen it since; she had
trouble even remembering the gender of it. The Mek
Kermak kinelders had welcomed the chance of binding one of the village chiefs by fostering the child out,
but there was no question of contaminating the godborn strain by keeping it.

Maihu shivered at the explanation. Among her people, as with the Kommanza, paternity within the kin-

fast was anybody's guess, but the thought of discarding a child like that . . .

It was no wonder they were as they were. It was a puzzle: the Kommanz, were perfectly fitted to their environment, but they seemed to break every rule of the Harmony that fashioned all things . . . Well enough, it was not her place to philosophize, merely to live within the Circle.

Dh'ingun walked across and settled down like a ball of midnight where Maihu's thigh crossed Shkai'ra's. Maihu worked fingers into the fur at the angle of his jaw and was rewarded with a purr, a hoarse rumble that she felt as a vibration where the feline's body curled against her leg.

The westerner pulled a book from a pocket on the fabric wall. "Read for me again," she said.

"Which one, Chiefkin?" The Kommanza's taste was strange. Maihu would have expected her to favor the blood-and-thunder epics most like the chanted-sung poetry that was the great art form of the steppe. Instead she had a child's appetite for marvels, princesses with eyes like the moon who rode on swans from domes of crystal, or the funny earthy animal tales Minztans used for amusement and instruction of their youngsters.

"The one about the talking animals," she said.

"A wizard coupled with a poor woman once, in the city of the king," Maihu read. "She bore a son with one gray eye and one black . . ."

Maihu propped the book against the curve of her hip and read on, the steady sound of her voice the loudest thing in the closed space, melding with the soft hiss of the stove and the sough of the wind.

"Enough," Shkai'ra yawned. "I've a day in the saddle to await." Drowsy, she continued: "While you sit on the sled and tootle on your flute. Although Dh'ingun doesn't seem to like it much; he yowled every time I rode by."

Of course, thought Maihu, cats have the *overhearing* too. But they can't talk. The Kommanza dropped away toward sleep.

Maihu watched her for a time. *What is it I feel?* she thought. Not hatred, although the Circle knows I have reason ... Perhaps I'm nearer to Enlightenment than I thought. Pity? Yes, pity, although I will bring this one to ruin and death if I can. But she has the remnants of a soul, and acts only as her training commands. She turned out the light and smoothed a braid back from Shkai'ra's face before closing her own eyes. Together the women and the cat drifted into darkness.

The commanders woke Shkai'ra early the next morning. She stepped out of the sled, looked around at their faces, and snarled.

"How many?"

"Two missing," the second-watch commander said. *"Get the spook-pusher!"*

The shaman came swaggering, chewing with pleasure on a piece of raw liver. His face was livid with bruises; to the experienced eyes about him, much like the wounds of glancing blows with a wooden club. It took a moment for the glares of the officers to penetrate his self-assurance.

"I thought your wisdom was going to stand over us 'like the shield of Zailo,' " a voice said. Shkai'ra was voiceless and motionless. Walks-with-Demons took a step back at the sight of her.

"I ..." He wet his lips. "I held the wood-switch in fight, this night past. He couldn't have made any strong magic—"

"Out of my sight!" Shkai'ra said, with cold deadliness. "Out in the woods; maybe you can do some good there. You ride outer scout."

"If he can find his own arse with both hands," one of the Bannerleaders muttered.

Shkai'ra rose and stood tapping her gauntlets on the palm of one hand. There was an unfamiliar taste in her mouth, like tarnished copper; it took a few seconds for her to identify it. Fear.

"Standard procedure," she said in the same steady tone. "Make speed; push it, kill any in the coffles that drag. Zailo shield you."

"Zaik lead you, Chiefkin."

The first scattered flakes fell from a sky the color of iron, and the wind began to keen.

The Minztans found the body left bound on a leather groundsheet pegged to the packed snow that covered the river ice. They had been finding bodies all day, huddled shapes under blankets of snow. It was a moment before anyone realized that there was no snow on the corpse; it had melted off. Narritanni's second-in-command pushed forward and knelt beside the spreadeagled form, wincing at the huge splayed-open incision in the gut. She carefully avoided looking at the face, and suspected that her single glance would stay with her far longer than she wished.

The interior of the wound was like a diagram, nothing missing but a slice of the liver. And there was impossibly little blood. A sudden suspicion formed. She touched the blood on the leather sheet: it had had time to dry before it froze, time to blacken. She stripped off a glove and touched the victim's flesh.

The warrior turned and ran half a dozen paces into the concealing curtain of the snowfall before falling to her knees again. Her sword flashed out, and she began hacking at the ice; flailing at first, then with steady methodical persistence.

Narritanni saw the band group around the body,

then suddenly back away as if from a fearful menace. He hurried forward, and stopped in puzzlement. The sight was foul, yes, but not enough to throw adrift the mind of one of his trained followers, who had seen far worse things.

He slid to a halt beside her. She was speaking, under her breath, in a tone like cursing, like weeping.

"No, no, no, oh Circle, *please, no* . . ."

He laid a hand on her shoulder before speaking. "What . . . ?" he began.

A face streaked with tears looked up at him. He waited in shock.

"The body," she said, breast heaving. Her sword rested in a pit of blue-green ice chips. "The blood was dried, hours old-from last night."

"The Eater," he said, lips tightening. "Well, we knew—"

"The body hasn't stiffened," she ground out. "Barely even cold. It's been ten hours, *and she was alive all the while.*"

The one who had named himself Man of Stone hid his face in his hands, then wheeled into the wind and forced down huge breaths of the damp cold air. His body prickled, with a fearsweat that was wholly impersonal.

"Ah, ah, ah," he gasped. Then calm settled over him. "We can't attack until . . . We'll have to ask the Wise Man, and try the Litany for *It* to help . . ."

She rose, checked the sword, and rammed it back into the sheath as if that was a body. "Tomorrow, then," she said.

Leafturn held the eyelids of the victim closed, long enough for them to stiffen in that position. He read the symbols painted on her body, with knowledge and a grimace of distaste, sinking back on his heels. Probing at his foreboding, he could not force it to become

more definite; but he had walked the Way too long
not to know the smell of fate. There was more here
than he had imagined, and more than the destiny of
these few scores of folk. He had an uneasy sense that
he and his opponent both ran on leashes.

What was it that the steppe peoples called tragedy?
His mind groped for the phrase. *The laughter of Zaik.*

Slowly, sullenly, the walls of the forest slid by as the
column moved down the thirty-meter-wide corridor of
the frozen river. Above, the low cloud roiled gray,
filtering the afternoon light to a pale monochrome.
Wind blew, smelling of cold and the hinting dampness
of snowstorm, ruffling the manes of the horses and
sending lance pennants snapping out. Shivering, the
slave coffles bent their heads and trudged. The sound
of their shuffling made counterpoint to the muffled
thudding of hundreds of hooves and the hissing of
runners. A crow launched itself from a skeletal maple
leaning out over the ice, its *grawk-grawk-grawk* loud
among the quiet murmur of the warband.

Shkai'ra followed its flight with longing eyes as she
cantered down the line. High it would fly, until the
struggling humans were a string of black dots on the
snow, ants lost in a wilderness of trees. She shivered.
Morale was bad; they had been losing the outlying
scouts by ones and twos for days, more casualties than
the battle had cost them. Her killers were not afraid
to face death, she thought. It was the unknown lurker
that frightened them. Her lips tightened. This morning, one of the scouts had refused duty. Her Bannerleader killed her on the spot, of course, the
traditional punishment for insubordination in enemy
territory. But the decay of discipline shook Shkai'ra.

And they had found the first dead scout's horse—
or the head, left by the riverside impaled on a pole,

with runes cut in its forehead. The Horse Curse, most deadly of all doomsayings.

She looked upward; the snow had lifted for a while, but there would be more soon, pulling at boot and fetlock, draining strength and spirit. There was a scuffle around one of the coffles. She pulled up. A Minztan had sunk to the snow and sat on his haunches; the guard reined in and leaned over to snarl and strike with her quirt. The slave looked up and shook his head with infinite weariness. The Kommanza pulled her lance out of its rest, flipped it up to the overhand grip, and stabbed downward with clinical precision. The man toppled over and flopped as she pulled the long razor-edged lancehead out of him with two swift jerks and cleaned it on his jacket. Without dismounting she used the edge to slice the body free and then left it to lie. The rest of the dead man's coffle stood, staring dumbly, motionless. The guard yelled, a shrill note in her voice, then prodded savagely with the butt of the lance. Still soundless, the Minztans slowly turned and resumed their weary plodding.

Shkai'ra shivered again, and debated getting out the bison-pelt cloak. *No,* she thought: *bad example.* It would be pleasant to go back to the sled and lie with her head in Maihu's lap and listen to one of those strange stories . . . even to that accursed flute that put Dh'ingun's fur up. But no, that would be weakness. It was more important than ever to set a standard; it was more than the lurker that was eating at her followers' hearts, it was this Zaik-forsaken, Zailo-damned country. Out on the steppe the sky was the most endless on earth, but in this forest you couldn't *see,* each *kylick* was the same as the next, and there was an infinity of places for things to hide . . . She jerked her mind out of that track as she passed the still form of the Minztan.

At least the ravens will be happy tonight, she thought dryly.

She had not been listening to the whistle calls, not consciously. They were a language of their own, woven into the fabric of the mind in earliest childhood. The background mutter was conversation; mostly routine, position changes, time checks, a running commentary on the terrain. You could always pick out something meant for you, the way your hearing could filter your own name out of the babble in a crowded room. And it was a marvelously compact language, stylized, each sound standing hieroglyph-like for a phrase or sentence.

Thus the first relay brought her head up. *"Gap,"* it said, and followed with identity and position references, all over in a few seconds. A chill of apprehension prompted her to send a signal of her own down the line of the column: attack-alert, left flank. And right on the heels of that came confirmation, a hostile-sighting call from the left-flank third-layer scouts—the ones next to the column itself, pacing it a few hundred meters out in the woods. That shocked her to her soul. How could anyone punch through the mesh that fast? Magic . . . unless the scouts were demoralized enough to close in and report false positions. Neither bore thinking about. She heeled her horse into a gallop.

13

Maihu and Taimi had been sitting inside the sled; there was little to see outside, and no point in enduring the cold without need. Both wore ankle tethers: linked sections of hardwood covered in sheaths of iron-hard rawhide slipped on wet and then warmed and greased. The ropes ended in maplewood rings fastened likewise, wound around with wet thongs in a massive knot that could be cut but never untied. Taimi crouched listlessly in a corner, staring fixedly at the opposite wall and picking at the bindings on his ankle.

Worried, Maihu looked up from her work. She had been carving a piece of antler for the hilt of a hunting knife, holding the bone between her bootsoles and attacking it with gouge and emery and polishing cloth. The sled was not really the place for such work—the occasional lurch set the tools awry—but it was better than letting her thoughts chase each other around and around on the same well-worn tracks. What the Circle gave would happen, and she could do no more than she was doing already. It was Taimi who gave her most concern; he had taken to copying the Kommanz isometric exercises, which was well enough, but . . .

It was a blankness at the back of her mind that
alerted her. Even with the Eater out of the camp she
was cautious, but a hint of familiarity emboldened her
to probe.

And that brought shock: *It*, there was no mistaking
it. Rage, and cunning, then concealment: no hostile
mind could likely catch that perception now, unless
perhaps the Eater's. Shouting resounded dimly through
the padded walls of the sled, as the Kommanz threw
themselves into ordered motion at the prompting of
the code-calls. Hooves thudded past, and there was a
neigh as a horse was pulled up. She heard the youngling driver call a question.

"The gutsucking bark-eaters have gotten up their
rabbit's courage and attacked," a harsh voice barked
in Kommanzanu. "Report to your duty station. We go
to our chiefs."

The youngster gave a yelp of delight. Taimi had
come to life, tense and quivering; he thrust his head
through the entry curtain to see what was happening.
The driver cursed and lashed him savagely across the
face with the loose end of the reins, then looked in
to check on their bonds.

"Good," she grunted, and dropped from the seat,
picked up her light bow, and trotted away to where
she would help with the wounded and shuttle spare
arrows. Her scalplock bobbed.

"Quick, kinmother," Taimi gasped. "This must be
the rescue."

"Wait," Maihu said. Reaching inside a concealed
pocket in the sled lining she produced a heavy knife,
tucking it inside her jacket. Restraining Taimi with
one hand, she listened cautiously. There was a slave
coffle behind them. Thence came only a low murmuring, rising now as the captives realized that something
unusual was in the offing. Ahead, around the bend in

the river, forest and earth cut off sight. Yells, first; then the humming snap of massed archery, the whickering of shafts. Then screaming, one voice at first and the others picking it up, a shrill ululating wailing falsetto shriek that raised the hairs along Maihu's spine. Madness, and death, and hatred, quavering through the chill restless air; the Kommanz warcry. Then all sound faded with surprising speed; wood-strained ears told her why.

"They're retreating," she told Taimi. "No, it may be a trick," she continued as his face crumpled.

They jumped down from the sled. Behind it the slave lines had turned into a surging chaos where the villagers heaved against their bonds and roared out anger and hope. Most of the Kommanz guards had been drawn forward to the combat at the head of the column, or into the left-flank woods in an attempt at counterambush. The few remaining Kommanza struggled with lancebutt and whip to keep the captives under control; only the unwieldy size of the coffles kept them from making a break for the woods a mere ten meters away. That had been the point; groups that size could walk slowly, if they moved in unison under direction, but in a situation like this where each individual tried to move in his or her own track, they hampered each other, jerked each other off their feet. Maihu saw one whole coffle go over in a tangle of limbs, with the guards lashing out as the slaves tried to regain their feet. One rider had his saber out. She knew with gruesome certainty that fairly soon it would be in use, and not the flat of it either.

They were on the right side of the sled, and so Maihu saw the Minztans come sliding down the opposite bank of the river a moment before the Kommanza did. There were many, perhaps thirty, Maihu thought. Taimi was yelling, frantic, jerking at the wood-and-leather chain that bound him to the vehicle, setting it rocking on its bone-and-fiberglass springs. The three ponies hitched to it were catching the infection, snorting and backing, their eyes rolling white against the shaggy brown hair.

"Quiet!" shouted Maihu, shaking him by the back of his jacket. "Quiet! If the horses run, we'll be dragged." On the third repetition that sank in.

The squad of Kommanza reacted swiftly. It was no part of their mission to waste their lives against impossible odds. Their squadleader shrilled out an order on his whistle, and they raced their horses forward toward the head of the column. All except one, whose horse was lapped by a wave of prisoners gone mad with the sudden hope. They pressed in regardless of hooves, a many-handed grasping monster terrible in its clumsy power.

The saber rose, its edge glittering even in the dull cloudy light, fell, rose again stained where the curved cutting edge had landed with a drawing slash. The horse sounded, loud as the rider's shrilling, lashing out with teeth and battering feet, rearing and plunging. It pulled free before bound hands had a chance to haul the steppe killer from her saddle, but by then the free Minztans had arrived.

Maihu saw who led them and leaned back against the sled, suddenly weak as her heart seemed to lurch under the confining breastbone. Most were Garnetseat villagers, but at their head ran two in light armor and helmets, armed with shortsword and billhook, their smocks of gray and off-white making them almost impossible to see against the snow. They swarmed around the Kommanza as she spurred to escape, brought her to bay near enough for Maihu to see the taut grin on her face as she realized her death. The two rangers spread, darted in. One of them engaged the westerner with a clang and clatter of metal on metal, parrying and striking with the long polearm. The other dodged in, reckless, and swung two-handed to hamstring the mount. He succeeded; cavalry are most vulnerable when they lose momentum. A human on foot is more nimble than a standing horse.

"The Seeker's people," Maihu thought, breathless. They came in time. And *It* must have come as well, for them to be this bold. *That* was what took the Kommanza in the woods.

The volunteers moved in as the Kommanza leaped from the saddle. She landed rolling and bounced erect. In that moment a tall hunter threw a cord around her neck from behind and closed strangling hands—but he had forgotten the gorget that guarded her throat. A spurred boot snapped up and back, ripped down, left him yammering anguish at his mutilated groin. Her hands went up and gripped, leaving the sword to dangle by its wrist thong. The armored body twisted and heaved, and the wounded Minztan flew over her head to land with breath knocked loose on his back before her.

"*Zaik!*" she screamed. "*Zaik with me!*" A single chopping motion of the shield stove in the man's larynx, leaving him to strangle slowly.

Leaping the body, she sprang into the midst of the enemy, forcing her way into the center of the crowd where their own numbers would hamper them, where they could not strike freely for fear of striking their own folk. No such limits hindered her. Lacking any hope except to make an honorable death, she had gone *ahrappan*. Her face twisted into a gorgon's mask that startled her foes into panic by its sheer hideousness. Froth dripped from her wide-stretched mouth, and she fought with sword and shield and feet, whirling and striking and slashing like a dust devil

edged with knives. Armor protected her, and what
blows did land she seemed not to feel.

Driven two-handed, the spike on the tip of a billhook drove through the side buckles of her gorget.
She turned, wrenching the point free with a twist that
brought blood gouting out in throbbing red pulses.
And even then she did not fall; the curved sword
flicked out, took off half the hand gripping the shaft
of the weapon that had killed her. The wielder
screamed and spasmed, sending it flying to land at
Maihu's feet. With a last thrust the Kommanza
stabbed her slayer through the throat and collapsed.
And died, still struggling mindlessly to rise as the last
of her blood pumped out on the trampled snow.

Not in vain. Distracted, the Minztans had no time
to free their landsfolk. Now around the corner of the
river bend came the shivering thunder of hooves. The
Minztans were about to learn why the armored lancer
and horse archer ruled the steppe lands.

"Into the woods!" screamed the wounded Minztan.
Most of the freed slaves followed him, but others burst
east in panic, down the open road of the river.

The space between the sleds and the north bank of
the west-trending river was just wide enough for ten
riders abreast to deploy comfortably in line. A full
Banner rounded the bend at a pounding gallop, and
checked the barest fraction of a second to dress ranks
before plunging forward. The front rank leveled
lances; the second kept theirs at rest and fired over
their comrades' heads, arching shots that fell among
the forest folk in whistling sheets. Then the charge
struck. Watching in fascinated horror, Maihu half expected to hear a crash of impact. Instead the Kommanz ranks passed straight through the loose Minztan
formation without slowing. The loudest sound under
the Kommanz wailing and the screams of the wounded

was the heavy massive thudding of lanceheads striking home with hundreds of kilos of swift-moving horse and rider behind them. Few survived such impact.

Then the riders were through, turning, sheathing bows. The lancers let the long ashwood shafts pivot free about the balance point of the grip, or shook their arms out of the elbow loops of broken weapons; and now the sabers came out, bright and long. Those of the Minztans near to the forest edge had some chance if they survived the first passage; a few scrambled back into the sheltering trees. Most broke in panic fleeing downriver, and the Kommanza followed them whooping with delight. Seven thousand years of history had shown that it was death to run from a lance; the principle had received another demonstration.

Maihu heard Taimi beside her, cursing and sobbing with frustration. Not far away on the ice a Garnetseat villager was crawling, dragging herself along on her hands; the bright-dyed fletching of an arrow lodged in her lower spine showed why, bobbing and jerking with the movement. A man sat and stared at the stump where a hand had been. With painful slowness he began to fumble at his belt, for a loop to twist around the wound, then he fell soddenly into the stain spreading around him through the packed layers of snow. The first swift flakes melted as they struck it, then began to draw a merciful curtain of white over the redness.

Maihu shook herself out of her daze. Taimi snatched up the billhook and began hacking frantically at the tether that held him, driving two-handed blows that might have done more good had he been calm enough to land two on the same spot.

"Come *on*, kinmother," he gasped. "Help me, oh, help me!"

She hesitated, looked up at the sound of a rider

approaching. "Quick, quick," her kinchild groaned. He
was driven, oblivious. But Maihu looked up, into cold
gray eyes under a plumed helmet. The bow was drawn
to the ear, the point of the arrowhead trained un-
waveringly on Taimi's stomach; at that range it would
nail him to the sled to die like a shrike's prey on a
thorn.

With a convulsive movement the Minztan woman
grabbed the bill. They wrestled for it, before smith-
strong arms wrenched it away. She threw it whirling
end over end, out beyond the reach they could follow
on their tethers. She gathered Taimi to her, cradled
his head on her breast in the crook of one arm, stared
over it into Shkai'ra's eyes.

The arrowhead sank; Maihu could hear the relaxing
string *scritch* on the bone ring the steppe-dwellers
used for the thumb-locked-under-forefinger draw of
their horn-stiffened bows. Their eyes stayed locked.

Then the Kommanza leaned to the right. Sensitive
to every shift of balance, the horse pirouetted, turning
in place. Shkai'ra drew and loosed without seeming to
aim; the arrow was only a flicker of head and fletching
streaking in a dead-flat line to the north bank of the
river. A Minztan was nearly to the trees, dragging a
stiffened leg; he slapped forward as if a giant hand
had struck between his shoulderblades, fell facedown
and slithered back to the surface of the river ice. Ten
meters beyond him the arrow sank a handspan deep
into a tree and stood quivering. Then Shkai'ra slid the
bow back into its case and drew her saber, heeling
her mount into a canter to join the chase. Maihu saw
a stumbling Minztan throw herself down to lie out of
reach of the meter of killing steel in the Chiefkin's
fist; the Kommanza guided the dancing steps of her
horse over the prone body and trotted back toward
the head of the column. Her horse left red hoofprints
in the snow.

Maihu sank down. Taimi was too stunned to move; she knelt clutching him, sobbing with soundless harshness and swallowing against the sour taste of bile in her throat.

Bannerleader Kh'ait heard the alarm floating through the relays, from the contact points where the scout-mesh linked into the column. That gave him the position: not far from his own at the head of the trek. Two Banners were here at the point, one back a little, screening the bend in the river, and his own Fang-Banner on guard in the lead; a chokepoint like this narrowing curve was always dangerous when a force was strung out without room to maneuver. And to see it was to think of possible patterns of attack and defense, alternatives and force ratios. The signal tripped the automatic process off, factors smoothly meshing with terrain and tactics to produce answers. His whistle sounded:

[Identity code]: FangBanner, HighKestrelBanner— out bows, left flank, prepare for massed fire on command or sighting.

Straight on the heels of the alarm came shouts and the hum of bowstrings from the woods. The inner link of scouts came crashing through the shrubby undergrowth, retreating toward the main force and trilling out their information. An attack in Banner strength or more, twenty fighters at least in the first wave. That decided him; the attackers would try for an exchange of fire from the bank, where the cover would favor them and their crossbows would be in effective range.

The last of the scouts paused, his mount poised on the lip of the riverbank; he turned and shot from the saddle. He waved the bow triumphantly over his head as the horse slipped and scrambled down to the surface of the ice.

"Shoot!" Kh'ait bellowed.

The two Banners responded with tiger precision, relieved to have an enemy they could fight openly. The arrowstorm raked into the trees, forty wheelbows loosing as fast as the warriors could draw and fire. One crossbow bolt whipped out of the scrub and slammed into armor with a hard *tock* and a trooper fell, shoulder pierced. But the plains wheelbow shot with equal force, and these were archers trained from infancy; they could deliver six times the rate of fire of the clumsy Minztan weapon. There were probably few hits, the Bannerleader decided; not enough targets were visible. But there was nothing the Minztans could do but hug the earth. To stand and fire up there was certain death.

That would only last as long as the contents of their quivers. Thirty shafts was the standard battle reserve, and a few had five-shaft quick-draw magazines clipped onto the side of their bows. Enough for two minutes of concentrated fire, no more; then they would have to wait for bundles to be brought up, and by then the forest folk would have established firing positions along the verge. And crossbows could be fired lying prone. At ordinary battle ranges the wheelbow had much the same firepower as a bolt-action rifle, except for the penalty of bulky ammunition. Kh'ait knew little of firearms, save as distorted legend, but he had an exact understanding of the limitations of his own people's armaments.

Yessss . . . he thought: they would have to go in and take them. And that knowledge woke the carnivore glee that had been building under the calm analytical surface of his waking mind. He slid from the saddle and shifted his shield to his arm. Sword? he asked. No, better the warhammer for this. It was his favorite weapon; you could feel the crunch and shatter of bone along the haft as well as hear it. Even more thrilling than feeling a human dying on your blade.

"FangBanner, up!" he shouted. "Zaik-uz wemit'chi! *Zaik with us!* In and take them—*killlllllllleeeee-eeeeeeeEEEEEEEEEEEEEEEEEEEEEEE.*"

The squads formed around him and they rushed the slope, toiling up under the continuous thupping whisper of the arrowstorm, chopping their shield rims into the snow to give put-chase. He could hear the panting on either side of him, the riding boots scrabbling on the slick surface. Heels dug through with a crunch, snapping the reeds and scrub that stuck up pale and brown and dead through the snow in the shadow of the trees. And as they climbed, fresh snow was flung at them by a wind smelling of damp and pine.

Crossbow bolts flipped by, but few and ill-aimed. Excitement hammered in his temples; now they would see how the woodsrats did when it came to hand-strokes. Just below the lip of the bank there was a final sheer rise of a meter height; as they reached it the flailing wind of shafts ceased, the archers below holding their last shafts on the string, scanning for a good target and waiting for the unblooded youths to come up with the spare shafts, fixed in their circular holders of hard leather. The attackers formed a shieldwall and surged through the screen of frozen undergrowth, into the comparatively open spaces under tall timber. They broke into the cathedral gloom and stillness like a horde of grotesque metallic wolves, their warcries rising to the insane trilling of the blood squeal. Kh'ait saw that he had been right; there were only a few bodies lying about, still or pulling at shafts anchored in flesh; the trees were thickly studded. The bulk of the Minztans were hanging back, below the angle that high-velocity arrowfire from below could reach, protected from dropping shots by the branches

overhead. Some fled at the approach of the Kommanz;
in ones and twos others tried to make a stand.

It made little difference. Those who ran died
quickly; no one can flee and fight, but a pursuer can
still kill. And for those who stood and fought, unarmored, untrained in group combat, death came
nearly as swiftly. The Kommanz wasted no time in
individual dueling; drilled teams moved in, one using
shield or blade to pin an opponent's weapon, the other
sending home a short economical thrust. Little ripples
of deadliness broke up and down the line; gaudy
enameled black armor closing around fur and wool, a
flicker of metal and then another sprawled corpse on
the trodden floor of snow and pine needles.

Kh'ait faced a burly farmer with a woodcutting ax.
The trooper next to him took the blow on her saber,
under the axhead, bringing her shield arm around to
immobilize it. The Bannerleader heard a grunt of frustration, then the sweep of the warhammer drove the
smooth stone head into a cheekbone, left one eye dan-
gling out of its socket and sent splinters into the brain.

This is going well, he thought. The main danger
was that too many would escape into the deep woods,
scattering before his force and retreating faster than
the more heavily burdened Kommanza could pursue.
He was about to give the order to disperse into squads
and garner more of the fleeing enemy when he saw
what waited ahead.

His eyes flicked rapidly down the line. Yes, a definite line; someone had finally taught Minztans to fight
in a well-ordered array. Baiwun strike whoever it had
been! Smocks with uniform blazons, corselets, helmets, billhooks, shortswords, crossbows—lakelander
light infantry kit, from the descriptions he had heard;
some Kommanza had wandered that far east,
horsetraders, and sellswords in the endless fratricidal

wars of the city-states that ringed the inland seas.
Hmmmmm, placed a little too close together for optimum effect—they would get in each other's way—but commendably steady. He waited tensely until the last moment before trilling out the signal—*down!*

The Banner threw themselves to the earth, under the crossbow volley; before their opponents could reload they charged, shrieking. The Kommanza prided themselves on versatility, and next to mounted combat this was the form of war they liked best. Numbers were even, thirty to a side; the plains killers stepped in, reckless of thrusts, keening between their teeth and hammering with edged metal.

The Minztans retreated calmly, a slow steady movement Kh'ait recognized as a controlled retreat to keep his fighters in play until the helpless villagers had a chance to make good their escape. Or, yes, if enough of those rallied, they could break his formation from behind with sniping. He growled with frustration. These bark-eaters were good enough to delay his Banner: there was one down, then another, and then one of his own. Heavier-armed and more skilled, the westerners were having the best of the encounter, but not swiftly enough. Not nearly. Battle-sound echoed through the lanes of the wood, dull thud of blade on shield, occasional harsh musical clang of metal on metal, warshouts, a wounded Minztan screaming endlessly, until unconsciousness cut off the sound sharp as a knife.

Snarling impatience, Kh'ait ran eyes over his opponent. Shield up and angled, short broad-bladed cut-and-thrust sword held hilt down; it was an effective stance, against an adversary armed in the same fashion.

He skipped back a pace and released the outer handhold of his shield, taking the warhammer in a two-handed grip. Then he stepped in, relying on his breastplate. That worked; the tip of the Minztan's sword darted out, struck, and slid off the hard smooth surface. The withdrawal was snake-swift to a ready position with the point just past the edge of the shield, offering him no target. But he was not interested in subtle fencing; he was going to break this line, and had the right tool for it. The warhammer's heavy granite head went up over his helmet. He planted his feet, swung downward in a lashing stroke, unstoppable. A mace was a strong man's weapon, but the arms and shoulders that drove this stroke had trained to war every day of his life, and wrestled young bulls for sport. The shield crumpled; the frame broke, and the arm beneath it. The Minztan wailed in agony, and Kh'ait giggled with pleasure as his backhand blow snapped her neck. He stepped through the gap, ready to turn and kill from behind.

A sword probed for his eyes, and he had to give ground to bring his shield up. He made swift evaluation. This was the leader: chain armor, longer sword, stance, balance. Greed awoke at the sight of that hauberk; this was one soon-to-be corpse that he meant to strip himself. The shield was oval, larger than the round plains buckler; it met his one-handed blows expertly, moving just enough to slide the force off the curves without giving him a clear solid impact that might have done harm even through protection. And the sword worked at him, over the top and side of the shield. The Minztans were backing faster now, moving like a huge door swinging open; he might have been puzzled at that if he had had the time to think about it. It was almost as if they were trying to draw him on toward something waiting in the woods. . . . He drove in, lashing at the enemy commander overarm and backhand; the warhammer boomed on the shield, a drumbeat sound through the trees. But he dared not use full force. The follow-through would leave him off balance, open for an attack, not a risk to be taken with an opponent of this caliber.

The trees were splitting the battle lines, the forest folk using the trunks to prevent the steppe warriors from coming at them more than one-on-one. Out of the corner of his eye Kh'ait saw a trooper charge a single Minztan, using the light one-handed plains ax. It whirled around her head in a blurred, rippling circle; she struck, driving him backward as chips flew from his shield. He tried a stab, relying on the pattern of attack; she stopped the ax in midflight and drove the head backhanded into his neck.

Kh'ait saw an opportunity. The mace was a weapon relying on sheer mass and battering for its power; chainmail gave more protection against cuts than leather, but it lacked the stiffness and fiberglass backing to resist a crushing blow. The enemy leader ... yes, it must be habit, using his sword as if the chain hauberk could protect his shoulder.

The heavy stone head halted in midair, then blurred down with amazing speed.

It was a trick. The Minztan dropped to one knee, throwing his shield up at an acute angle to catch the macehead. Kh'ait saw it even as he began the stroke, but by then he was committed and the momentum was too great to stop.

This one is really not too bad, he thought with surprise. At the same instant the sword snaked out, angling up under the skirt of his hauberk, through the slit that let a horseman bestride a saddle; a frantic twist deflected it a little, but the point plowed painfully into the back of one thigh, above the greave. He crumpled backward, for a heartstopping moment certain that the blade had parted his hamstring. It hadn't, but the wound was still serious. He rolled backward, curling himself under the protection of his shield and struggling to draw his saber. The Minztan followed, striking cautiously, then skipping back as the Kommanza's followers closed in. The forest war band was in full retreat; their leader joined them, darting from tree to tree.

"After them, kinless bastards!" he snarled. "Pursue until they scatter, then rally to me."

Humiliation burned him worse than pain. Someday, he thought, I will take that one's scalp, then kill him for a day and night. His hands probed the wound. Not as bad as it might be; the blood was coming in a steady flow rather than gouting as it would have if one of the big arteries had been cut. From his belt he pulled a field dressing in a leather pouch; it had been boiled and soaked in pure wood alcohol, as the shamans prescribed, a powerful ritual against the demons who brought pus and the green rot. Of course, the shamans could usually lay a deathspell on the little demons who infected wounds, but it was better not to take chances. Absently, he bound the wound, his mind focused on his report. This was an important development, Minztans trained and armed as regular troops. They would have to get to the bottom of it. He hoped his killers had remembered to take a prisoner for interrogation.

He brightened. That would provide amusement, even if he had to stay off the leg for a while.

Deeper in the woods, a consciousness wavered in indecision. The *calling* drew it, and the rage of territory violation; but wariness had been ground into its breed for generations past counting. It hooted softly.

A mind touched it. *Reassurance-familiarity-confidence,* it projected. The flavor was not familiar, but it had the right resonances. Slowly, cautiously, it drifted forward. The Wise Man came in its wake, alone of the forest people able to sense any trace of it at all. The exultant screeching of the plains raiders turned to shouts of alarm as the Minztans turned; and as they did axemen sent the final strokes through trees already nine-tenths cut. The huge pine-trunks thundered down in a crackling of branches that was like volley-fire. Not many of the Kommanz were caught directly by the latticework of fallen trees, but it disrupted their formations and each trunk was a breast-high fort. And the pursued turned back to worm their way through the tangle of fallen wood, as at home in the under-brush as their enemies were clumsy.

Shkai'ra spurred down the line of the column in the wake of the alarm alert, past sleds and horses and warriors reined in by discipline but longing to join the distant combat.

"Eyes on the *woods*, you kinless lumps of nomad shit," she heard the officers shouting. "Bows out! Fire at will on sighting!"

She reined in at the head of the column, to see the warriors of HighKestrelBanner stuffing fresh arrows into their quivers, each bundle of thirty held in alignment by two pierced leather disks at point and midshaft. She pulled up and called to the Bannerleader: "Report!"

The woman replied without taking her gaze from the trampled underbrush where FangBanner had vanished.

"One casualty," she replied, clipped and impersonal. "Attack in Banner strength or more, but we won the shaft battle. Senior Bannerleader Kh'ait decided to exploit fire supremacy with FangBanner, ordering me to remain here with the reserve and await your orders, Chiefkin."

Down on the hoof-pounded snow two unblooded

youths and the shaman were attending to the wounded warrior. The crossbow shaft had been cut across flush with the cuirass before the breastplate was removed, and they were hacking a clear area around the wound, slicing away gambeson and tunic. Walks-with-Demons put his ear to the man's mouth, listening for the telltale bubbling.

"Good!" he grunted. "Missed the lung." A preliminary tug at the stub of wood produced a stilled grunt and quiver from the victim. "So, yes, have to cut."

The shaman halted and turned his face to the woods. There was something ... but no time. They placed the warrior's knife hilt between his teeth. The shaman took a small crook-bladed tool from a pouch and swabbed down the edge with alcohol from a flask, scrubbed the area around the puncture, and began to probe.

"Have it out in a minute, yes, Rh'ivvuk," he muttered: Healing was not the most dignified part of a shaman's work, but he was proud of his skill; the dhaik'taz learned anatomy and the healing skills as the first part of their training. And it served to keep the warriors feeling less hostile, to have them reminded of their dependence on his knowledge.

"Sssssa, caught on the joint, yes, as I thought." He made another cut, gripped the wood firmly, and pulled. The man lay panting, wide-eyed but soundless, as it came out.

"Ahe-he-he-we," he hummed, putting more of the disinfectant on his fingers and probing for bits of cloth and armor in the deep narrow wound. That done, he poured some of the clear liquid into the puncture, packed it with the special wound powder made from potato mold with secret rites, and covered it with a pad of boiled linen and the iodine the southron traders brought.

"Good as new, yes," he said, grinning, as he strapped bandages around the shoulder. "Don't put any strain on it for a while." Playfully, he gave a slap on the shoulder and rose to a torrent of scatological abuse.

Shkai'ra had been using them as a focus, her eyes blank as she weighed factors. Now she threw down a pouch from her saddlebag.

"Dreamweed," she said. "As much as you like of that, but no more once it's finished." To the officer: "This smells of a diversion; no sense to a weak attack like that, otherwise. I'll take your Banner—you whistle in the odds-and-sods on guard duty and the two inner ranks of the right-flank scoutmesh, and hold them here as reserve—"

At that moment the four slave-guards from the coffles came pounding around the bend of the river; the details of the Minztan attack floated ahead of them in an intricate sequence of trills. Shkai'ra wasted no time; she fluted HighKestrelBanner into double line and chopped her arm forward. Seventeen horses rocked into motion, the whole mass curving down the ice in a hard, controlled arc that would bring them around the narrow bend and into the slightly wider area behind in perfect contact alignment.

Shkai'ra suppressed excitement; this was no time to lose the self in battlejoy, no, she must remain alert and clear-witted. The lance was held loosely in her hand. Under her the horse rocked into a long, loping gallop, seeming to float across the surface of the frozen river, touching its hooves down at intervals to keep speed in that weightless trajectory. On either side, narrow leafshaped steel slivers jutted hungrily, the pennants streaming in the wind of the riders' speed. One with her mount, she leaned gracefully into the curve as they turned, their ranks rippling as instinctive skill

maintained exact distance between riders. Overhead
the arrows went whistling, *whup-whup-whup*, hoi-ah,
the Breath of Baiwun streaming out over the battlefield! Exultant, the troopers screeched, couched their
lances, each transformed into a hammering, sharp-
pointed projectile of flesh and bone and armor.
Hooves tossed gouts of packed snow and blue-gray ice
into the air; white-eyed, flare-nostriled heads pumped
with the effort of the gallop, huge muscles bunching
and coiling between tight-clamped thighs.

Shkai'ra felt the keening welling past her clenched
teeth, felt the shivering desire to kill rising in a hot
tide in her throat, a warm rank taste like blood. Even
then she was freezing the scene before her into memory: the last slave guard falling among the Minztan
blades (and that was a good death: that one would be
reborn as *ofzar*; she herself would raise a tablet in her
kinhearth). Thirty or so of the forest warriors running,
scattering before the unstoppable horror avalanching
down on them. More scrambling up into the woods,
but that was beyond control.

Time slowed. A moment stretched as the lancers
braced their feet. Time was . . . *now*.

Her lancehead dipped to spear one Minztan through
the back, low. His speed lessened the impact; she was
able to jerk the weapon free without pivoting it, the
sharp reverse shoulders of the blade completing the
bisection of his kidney as it pulled free of the ravaged
flesh with a shower of drops. White shreds of fat clung
to the rivets through the tangle. With a continuation
of the same movement she flicked the lance backward;
the ceramic buttknob connected with the skull of a
woodsdweller four paces behind her horse. There was
a hard thock, a wood-on-wood sound, and the Minztan
halted with an egg-sized depression in her skull that
glistened like a third eye, dark red in the whiteness
of her forehead.

Shkai'ra did not bother to look back again; instead she tossed the ashwood shaft up, twirling it over her head like a huge baton to poise point down to her left. There was an enemy there, running with terror-wide eyes, so intent on flight that he did not see his own death. She rammed it down with a snap, surgeon-precise, in the spot just over the collarbone. And then cursed; his dying spasm clenched the metal hard against bone. She wheeled the horse in a near half-circle and freed her arm from the twisted half-sling. A strong pull brought no result, and she had no time to dismount and brace the body with her foot. She abandoned the lance for the cleanup teams.

Far enough, she decided, looking up. The snow was about to begin; the crisp floury smell was unmistakable. Once the easterners were over their panic they could hide, and strike back from cover. Not much chance that they would rally, but ... Her whistle trilled out, authorizing a half-*kylick* of pursuit before rallying to the main column; she herself turned back, pulling out her bow and scanning quickly over the field of battle. Bodies scattered about, all Minztan except for the one guard; infantry had little chance against a charge like that, none without pikes and bill and missile weapons. Some of the wounded were still moving, and she decided to take care of that; it would not do to have any escape, or sham dead long enough to get within knife range of a trooper collecting scalps. These damned trees again, she thought disgustedly. Even when you had a decent fight like this the nearness of cover interfered.

Shkai'ra saw what was happening at the travel sled before the preoccupied Minztans glanced up. Her mount halted to the clues of knee pressure and balance that signaled her command. She curled her thumb under the shaft, locked two fingers over it, and drew to the ear. They were no more than fifteen meters to her left, a clear shot; the stave of the bow flexed against her arms as she threw back and shoulder strength into the draw, familiar pressure falling off as the pulley wheels at the tips flipped over on their offset pivots and levered against the pull of thick wood and horn and fiberglass. The rigid central handgrip pushed its molded curves against her left palm; the arrow slid smoothly back through the grooved cutout until the base of the head rested snugly against the front of the rest.

She hesitated. Taimi was chopping madly at his tether with the cutting blade of the weapon; Maihu was dithering, uncertain. *I should kill him*, Shkai'ra thought. *More trouble than he's worth, and he's trying to run.* Maihu saw her; she seized the billhook and threw it pinwheeling away, caught her kinchild to her. The blue eyes met hers. There was a long moment of tension.

The Kommanza lowered the bow. *Glitch*, she thought. Then: *don't want her made sullen again, anyway.* The thought frightened and disgusted her, to be shaping her actions for the approval of a slave. For a moment she thought of witchcraft, then pushed it away. Besides, the other's actions were a good sign that the taming was going well. And why shouldn't she do as she pleased with her own, to kill or to spare?

"Enough," she muttered softly to herself. There was work to do. She turned the horse and scanned for a target.

A double hand of minutes twice repeated had passed by the time Shkai'ra came trotting back to the reserve unit, wiping the blood from her saber. The Bannerleader had whipped the small detachments on guard and scout detail into tight formation, ready to strike in any direction. An energetic officer, Shkai'ra decided. But the sight reminded her that she had lost two-thirds of a Banner on this raid; it was turning into a running dogfight on unfavorable terrain. That would reflect on her, despite the rich booty; treasure was good, but the Kommanz were not a prolific people, and they needed every lance to keep the nomads at bay. That was a matter of survival, not wealth. It was luck that the Sky-Blue Wolves of the High Steppe bred no faster, she reflected, or there might be hard trouble.

She returned the nodded salute. "As I awaited," she said. "This was a diversion, up here. The main effort was to free the slaves and get them into the forest while we were occupied here. A close thing, but we stopped them and killed most, few losses. Best you get a detail back there, before the ones in the coffles start getting ideas again."

"Good killing, Chiefkin," the officer complimented her. "No word from Bannerleader Kh'ait yet. Do you think there's any cause for concern?" She sounded worried. Not at any effort the bark-eaters might put up, of course, but over the unknown force that had been killing the sentries every night. It was daytime now, but it was still out there.

There was a sudden gust of wind, hooting through the trees and down the river, flicking snow into their eyes. It was thickening as they spoke, cutting visibility. Shkai'ra's horse snorted and tossed its head; she smoothed a soothing hand down its neck, annoyed.

"Nia, if they had something better they wouldn't have tried such a half-arsed plan. It needed twice the force they had to work, and they'd have had to be dead lucky as well." She scowled. "They shouldn't have been able to get the degree of surprise they did, either."

The shaman started up, caught her eye. He nodded,

closed his mouth, and sank back down in a crouch, fingers dancing over his drum and eyes shut. One does not spit on the tiger's tail. His consciousness groped out again, puzzled. The woods wizard was blocking him, yes, but what was the *other* thing?

Shkai'ra bared her teeth at the sight of Walks-with-Demons and swung a foot out of the stirrup. "Kh'ait has a grip like a greatwolf," she said to the Bannerleader. "I'd better go and pull him back before he chases them all the way south to the Middle Sea; it's not safe in weather like this." She dropped to the ground.

"Alone, Chiefkin?" the officer asked. Shkai'ra nodded and transferred her bowcase and quiver from saddle to back.

"*Ia*; we don't have enough troopers to spare, at the moment. Get the guards in order, put the right-flank scoutmesh back in place, and patrol the river upstream and down with your own Banner until I get back. And see to the usual things, collecting spent arrows and so forth." She looked up. The short winter day was ending above the white fog of snow, and she suddenly realized that she was reluctant to venture into the woods with . . . whatever it was.

Disturbed, she turned to go quickly. "This looks like heavy snow. We'll camp hereabouts. Zailo shield you."

"Zaik lead you, Chiefkin."

She drew blade, trotted past the FangBanner horses where they stood drop-reined, and climbed the bank. The underbrush was trampled and crushed, paths plowed through the deeper snow on the bank. Beyond, the trees were pincushioned with arrows, and dead and wounded were lying about. All Minztan, she was pleased to see; only to be expected when so few of the enemy had good harness, or training in war. She loped on, wondering if the left-flank mesh had been able to cross-connect through the middle rank, and close in westward to trap the fleeing Minztans. That was the standard procedure, but difficult to accomplish in this terrain. It still puzzled her how the attack had been able to punch through in the first place, with so little warning.

She was well back when the trees fell. Thunder rolled through the woods, but she could see little. Through a gap in the treeline the pointed tips of the white pine quivered as trees swayed and began their crashing descent to the ground; then more, trying to cut off the Kommanz line of retreat to the river. *Glitch*, she thought, in reluctant admiration: her whistle shrilled out a warning back to Fangbanner, lest the Minztans try to punch through to the coffles again.

"Thought they wouldn't come back once they started running," she mused to herself, and spat. Momentum was everything; if Kh'ait thought he was pursuing and ran into a surprise like this ... She had better get forward and put things in order.

An animal snarl alerted her. Whirling, she managed to get her shield up in time to catch the leaping hound on the leather. Impact sent her staggering back and gave the beast time to dodge her return thrust; it had the weight of a small human, a great shaggy-brown hound with the blood of timber wolves in it. The jaws snapped shut scant millimeters from her face, spattering slaver, and carrion breath puffed at her. A brief wild gust of humor ran through her mind: that its breath was still better than the shaman's—and then she bent to her task.

The beast danced back from the whirring menace of her blade, and Shkai'ra knew she had to kill it before its master came. This was a hunting dog, trained to obey; in her harness she had little to fear even from jaws strong enough to rip the face from a human skull, but it could hamper her fatally. In the open few had any chance against two opponents; the hero songs told of such things, but the warmasters taught that two had eight times the strength of one.

The forest was lit by a dim white glow, slowly darkening. Not much of the snow was falling through the dark green ceiling twenty meters above, but it filtered the dying light to a soft luminosity. The soughing rush of wind in a million branches filled the air, louder than panting breath or the creak and slither of feet in the snow.

Skipping back, she went down on one knee, hoping that temptation would overpower learned response. Instinct made the hound take the bait, come rushing in a charge that ended in a soaring leap. She rose to meet it, shieldboss to muzzle, and stabbed low for the belly. The saber slid through flesh, grated on bone, and the dog's baying roar turned into a scream of pain that ended in a whimper. The twisting steel severed arteries and flooded its lungs, and it flopped, drowning. For a moment she wondered mildly at how human its blood smelled.

The Minztan came up at a run, and halted when he saw the dead hound, anger flaring in his eyes. He was tall for the forest folk, shaggy in his furs, probably a trapper by calling. A javelin in one hand rested in a throwing stick—a simple grooved lever with the butt of the spear resting against a notch. Throwing, he would release the javelin in midcast and continue to bear down on the spearthrower, adding enormous leverage. The honed edge of the spear glinted blue. In his left hand was a spike-ax, broad half-moon blade on one side, tapering conical spike on the other, shrunk onto a meter-long wooden shaft covered in thick leather and bone rings. He wore a coat of interwoven leather strips, boiled black in vinegar for strength and reinforced in strategic spots with horn plaques; his helm was similar, and heavy gloves with laminated wood and bone splints covered his hands. Not nearly as good as her armor, but vastly better than nothing. It would take a solid cut or thrust to do harm.

Shkai'ra circled, shield forward, sidling closer. Her boots scuffled through the crust on the snow as her feet came down with neat, precise movements. Elation filled her; here was something concrete, not shadowy terror that slipped away from her grasp. The Minztan feinted with the throwing spear.

"Not as brave as your dog, bark-eater?" she gibed, low and throaty. "Sa, sa, ssssssssssa, come closer, so I can *cut* you, man." Her blade tip twitched through the air with a tearing-cloth sound of cloven air.

The forester ignored her. A cool one, she thought, belike with some combat experience; there was always a little skirmishing along the frontier fringes, between hunters of the two peoples. She grinned into his eyes and waited. He would have to strike soon; these woods were full of Kommanza, and FangBanner would be coming back this way at any time.

He realized that time would work against him too. His throw was blinding-fast, with the leverage of the spearthrower behind it and no warning in his face. But his stance had changed, a slight twisting in the torso, toes digging into the snow. She blocked with a reflexive movement of her shield, bringing it up and around at a slant, batting at the flung weapon from the side. The spearhead gouged a line across the lacquered leather and skittered away in a flurry of snow. Metal clanged on treeroot.

He lunged behind the throw, body almost horizontal, chopping at her legs as he shifted to a two-handed grip in midleap. Surprise almost froze him as she bounced back in a standing jump to land poised and ready just beyond the swing of his ax; he traded momentum for distance in a forward roll, and felt his jerkin turn her overarm cut. He rolled to his feet and came up in a defensive crouch, sweating. He had fought the steppe-dwellers before, but that was mostly distance skirmishing. And herders and farmers did not work in full war gear.

The Minztan knew the harness must be half her own body weight or more, helmet and shield and thick strong leather, but it seemed to slow her less than his own jerkin of woven strips did him. She moved easily under it, like a lynx, no, like a great machine of joints and bearings and steel springs, one movement flowing into another in patterns as precise as compass-drawn curves on paper. Mad, and bad, every one of them, he thought, watching the slitted eyes in the high-cheeked plains face. He could read a little of the insect-bright patterns on her armor. And the chiefs worse than any. Reluctantly, he began to move forward.

Shkai'ra studied his stance; feet at right angles, one hand at the end of the halberd, one a little above the middle. The set of his muscles, the heavy blocky shoulders, thick wrists and arms.

So, this one has been to school, she thought. The surface of her mind was like a pool of still water, blanked to allow trained reflex to function faster than possible for conscious thought. Beneath that ran knowledge, weighing the strengths and limitations of the weapon she faced. Less reach than a saber, no point, but plenty of momentum, and the spike would punch through a breastplate with a solid hit. She knew the counters for it, of course, but it was too difficult to use from the saddle to be popular with her folk. Besides, although hugely strong for her size, she had never felt she had the heft for it.

They flowed together, seeming to cooperate in

dance of shield, ax, sword, halberd-butt, boom and clatter and deep quick breaths. He was using short hard chops, sacrificing sheer battering mass for control, parrying with the bone-covered haft. He feinted with the butt, then reversed and cut full-swing for her head; she jerked her body back from the waist, just enough to feel the ugly wind of a bright blade passing close before her eyes. Her return thrust was blocked with a daringly simple twist that deflected her point over one of the reinforced gloves. The flat top of the ax snapped out at her throat, driven with one palm cupped on the bottom of the ax-handle; it did not need an edge to do harm with all his weight behind it. Her shield darted up and caught it, but the blow forced her to cat-jump back to regain balance.

Shkai'ra tasted exultation, a warm coppery tang in her mouth; she felt totally alive, doing the thing for which she had been born. The passage of arms had taken a scant ten seconds; data flowed into her mind, extrapolated subconsciously, produced a gestalt-picture of her opponent's fighting style.

Never forget the shield is an active element, not passive like armor. The warmaster's remembered voice curled through her mind.

She edged her target up, a tiny shifting that would input into the other fighter's awareness and influence his strategy. He came in quickly, blade edge curving up for the angle of her jaw. It was a feint, to draw the shield to the area of sensitivity he had sensed. The ax looped over, down, back to the left, then struck horizontally as he shifted his hands and drove the spike in a line that would have ended in her gut.

The man had potential, she mused. Perhaps he would be reborn a Kommanz war-horse, or even a zh'ulda, and have a chance to realize it.

The ax fanned by. And her shieldboss punched out

in a straight line, into his mouth. There was a hard smack, and a sound like sticks crunching. The axblow lost force, and she was inside the curve of danger now anyway. She caught the shaft of the ax on the guard of her saber; the force was still enough to shock her hand, but she held it and pinned the weapon down. She used it as a fulcrum for her own movement; her left leg straightened, driving her forward like a hydraulic piston; her right knee smashed upward, driving the hinged cover of her greave into his groin. And the shield struck again, upward this time, the metal-shod edge whipping up into his jaw. Bone broke, and shattered teeth were driven agonizingly together. Blood sprayed out of the corners of his mouth, and he spasmed backward, arms flung wide and body locked rigid as the automatic bend toward the savage pain in his crotch was balanced by the blow under his chin.

Shkai'ra let him put a little distance between them, hugged the shield to her, and lunged, in a perfect line from left heel through locked wrist to point. It went through the leather with a slight hesitation, through wool and linen and hard belly muscle, a familiar soft, heavy resistance. She held the thrust until the point slid out beside his spine, the blade grating on a vertebra, then withdrew with a vicious wrenching twist to open the arteries and let the lifeblood out.

"Uhhhhhhhh!" the man grunted at the chill shock gliding through his gut. He put his hands to the bubbling redness, felt a soft give he knew was a severed loop of intestine. The cold seemed to knock the pain-haze from his brain for a second. The withdrawal had jerked him almost face to face with his killer, and for a brief instant he was sickened by the sudden flare of orgasmic pleasure in her eyes. Then he crumpled to the ground, the noises from his broken mouth growing louder as pain seeped through shock.

Shkai'ra stood cleaning her saber and watching the awareness of death seeping into his eyes as he lay making the little animal sounds of agony. He might live for a few minutes more, but deep stab wounds in the gut were always fatal, even without heavy bleeding. She sighed with a heavy, sleepy satisfaction that gave a feeling of warm relaxation, then forced herself back to alertness.

She was wiping the last flecks from the difficult areas around the guard when the first warriors came trotting back; if you let blood run under the guard . . . well, blood was salt water and the tang could corrode unseen. She was not one of the ancient heroes, or a god, to have steel that did not rust.

"Hai, how went it, killers?" she called, running gloved fingers down the edge to check for nicks and sheathing the blade without glancing down.

"Good at first, Chiefkin," the squadleader said. "We caught them before they could disengage, and they turned their backs." That was the signal for massacre in any battle on foot. "Not more than twoscore, anyway, and hardly a match for us, even the ones with some armor."

She pricked up her ears at that. "Then they dropped the trees on us and attacked again. We regrouped and sent 'em back bewailing their dead. Bannerleader Kh'ait is bringing up the rear; we go to our mounts."

But he did not meet her eyes, seemed to look anywhere but at her face. Idly, he kicked at the fallen Minztan's kneecap; the body jerked.

She waved them onward, worried. They had not sounded as exultant as they should; quiet, almost subdued, rather.

When the last came up the Bannerleader was being helped between two troopers, grunting every time his right foot touched earth. Behind came others, wounded but still able to walk, and two pairs carrying bodies. Shkai'ra wondered at their silence; a Kommanz zh'ulda was not likely to be upset by a corpse. Then she saw what they bore.

The head of the first rested on his chest. The neck had not been cut through: the ragged edges and gobbets of hanging flesh, the twisted and broken laces of the gorget, made it clear that the head had been *twisted* off.

"Jh'unnd Zaizun's-kin," Kh-ait said thickly. "Always a reckless one." He jerked his cropped red beard at the body. "In the van of the pursuit, that one. He and Bh'uda ran ahead out of sight. We heard him cry out and found . . . that, and tracks . . . bigger than human feet could be, Chiefkin."

She bent over the second body and hissed in awe; the whole side of the chest had been crushed, the stiff fiberglass-backed layers of leather shattered and the bone and flesh beneath pulped to a soggy mass.

"It's what took the sentries, isn't it, Chiefkin?" he asked. "The woodswalker." He looked around at the woods with hatred. "Zaik, these trees! They're crushing us!"

Shkai'ra did not think he meant the Minztan trick. She grabbed him by the nasal of his helmet, an iron calm upon her. "Whatever's out there can only kill you," she said coldly. "Are you a killer, or a lamb bleating for the ewe? Are you afraid to die?"

For a moment he stared at her with the eyes of a stricken beast, then clamped control, shook his head, and straightened.

"Get back to the column," she snapped. "Kh'ait, they may try to punch through to the coffles again. Watch for it."

For long moments she stood. The weight of the forest pressed down on her helmet, until she wanted to run screaming, to burst out on the steppe and feel *space* around her again. Out where the demons were ones she knew. At length she won herself back to an attitude of acceptance; what would be, would be. She would be a Mek Kermak still. She looked down at the form of the Minztan, using his body as a focus for the Warrior's Way, reaching back into her mind.

"I hate," she whispered. "I hate you all. I hate this shitpile forest, and the incompetents I have to command, and the useless twitching spook-pusher . . ."

Her voice sank into a singsong half-chant, and she felt the familiar black tide of strength filling her. She knelt and tore off his helm, drawing her knife and gripping his hair. "And I hate *you*," she hissed, as she prepared for the ritual scalping. "But I live, you die. You go, not me. I'm strong now, not weak. No one will hurt me again; I'll kill and kill, until the gods come to eat the world. And I'll dance in the flames . . ."

The man's eyes opened. He looked up into a face bent of shape, lips peeled back, lines of spittle hanging down. He jerked, and a degree of humanness returned to the glazed gray eyes. He was clear-headed now, with the odd lucid calm that sometimes comes in the moments before final blackout, but speech was an enormous effort.

"Plains . . . dirt," he said. Shkai'ra forced her breathing to slow. Her left hand stayed in his hair; better to wait for the moment before the scalping, for this one had fought well enough to make a strong ghost.

"Aye," the thin voice continued, mushy past torn lips and broken teeth. "Kill me . . . but I saw. Snowbrother comes for you . . . she summons well. Never leave . . . woods . . ."

"Zoweitz eat you forever!" she shrieked, springing

erect. Control snapped; she trampled and hacked, screaming, until a limp pile sagged redly to her blows, bootleather pounding into it with the sound of a hammer on wet liver.

Presently she stopped, ashamed of letting fear drive her. She gripped a lock of the hair, traced a circle on the scalp with the point of her knife, and ripped the clump of hair loose with a quick jerk. Shkai'ra stood over the body, puzzled. Fear she felt; well, it was no great disgrace to fear demons, any more than to fear thunder. But she was . . . she groped for the word . . . yes, sad. Shaking her head, she turned to go.

14

"We made a mistake," Narritanni said.

The remnants of the Minztan force huddled together under a deadfall of interlaced trunks. There were thirty here, none unwounded, but all could still run and fight; those too badly hurt to move had had to be left for the Kommanz. Some might have hidden themselves. The snow would have helped; it was still falling, flakes swirling around under their shelter, falling down straight and thick and fleecy. Leafturn stood just outside, motionless, as the flakes hissed into their small and carefully shielded fire. There were a half-dozen other parties this size, fallen back on the prepared hiding places.

"Mistake!" spat the one whom unspoken consensus had made leader of the remaining Garnetseat villagers. "More than thirty of us dead, and only that many of the prisoners freed! How many came back from the fight on the ice? Five, count them, and you wouldn't send more of those precious 'soldiers' of yours. No, you kept them safe in the woods."

Narritanni raised his head. "For the second attack,"

he said flatly. That had been a fiasco—although they had dropped more trees across the Kommanz pursuit, and the plains-dwellers had been visibly nervous about scattering in the woods.

There were shadows like purple bruises under his eyes, and his shield arm ached to the bone, pain deep in joint and marrow. Vomit rose to his throat at the sight of the woman's face. He did not think that the other one would have spoken thus; that one had had at least the wit to recognize his own ignorance. But he had gone missing in the retreat through the woods; his scalp probably dangled frozen on a plains-dweller's weapon belt.

"Yes, *mistake*," he said. "Mistakes. To try it at all, we let sentiment override reason; it was too soon. And I told you, I told you that everything depended on getting through fast to the bank and holding the bulk of their force in play. A few minutes more and *most* of the slaves would have escaped, and all the attack party. But you couldn't keep up the pace, *with the Circle itself turning for you.*"

"And you held your people back at the riverbank too—"

"*To cover your retreat.* If we hadn't been there, and ready, none of you would have gotten away when the westerners came up the slope."

There was a stir and mutter from the villagers; most could see the sense in that. The memory of the fight, bright blades and the squealing warcry at their heels, was still fresh. But the moment he had said it, Narritanni wished it back; he could see it in their eyes, how the thought daunted them. And the losses were shocking: a fifth of the band, a tenth of the adults in Garnetseat. There would be more than grief come spring. There would be hunger, for want of those hands and skills.

And nearly one in three of his trained rangers. That was far more serious; not just that those eager youngsters had been friends and surrogate family to him, that they had trusted his word, but their value to the New Way had been great. Suitable recruits were scarce. So few of those who had the desire had natural aptitude, and the cost of training and equipping and supporting them through the year was crippling. And, too, the Kommanz now knew that they existed.

He sank back against the log, hands resting on the long bone hilt of his sword. The desire for sleep was like fire playing on his nerves; nausea burned acid at the back of his throat, and he could feel the cold dragging at his body's inner reserves.

The villager had heard the sound in her hearthfolk's voices, and responded with a sneer she hoped would divert hostility back to the Seeker's troops.

"*We* made the mistakes, then."

"No." They all turned in surprise; it was always a shock when the Wise Man spoke, as if a tree or rock had done so. "Snowbrother aids us; the westerners are in fear of *It*." He withdrew his presence; not physically, but they could sense he would not speak again. He turned to watch the night. They were thankful for that, knowing what might run there.

From somewhere, Narritanni found the strength to rise. He knew the advantage of height and used it to the full, looming over his opponent. Red firelight flickered on his stained and battered armor, cast highlights from below over the curves and planes of his face, threw his eyes into shadow. He felt anger coiling like a snake under his breastbone.

"Think, then, if you can. If the Circle and the Harmony do not flow with our mission, how could the Snowbrother fight for us? Is it misfortune that the Initiate survived, and can call to *It* from the enemy's camp?

It is a symbol of the link between humans and the living earth, sharing the Natures of beast and human."

Shock rode their faces, to hear holy things spoken of thus openly, but they could not deny the truth of it; had not the Enlightened One said so? Heads nodded gravely. Narritanni flung out a gloved hand, to the Wise Man, the night, the presence that dwelt in it. Huge it lay beyond the circle of their firelight. In the little villages, in hunter's camps, in solitary vigil, they had lived with that immensity all their days. It was for that timeless unity they fought.

"*Next* time, we use that aid *properly*." He could feel the conviction behind his words, knew he would rally them. "Didn't the Wise Man tell us? The raiders are afraid of *It*, not us. Next time we go to them behind *It*, not before, at night, in the darkness, after fear has had more time with them. And not one of the barbarians will return to the grasslands."

The discontented villager sprang to her feet also. "*Next* time?" she yelped. "*Next* time? When you can kill us all? No. No. Tomorrow I and my kinmates— those you've left alive with your warmaking—we go back to our homes. And I think some at least of those here will return with us."

"That would be an offense against our people, the Seeker's oath, and the Way of the Circle."

"So you say. No soul can walk another's Way."

"So, then I will save you from your own misjudgment—" the soldier continued, sadness overcoming anger on his haggard face. His sword rasped out of its sheath and flicked forward. The tip suddenly rested on the woman's throat, just a tensing of his wrist away from the jugular.

She gaped in astonishment, rolling eyes down in an unmoving face to stare at the edged metal. She could feel it dimpling her skin, cold and hard, with the unmistakable about-to-cut sensation of something very sharp. Her mind refused to believe the information her body presented. Minztans had no government, had never had; their laws were enforced by public opinion. Force was used, with extreme reluctance, only against foreigners and the very rare violent criminal. Strong disagreements were settled by one party or the other moving away; there had always been room.

There was nothing she could say to the sight of a naked sword in the hand of a fellow traveler on the Way, prepared to imperil the Harmony by infringing on the integrity of another.

"Mikkika," he said. His second in command looked up, face pale but set. "Alert the watches tonight. If this one"—he jabbed very slightly—"or any other tries to leave, to desert"—he used a foreign word perforce—"call me. If I'm asleep, kill them yourself."

Shaken, she nodded wordlessly. He sheathed the weapon again and continued more gently. "Believe me, I do this only for the good of us all. For the Minztan folk. Don't you see, we must?"

The other gathered herself. When she spoke again the petulant whine was out of her voice, replaced by a curious dignity. "So you may think, Narritanni Smaoth's-kin. But if you think you can save what is by breaking and remelting it, you are no craftsman, and a fool, and I think your feet walk a different Way from any I would choose." She glanced out at the Adept. He stood silent and immobile; the Harmony was also the wolf in winter and inexorable decay. She turned away and sat down, wrapping herself in her bedroll.

Narritanni did likewise, but his open eyes reflected the fire for long and long.

Shkai'ra rose from the corpse of the prisoner, scrubbing blood from her hands with snow. The Minztan had kept them busy for hours, not so much from hardihood, but because his wounds put limits on what they could do. It was difficult to further pain a man with bone showing in half a dozen places, and there was always the risk of snuffing out life too soon. Added to that was the fact that Shkai'ra alone of them spoke really fluent Minztan, and she was less confident of her command of the tongue than she had been.

And the man had resisted cleverly, using his own weakness, blood loss, shock to ride out the pain; several times he had almost succeeded in throwing himself into trance, had been roused only by holding his mouth and nose underwater. Also, he had already known his death was imminent; that made mutilation, the slow irreparable damage to one organ after another, considerably less effective in breaking the will and mind. Altogether, it had been unsatisfactory; he had spoken a little, and the shaman had been able to pick up somewhat more from the disintegrating mind, but . . .

And I didn't enjoy it, she thought, puzzled. "Well, so much for that," Shkai'ra said aloud. It had not even been very exhilarating, simply messy and boring.

"We know they've loosed a woods demon on us, yes," the shaman broke in.

"And that the sun will rise tomorrow," Eh'rik added, and looked up into the blackness above them. Snow pelted into his chinbeard and caught on his eyebrows, making a winter troll of him in the hissing, popping glow of the pinewood fire. Camp hearths only ten meters away were red glows muffled in white. "Best we stay up and check on that. He might have lied."

The shaman stalked away. "But this thing about the Minztans' setting up standing warbands," the warmaster went on, "this Seeker, this New Way, that's serious.

The High Senior must know, and the *Kommand'ahan* in Granfor."

"I have every intention of telling them, when we get back," Shkai'ra said.

"If," one of the Bannerleaders grunted.

Shkai'ra whirled on him. He fell back a pace, crouched, relaxed as he saw her beat down the murderous flare of killing-lust. You never knew when someone would go ahrappan, especially in a time like this.

"The day of our deaths is woven by Zailo," she said icily. "But I think there's a good chance some of us will make it."

"Who can fight witchcraft?" The words were heavy with dread. The wind hooted around them, laden with hungry ghosts, the ghosts of the slain, longing for the hell-wind of their slayers' deaths to blow them free into the afterlife and rebirth.

"We can, the children of the gods! Do you think the Mighty Ones can't aid us here, or that branches can hide the Sun? If live bark-eaters can't keep us from slaughtering them, then say boo to their thin ghosts, and their tame spook too. The Sun sees all the lands."

"And leaves them all, the Zoweitz rule the dark."

Shkai'ra pressed fingers to her brows, closed her eyes, composed herself, then looked up with a smile.

"Tactics," she said. "Listen, today we *defeated* them. And killed ten to one or better. If they had overwhelming might, earthly or ghostly, they would have overfallen us. Instead, we butchered them like sheep. Scant losses, even counting those ... not killed by blade. So far the spook, whatever it is, hasn't dared face more than one or two warriors at a time.

"What really worries me is the troops." She looked around at the officers. "This has taken the savor off their victory: They aren't ofzarz. A common zh'ulda doesn't feel as close to the gods as we do, and fears nightwalkers more. Go among them, hearten them, tell them we *did* win. And don't the Sayings of the Ancestors tell that victory is the only aim, whatever the price?

"Make them believe we can win through: we'll suffer losses, yes, but when were the Kommanz ever daunted by that? And think of the undying fame and envy, if we overcome spellcraft. Heroes have beaten wizards before, and their Names lived. Folk have had hero-shrines dedicated to them for less!"

They rose to go back among their followers; heartened, or at least giving a convincing show of it. She would follow, later; it was fitting that she maintain a little more distance than the village chiefs. They were woven into the everyday life of their fiefs, but the ruling kinfast of Stonefort had some of the glamour of remoteness; they interceded with the high gods and the far-off rulers in Grantor. Both together would be best.

Eh'rik alone remained. "Do you really believe that, Chiefkin?" he asked, almost gently. She was startled; it was not a note she often heard in a warmaster's voice.

She smiled wearily at him. "Well ... yes and no, old wolf. There is a chance, always some chance until they throw you on the pyre and cut the horse's throat over your ashes. But we're still too far from home for my taste." They sat silent together, a companionable quiet. "There's no better company to depart life with, anyway; I never expected to die in the straw."

He went down on one knee, hands crossed on brow in the formal gesture of homage. Touched, she reached out and clasped his hands between hers, in formal acknowledgment. She was too junior to merit the salute in strict law, but it was a gesture of profoundest respect. "Come," she said. "Let's make our rounds. And *t'Zoweitzhum*, you know the saying: 'It *must* be done, therefore it *can* be done.'"

They rose and walked together into the restless night. The waving treetops were half seen, half sensed, always heard. They drew their scarves over their faces and bent their heads into the wind. From the slave lines came the sound of singing.

Maihu had gone to some trouble to make the sled comfortable these past few days. A jug of mead bubbled on the tile stove, and she had added cedar branches to the fuel; the spicy scent of the honey wine blended with aromatic wood and warm fur to fill the space between the padded leather walls. The lantern guttered, sent shadows flickering on the porcupine-quill embroidery of the sled's lining and the patterns woven into the cushions. She smoothed a quilt, fluffed a pillow, dropped a few grains of precious cinnamon into the heating mead, before settling against the wall with Dh'ingun curled on her lap.

Taimi looked up in sullen puzzlement. "Kinmother, why? Why did you stop me? We could have—"

"Died!" she snapped. It was tiresome; couldn't the boy see that there had been no time? And it was worrying, as worrying as the long silences; both had been growing worse in the half-week since the fight.

"And the way you play up to her, it's—"

"Necessary."

"Not ..." He frowned, hunting for words. "I've done that too. But ... you don't seem to ... hate her enough."

Maihu turned and slapped him across the face, hard. He recoiled in shock. Minztans never struck their children, and he was still young enough to be accounted such. It was the first time his mother had ever hurt him.

"Shut your *mouth!*" she hissed. Then she froze, appalled. After a moment, she reached out and touched him on the face, hesitantly.

"Taimi, child of my womb, I'm sorry. Put it down to the company I have to keep, these days. But no, we're not supposed to hate; it's against the Way. She's . . . not as bad as some of them. I pity her, really—"

"That's sheepshit!" he cried, using the Kommanzanu oath. "I hate them all, I—"

She grabbed him by the shirtfront and held up the symbol-carved flute. Even now his eyes slid away from the carving on it, the curious bulbous mouthpiece.

"I got this by playing up to her," she said coldly. "Do you understand that? Do you understand that this is our only hope of ever being free again?"

"It—it didn't help our folk during the fight." He stopped in fear, glancing at the front flap of the sled. The Kommanz driver was still out there, seeing to the horses.

Maihu laughed, a she-wolf yelp so unlike her remembered mirth that Taimi felt his skin crawl. "No worry," she said. "I've been calling that one every filthy name I could, for days. Not a word of Minztan."

"Listen, kinchild," she continued earnestly. "Do you know where we are?"

"Close to the forest. Closer than we were when you stopped me from cutting the chain."

"We're at the *Place of Summoning!* Here, or close to here. And we're not moving very fast anymore. It will come right in among people and lights, here."

"Are . . . are you sure?"

"Here? And at this time of year? Oh, yes, *It* will come. Now run along, kinchild. I don't want her seeing you here if we can help it; she's harder to handle when she's been on you, and I can't trust you not to anger her." She gave him a brief hug. "Not long now, I promise. Then everything will be good again."

Her smile faded as he left. *I hope that can be true,* she thought. *I mean it to be, but . . . why does my life before these weeks seem like a dream? Is it only the contrast? It does,* she mused. *There are moments when it seems incredible that there was a time before her . . . Hate is a more complicated emotion than I thought. It lets her into my mind. I want to be free, I wouldn't be surprised or sorry if she dies, but will it be empty without her to fight? And if I am free again, will I be the same person?*

Her mouth quirked at that. There was a very old saying of her people, that you could never step into the same river twice. That was an aspect of the Circle, always returning to the same spot, yet never the same. But there were changes she had not expected. *Are humans chameleons, then?* she thought. *I could never have hit him, for anything, before this.*

It was warm in the sled. She shivered, and pulled Dh'ingun closer to her. He squirmed sleepily and then settled back to sleep as she rocked him gently. It was too lonely a time not to have life by her.

Shkai'ra rolled into the sled in no pleasant mood. It had become easy for Maihu to follow her emotions now; she sensed boiling frustration and a despair that was murderously ready to lash out, and kept silence for long moments as she refastened the flap and handed the Kommanza a cup of mead. The Kommanza sat cross-legged, inhaling the warmth and fragrance of it. Slowing her breathing, she forced muscles to relax, mind to unknot, pulling strength around her like a cloak. Presently she opened her eyes and spoke:

"If I live to threescore, may I never have to bed down eighty whining Minztans again! They'd have stood and frozen if we'd left them. Wasteful." She drained the bowl and held it out for the slave to refill.

Maihu served her and drew some for herself, before reaching out and touching one of Shkai'ra's braids. "Do you want food, Chiefkin?" she said softly. "Of your pardon, you look cold and tired. I could help you out of the armor, give you a massage, or we could lie together. You look as if you could use some relaxation."

Shkai'ra sighed and laid her head on her knees. "That's true enough, Zailo Protector knows. No, nothing to eat, and I have to stay in harness—a staff meeting, and then a tour of the posts." She did not mention that that was the only way she could be sure of making the troopers keep to their posts. They had lost more scouts every night since the ambush; it was a sentence of death to be alone among the trees, and the grisly trophies the shaman had brought back once or twice were not much consolation. Not death alone could have wrought such fear; the zh'uldaz were whispering "souleater," when the chiefs could not hear.

"You're being more sensible than the other slaves, at least," Shkai'ra said.

"The Way of the Circle is to move with the flow of the world," she said. "You're the current around here, right now."

The Kommanza stretched hugely, and yawned. "And if Jaiwun Allmate appeared, all I'd want to do is *sleep.*"

Maihu shrugged and turned down the lantern. "The Chiefkin wishes," she said in the western tongue.

"You're picking up Kommanzanu faster than most," Shkai'ra said approvingly. "The sounds are difficult for outlanders . . . not many in Stonefort speak enough sheepblea— Minztan to be useful." She turned her head from the coarse wool of her trousers to look up at Maihu's face. "You look peaked yourself, little smith, and you're more silent than you were at first."

Oddly, there seemed to be genuine concern in the voice; the forest woman could sense it. *Probably doesn't even recognize it herself,* she thought wryly. And the Kommanza was haggard as well, she noted with ironic sadness. *We both have our battles to fight, and folk to wear the mask of confidence for,* she thought. *Only with each other can we be weak.*

"Oh, I'm well enough, Chiefkin; the traveling is wearying, that's all."

"I'm worried," Shkai'ra said. "We can't lose too many more warriors, or this raid won't be worth it at all. Punishment aside, I can't weaken the People like that, I just *can't.*"

Maihu made an inquiring noise, and the Kommanza went on: "The elders think the *graizuh,* the cannibals, may try to break the border again soon. We'll need every warrior, every trick and advantage we can buy from the southrons, for that."

"Can the savages prevail against you?" Maihu said, smoothing a lock back from the other's forehead. Shkai'ra's eyes were closed.

"Not usually. They've no order, and only their nobles are full-armed; they fight by clans and tribes, among themselves mostly. But they're pressing on their pasture, and when they get a strong warlord . . ." She bit at a lip.

"Long ago—the stories say, fifteen generations after the Godwar—the graizuh pushed us east out of the short-grass country." Her voice took on a slight singsong note, unconscious imitation of the bards. "No more than two or three hundreds of us." That was probably true; humans had been very rare, in the centuries right after the Fall.

"We found a few farmers in the Red River valley, and became their lords and married with them, and we made them folk of the horse and lance and bow. Then we multiplied and we spread; from Granfor was born the Kommanz of Ihway, and the Kommanz of Maintab; and Maintab sent warriors north and west into the aspen grove lands, and founded Rh'eginz around a ruined city of the Ancients; and then Paizrav, and together they made Kai-Gara under the Westwall range, in my mother's mother's mother's lifetime." She sighed, dropping back into normal speech. "I've met Kommanza from Paizrav; they talk funny and shave the back of their heads."

A moment of brooding silence. "But now the Wolves grow stronger. They've driven the Mek nomads off the southern shortgrass plains and over the Red River of the South. They trade with the southrons of Senlaw down the Zoura River, and we can't keep them from getting metal weapons any more. We *must* have more strength, more metals and weapons."

Another pause. "Senlaw," she said after a moment. "They say it makes even the cities of the Pentapolis look small. I'd like to see it . . . see the Great River, and the sea." A shrug. "I'll never see anything but Granfor, fighting every year to keep the nomads off the crops—if we're lucky."

Maihu stroked her forehead again. "Sleep now," she said. "Think of it later."

Shkai'ra sighed again and leaned back against the Minztan with her head resting under the older woman's breastbone. She wiggled her shoulders comfortably and Maihu held her, with her knees and arms around the hard slick surface of her cuirass. The weight was heavy, but not uncomfortably so.

"Hmmm, that feels good," Shkai'ra said. "Don't know why. I usually hate having anyone this close except for fighting, fucking, or warmth on cold nights . . ." She paused, and continued sleepily, thoughts drifting as she allowed herself to linger on the edge of sleep. "It reminds me of something . . . long ago. Can't think what. Someone held me like this."

Then: "Why do they sing?" she said, more alertly.

"Who sings, Chiefkin?" Maihu asked, rocking her slightly, deliberately casual.

"The slaves, the ones who haven't just given up and gone passive. Every night, they sing; you can hear it from here. Even in that sheep-raping snowstorm, now that it's letting up." It did come through the walls of the sled, very faint, easy for the mind to filter out as it wove itself into the background noise of the camp. But one who knew the full meaning of that song was unlikely to ignore it.

"It's . . . prayer, Chiefkin. They pray to Harmony, for deliverance."

"They talk to spirits?" The narrow blond head came up a trifle.

"Oh, no, Chiefkin. They only ask. No one can force the Harmony; it moves as it must."

Shkai'ra's curiosity subsided. "Our gods are more sensible; obedience and offerings, you bargain with them. Minztans! I'll never understand them."

Maihu risked a barb: "How would you act in their place, Chiefkin?"

"Mmmmm?" Shkai'ra murmured absently. "*Ahi-a*, a Kommanza falls on the Sword of Apology, or bites through her tongue and inhales the blood; we're never taken prisoner for long. Not by foreigners, that is. It's against the Bans and the Law. But," she continued generously, "it's no use seeking an outlander who understands honor. I don't expect it of you."

She snuggled back. "I can sleep for an hour, no more. Wake me then. Can you play like this?"

Maihu shifted slightly, took out the carved flute, and began to play, the same slow minor-key tune that sounded over the camp. Shkai'ra grinned at the jest and fell instantly asleep; she could drop off in almost any position, an ability common to both cats and experienced warriors.

The Minztan laid down the pipe and held her, considering. *Bites through her tongue*, she thought. *What must they do to the little children, to make that natural for them! And how dangerous they are because of it.*

She remembered stories her captor had told her, of her own childhood. And of her people: raid and feud, arrows out of the long grass, poison and fire and knives in the dark. The Kommanzanu word for summer was "makes-war-time"; it was then that the *graizuh*, the nomads, came down off the short-grass plains every year. That was in normal years . . .

She reached down and brushed a lock of loosened red-blond hair back from Shkai'ra's forehead. *Doesn't even know why it's nice to be cuddled,* she mused. *Poor wolf, you have your chains, as heavy as the ones you've put on me. You've just worn yours so long you don't notice them. May they sustain you, at the last.*

Narritanni sketched quickly on the scroll of birchbark. "We hit them from three sides, as soon as the signal's given," he said.

The forest folk leaned on their spears around him; dim light from a bull's-eye lantern caught their faces from below, casting shadows across beards and cheekbones, glinting off eyes and the whetted steel of their weapons. Most were munching maple candy, concentrated food for energy in the draining cold.

"It'll be snowing, thick," the commander went on. "They're not in good spirits. The Snowbrother will come in at the head of the caravan. We *wait* until enough have had a chance to see and be terrified, but not enough that they recover their wits—I doubt any will dare stand against it, and if they do, fear will weaken them. *Then* we attack. Remember, our first task is to rescue the rest of our people. Push hard, though—if they break, we may be able to wipe them out."

"The Eater?" someone said. That one had been hard enough on *their* morale.

Leafturn rose. "He and I have a meeting," he said. "I shall not return from it."

Gasps of dismay; Narritanni felt a stab of sorrow mixed with deep anger.

"I did not say I would die," Leafturn continued dryly. "There is a fate in this; and fate is something best met as early as possible. The Eater will not trouble you; you have my word on that."

He rose and moved into the darkness beyond the lantern's circle. Narritanni's mouth quirked in a smile as he looked around at the others.

"Time to fight," he said. "Each of us with our own Way." His sword rasped free. "We go to rescue our kinsfolk. Let's *go*."

A chorus of growls answered him.

15

"Four *kylickz* today," Shkai'ra said, looking around the circle of the commanders. "Four days since the ambush, and not twenty *kylickz* nearer home, and it's not just the *zteafakaz* snow, either. At this rate, we'll be here until"—she made a gesture past the fireglow at the forest—"takes us all."

Some shuddered openly. All made the sign against ill luck and foreign magic.

"Chiefkin," the caravanmaster said, "I've had more dealings with Minztans than most, and not just trying to let each other's livers see daylight. If this . . . 'Snow-brother' is like most of their spooks, they think it guards the forests in the name of the, what do they call it, the *heka . . . ehaka . . .*"

"*Ehakalagie,*" Walks-with-Demons supplied. "Harmony. Another of their rabbit's notions, that life is more than eating and being eaten."

"Minztan childtales," Shkai'ra snarled. "Caravanmaster, tell me why we aren't making more speed."

The caravanmaster licked chapped lips. "The slaves," he said, and held up a hand to fend off the explosion

277

of anger. "I've tried it!" he cried. "Chiefkin, you *know* I have! Burning, pinning . . . too many of them won't *frighten* anymore."

"Cut all their throats, and be rid of them," someone suggested.

"Destroy our loot?" Eh'rik asked. He continued with a feral snarl: "And it would let them off too lightly, anyway. Being dead doesn't hurt too much."

A chanting came from where the coffles of Minztans were herded for the night. Shkai'ra ground her teeth, remembering where else she had heard it that very night.

"And they won't stop that, either," the caravanmaster finished.

"And morale is worse than ever since you pulled the scoutmesh in closer, Chiefkin," Eh'rik said. "Half the band are staying awake all night, then sleeping in the saddle the next day."

She looked at him coldly for a full half minute, until he dropped his eyes. "I did that," she said slowly and deliberately, "because the effect on morale would be even worse if I gave an order and couldn't enforce it. Which would happen, if I tried to send them out into the woods alone. So we have to double up, which means less territory covered."

There was silence. They had all known it, after a fashion, but it was still shocking to hear the words spoken among a folk who would fall on their own swords if commanded on campaign in enemy territory. Eternal shame, miserable rebirth, would be on them if successful mutiny occurred. And the example . . . Discipline was life to the whole folk.

"Go ahead," she said. "Somebody propose it."

The silence stretched. Each officer glanced sidelong at the others, waiting for someone to speak. This was the moment that would be recorded in the song, if there was one, and none wished to be the one remembered as the first to say the naked words.

At last, Eh'rik spoke. "Some think," he said, using the distancing unpersonal mode, "some think that if we released the slaves, left the rest of the booty, we could get out alive. There have been warbands that never came back from the forests. Not often, but it has happened."

The wind in the trees and the singing of the slaves were the loudest sounds, and the hissing of fresh snow as the air blew it along the surface of the ice. He paused to look each one of them in the eyes before going on:

"I say no. It would be against honor. The gods would turn their faces from our ghosts at the Judging. We all die, soon or late, but we are the children of the Ztrateke-ahkomman. We do not concede, we cannot be defeated. Killed, yes, but we do not bow the neck. Even if none sees our endings and returns to tell how we die"—that was a dreadful prospect, to be deprived of the praisesong—"Zaik Godlord and Baiwun Avenger will know."

Shkai'ra felt a warm rush of gratitude; he would back her to the end. There was a rustling and settling around the circle. It was done, and they were relieved. Now they could abandon hope, and set about seeing that they and their followers died well. The best grave for teeth was a throat, went the Saying.

The shaman shook his head. "This woodswizard—stronger than I thought, yes. Every night I fight him, yes, until my magic falters, yet still he has the strength to summon the demon." He rubbed a hand over the scars and bruises on his face. "So well I know him, that I see each bristle of his beard—"

Shkai'ra flung up a hand for silence. A thought nagged at the corner of her mind: she saw Dh'ingun

bristling at the sound of strange music, heard a dying
forest warrior speak . . . Kommanzanu had a single
pronoun for both sexes. Minztan was more archaic in
its grammar; it had three, and used the specific as
often as the general one when speaking of a particular
individual. And the Minztan in the woods, as he lay
bleeding . . .

" *'She* summons well,' " Shkai'ra quoted softly. She
came to her feet. "General attack alert: to your posts.
Kh'ait, Eh'rik, you, spook-pusher, come with me!" She
plunged toward the sled.

Maihu dropped the contact as she watched the
camp, after Shkai'ra left. It was strong, and growing
closer. Soon now. That gave her a tightly reined-in
satisfaction, and so did the sight of the camp itself.
The Kommanz warriors no longer sang or talked at
their tasks; they were quiet even for a taciturn people.
Few bothered with sex, and none was pulling partners
out of the slave herd; most ate their jerky cold in an
echoing silence, then rolled themselves in their bags
and sought sleep. Many stayed squatting upright in
pairs, back to back with their bows across their knees,
listening in haunted fascination to the singing of their
captives.

When she saw the Kommanz leaders walking
toward her, Maihu knew a moment of wild hope. If
they were going to ask for terms . . .

She could sense their fear. Perhaps no one would
have to die after all. She struggled to put down a
sudden hot longing for revenge; to so repel the raid
would be a blow for the New Way, and she had always
felt that the ultimate goal of the Seeker's movement
was not just to defend, but to bring all the peoples
into the Harmony.

And is that all my reason? she asked herself.

Kh'ait wasted no time as he hobbled up. Maihu felt his hands grip the front of her jacket, sweep her into the air, and smash her as easily as a jointed doll against the side of the sled. Through the roaring in her head and the coppery salt taste she knew sickly that she should have remembered—in a steppe-dweller fear bred ruthlessness.

Shkai'ra stepped close. Firelight gleamed on her eyes and teeth, lips drawn back in a rictus of carnivore fury. She motioned the Bannerleader aside and reached out to grip the Minztan's upper lip in one gauntleted hand, twisting until lances of pain shot out from the sensitive flesh.

"We've guessed," she hissed in the Minztan's own tongue. "We know. Tell it all now, and you can still have your life. Balk and we'll rip you and your sprat apart."

Even in the midst of her fear, Maihu noted the offer. Almost sadly, she shook her head, braced herself. *It* needed only a few more minutes now, and the Seeker's force would be close behind *It*.

Shkai'ra shrugged and turned aside. Eagerly, Kh'ait gripped her by the back of the neck. But he struck no blow. Instead, he forced her face down to the level of the Eater's, and the fingers of his other hand remorselessly held open her lids.

The eyes . . . the pupils grew until they swallowed the blue of the iris. Then they swelled, swelled until they consumed her field of vision. They were black, and empty, but the emptiness knew and hungered. Slowly, effortlessly, something began to peel back the layers of her mind like the skins of an onion. And she knew when that was done, she would still be standing there, but that same bottomless nothing would be staring out of her eyes also. . . .

When the alarm came, she barely heard it. She tried

to struggle, but her arms and legs were very far away. The red-bearded Kommanza dropped her and tried to whirl. His wounded leg gave under him, and he clutched at the side of the sled for support. It rocked under his weight.

A horn bellowed through the night; there was panic in the sound. A sled near the head of the column went over on a campfire and exploded in a gout of blue flame as the shattered barrels spouted potato-spirits. Voices rose in the shrilling Kommanz war-cry, then cut off sharply as if a knife had sliced across that eerie keening. In their place came first a confused murmur, then a single hoarse scream of terror and the agony of death.

"Stay here!" Shkai'ra yelped at Kh'ait. With a convulsive wrench she seized the shaman by his drum-laden belt and hurled him spinning a dozen paces, staggering as he struggled to keep his balance in the savage backlash of interrupted sorcery.

"Get your spelltools! *Do* something!" she ordered, cuffing him away. To Eh'rik: "Come *on!*"

They ran through a camp thrown into chaos; horses on picket lines screamed fear as they caught the whiff of terror from their masters, and a deeper alienness from beyond. The slaves milled about, nerving themselves for a break to the woods but not quite daring; not yet. Walks-with-Demons darted among them, cut a child free with a few economical strokes, and ran for his tent with his kicking burden, almost unnoticed in the milling confusion. There would be a conventional attack soon, he calculated, and he meant to be ready for that, at least.

Walks-with-Demons gave a mental howl of anguish as he burst through the Veil, anguish and bitter pleasure. His body remained motionless in his tent, one hand thrust through the child's cracked breastbone; there had been no time for careful preparation, and the boy's piping scream cried counterpoint to his. The shaman's *essence* twisted, preparing to impose itself on the world. The currents were wild and dark tonight, amid fear and the sorcery-driven currents of the gathering storm. Belief was stretched to breaking-point as hundreds found themselves drawn into waking nightmare; that strengthened him.

Now they will know terror, he thought, as he prepared to walk out among the enemies of his folk. His consciousness fountained up through red-shot darkness, tearing through the fabric of reality like a great shark savaging its way to the surface behind an open grin.

no.

The shaman struggled, but the grip was too hard. Behind it was the strength of a belief as strong as his. He threw malevolent chaos at his enemy, and felt it met by an intricate ordering of music, surrounding him with a Dance that went on forever, driven by coruscating ropes of sunlight.

i will eat, eat your soul! he screamed, lunging forward.

indeed. yet there is more at work here than you or i or the one you serve. i do not contend with you. The sudden absence of resistance tricked him, and he felt himself tear loose from handholds of concept and intention, spiraling down into brightness. *i make you a gift of my soul. come to me.*

—and he saw—

—Shkai'ra before a city wall that rose like a mountain—

—looking across a campfire at a small dark-haired woman; there was a silver streak in the black mane, and witchsight showed energy crawling over her in a curtain of blue-red—

—holding to a great wooden pole in a lashing wilderness of storm-driven waves—

—on the deck of a ship, looking up at a city carved into the side of a mountain as snow feathered down—

The vision became closer, threads of fate connecting lives. For a moment the snowflake beauty of the pattern entranced him, and then he fled. This time his scream of pain was quite sincere, in world and Otherworld. His body fell forward over the dead child.

The war leaders ignored the shaman in their pounding run toward the head of the column. Shkai'ra passed a Kommanza running in the other direction, weaponless, mouth gaping in horror. She killed him without even breaking stride, and it was only as she was shouldering and cursing through the immobile ranks that stood facing the treeline and what stood outlined against it that she remembered him. It was the one with green eyes, Dh'vik.

The useless fact crawled through her mind as she stood, riveted. There was light enough from the bright burning of the lifewater-soaked wood to see It clearly. With all her soul Shkai'ra wished that there was not. Here was what had eaten her killers.

Tall it was, near three meters, and the outline was that of a man. But it was broad enough to seem squat, feet wider than snowshoes upholding legs like tree trunks; the arms hung lower on its thighs than a human's would. Dirty whitish-brown fur covered it, thickening to a mane around the head and down the spine. It was male, and she could smell the rankness of its scent across twenty meters of frozen lake. In some crazed stockbreeder's corner of her mind she estimated the weight of the thing to be at least four times her own.

Worst was the face. The skull was long, rising to a

ridge along the crest, set on a neck thick to vanishing; there was no chin under the thin-lipped mouth. That was open, showing yellow dog-tushes between puffs of white breath-fog, and it drooled. The nose was vestigial, a knot of flesh below eyes that were utterly out of place, long-lashed, golden brown, mild and curiously gentle. The creature called, in a high tone hideously unlike the bull roaring she expected. It was modulated; it was an echo of the chant the slaves had sung, and part of it was in registers not meant for the human ear, and part of it was not speech at all but a something *else* that woke feelings as old as the race, that bristled the hairs down her spine under her gambeson. She remembered that tone-series played out over her head, and her cat bristling at something she could not hear.

It strode forward. A Kommanza stood before it, frozen, as helpless as those it had approached unseen in the woods. The huge hands stretched out, clenched into fists, swung bunched through the air to connect with ponderous force. The crunching sound came clearly, and the warrior made a rag-doll flight through the air, to land flopping and broken.

A paleoanthropologist of another era might have been fascinated to see the sight, if she could have believed what no fossil recorded. Shkai'ra felt the pulse of her warband like blood in her throat; the face of the thing before her was an intolerable affront, the kinship to her own kind a thing that demanded the blotting-out of death, hers or the thing's. And in a moment the warriors would break. This was too much to ask of them. They would break, and the Minztans would hunt them through the woods like deer.

Ancestors, receive me, she prayed silently, in that moment of transcendent fear become rage. *Ahkomman, judge me.*

Shrieking, she ran forward to meet it. Yet even then the Kommanz battlemind did not desert her. Despite fear, despite despair and killing-lust, the habits ground in by a lifetime prompted her to remember the beast's fighting style.

Lunging, she went in *under* the hammerstrike of the great fists, stabbing for the thigh and the snakelike vein that showed through sparse fur. Speed saved her, and luck, and the reflex that kept her shield clenched hard against her left side. The slanted-chisel point hurt the beast, and the blow was glancing, and the protection enough that she merely flew through five meters of space, landing without the splintering of bone through heart and lungs and kidney that might easily have befallen.

Flashing before her eyes, taste of metal and salt in her mouth; with a strength she had not known was in her, she rose to her feet and waved the blade. The world reeled drunkenly and showed double before her as she shouted, over the hooting of the animal and the crackling of the flames.

"If it can bleed, it can die! It's only a beast, a strong beast! Kill it! Kill! *Kill!*"

There was a deep base throb, a whirring thump. The arrow sank feather-deep between the huge ribs. The creature gave an almost human moan of bewilderment and pain, plucking at its chest. There were too many humans, too much light; it could not hide. Among the Kommanz fear turned to fury, as a dozen shafts flickered toward the thing that had made them admit they were afraid.

Safest it would have been to stand off and kill it with arrows, but their hearts demanded a closer ending. Screaming, maddened, they swarmed over it with sword and knife and warhammer. And though it killed two more and wounded many, though some would never walk hale again, at the last, they got it down and gave it its death.

None had much attention to spare for what passed elsewhere.

The first of the attacking Minztans nearly ran into a small horsehide tent in the darkness. Pragmatic, he slashed the guyropes to imprison the Kommanza within. He did not succeed, but what flowed forth was only a momentary chill. Shaking it off, he plunged on.

Maihu struggled to her feet as she heard the call of the Snowbrother, fighting off the sense of glassy detachment that lingered before her eyes. It had come; her people would be close behind, but there was no sense in remaining, no need for further risk now that duty was done. She was not tethered. Taimi was; he dropped from the end of the sled and thrust a hammer into her hands. It was one of her own work tools, a long iron-headed sledge. Two quick blows against the back of a knife held down on the link of wooden chain nearest his ankle cut most of the way through; only the leather casing held, a slender thong of it.

Kh'ait turned from the dim outline of the struggle by the fire and saw them. The pale eyes lit in his narrow red-bearded face, under the braids; here was something that could not run, that he could slay before he fell. The deepest, buried wish of all his kind, to kill and kill and kill and kill and die. He drew blade. Maihu faced him and called to her child.

"Taimi, run for the woods. Go to the Seeker—she will find you a place." He sawed at the last link of leather, then hesitated. His face twisted.

"Oh, please, run!" she said.

Kh'ait lurched forward, and she prepared to delay

him, no more. Then something woke in her. She remembered a sacked village and dead kinmates, rape, and laughter, and Sharli pinned living to a door, and the knives driven through his flesh. The first blow knocked the saber from Kh'ait's hand. He yelled in surprise, lurched, fell to one knee, snatched for his dagger left-handed. The second stroke crunched down on his collarbone. The third landed on the back of his head.

She saw a shadow moving out of the corner of her eye. The world ended in darkness.

The shieldwall halted. Narritanni hacked over his shield, swept it up and around to catch the blow, then stabbed underneath it. The snarling painted face disappeared, but another took its place.

"Ward me!" he snapped, leaping backward.

Two others crowded in, and the line stayed intact. The Minztan strained his eyes into the night; the snow made the darkness almost impenetrable, like fighting in a closet that threw ice in your face. He looked left and right. The attack had stopped, and as he watched the Minztan line took a lurching half-step backward toward the east. More and more Kommanza were running up to take places in it; a mounted squad appeared, distant firelight glinting red on their lanceheads above the dark mass of foot that shoved and smashed and grappled across the surface of the river. His second ran up panting behind him.

"Got them loose," she shouted in his ear. "All we can find!"

A smaller body collided with him out of the darkness. Narritanni's sword turned aside its killing arc barely in time.

"Who the *ahlspl* are you?" he said.

"Taimi—Taimi Jonnah's-kin," he gabbled, grasping at the soldier's shoulders. "My kinmother—Maihu—"

"Where is she?" Narritanni asked eagerly.

The boy pointed west, beyond the Kommanz line. Then he screamed as Narritanni shook his head.

"She'll have to make her own— Circle, grab him!" Between them they wrestled the boy to a halt. "Get him out of here," he went on. "I'll manage the retreat."

He doubted very much the raiders would pursue them into the woods . . . or do anything much in the morning but head west at full speed. "An expensive lesson," he muttered to himself, readying his hoarse throat for the bull-bellow it would need. "For all concerned."

It was near dawn when Maihu woke. She was lashed to the side of a sled, spread-eagled; the returning feeling did not spread to her hands or feet, and she knew they were frozen.

Shkai'ra stood before her, silent, her eyes gray and hooded. The first rays of the sun rose over the treetops, a stray beam turning her hair to molten copper. It was minutes before she spoke, softly enough so that the warriors circled at a respectful distance could not hear.

"Most of the slaves escaped in the confusion. Your people hit us hard while we were disordered, and we couldn't pursue. Taimi went with them."

Maihu slumped. It was something, she thought dully. Beyond the ring of Kommanza the head of the Snowbrother looked down blindly from a lance, high enough to be in full light while they waited in darkness below.

"You fought us well, Maihu," continued Shkai'ra gravely. "You made us think you weak and cowardly, then your plan nearly destroyed us. It'll be long years before we ride a raid as lightly as we did this one. A killer like you deserves to live again as a Kommanza; when you go before the gods, tell them I sent you with honor."

"I move with the Circle, into the Harmony," Maihu said with quiet dignity. She turned her eyes to the rising light in the east, ignoring the knife in the other's hand.

The Kommanza leaned closer. "I never really knew you at all, did I?" she murmured.

Maihu met her eyes. "Do any of us?" she said. "Make an end, Shkai'ra." It was the first time she had said the other's name.

"As you will," Shkai'ra said. There was a moment's coldness, then nothing.

Shkai'ra withdrew the knife from between the Minztan's ribs. The warband cheered wildly as she turned. *Witchkiller*, they would call her: *Demonslayer*. The shaman told her that there was a fate in this, or the hand of a god; that she would return here one day, and do greater deeds. He had seemed only half himself, though. Whatever the truth of that, this fight would keep her Name alive; the songs would be sung for centuries. If the slaves were mostly gone, there was still more than what her kinmother had sent her to reave, and knowledge that was more precious still.

I have glory, and my Name, she thought with bewilderment. *Why do I feel no joy?* She reached out and brushed fingers on the cold cheek.

"Eh'rik," she called. "Bring a torch. We're going to burn this. Scatter the ashes among the trees."

He gazed at her with shock: cremation was the warrior's rite. "What will I tell—" he began.

Her palm chopped down. *"That I will it,"* she answered, flatly.

He bowed salute. "The Chiefkin wishes," he murmured. She stood immobile, waiting, staring into the west.

S.M. STIRLING
and
THE DOMINATION OF THE DRAKA

In 1782 the Loyalists fled the American Revolution to settle in a new land: South Africa, Drake's Land. They found a new home, and built a new nation: The Domination of the Draka, an empire of cruelty and beauty, a warrior people, possessed by a wolfish will to power. This is alternate history at its best.

"A tour de force."   **—David Drake**

"It's an exciting, evocative, thought-provoking—but of course horrifying—read."
     —Poul Anderson

MARCHING THROUGH GEORGIA
Six generations of his family had made war for the Domination of the Draka. Eric von Shrakenberg wanted to make peace—but to succeed he would have to be a better killer than any of them.

UNDER THE YOKE
In *Marching Through Georgia* we saw the Draka's "good" side, as they fought and beat that more obvious horror, the Nazis. Now, with a conquered Europe supine beneath them, we see them as they truly are; for conquest is only the *beginning* of their plans ... All races are created equal—as slaves of the Draka.

THE STONE DOGS
The cold war between the Alliance of North America and the Domination is heating up. The Alliance, using its superiority in computer technologies, is preparing a master stroke of electronic warfare. But the Draka, supreme in the ruthless manipulation of life's genetic code, have a secret weapon of their own. . . .

"This is a potent, unflinching look at a might-have-been world whose evil both contrasts with and reflects that in our own." —*Publishers Weekly*

"Detailed, fast-moving military science fiction . . ." —Roland Green, *Chicago Sun-Times*

"*Marching Through Georgia* is more than a thrilling war story, more than an entertaining alternate history. . . . I shall anxiously await a sequel." —Fred Lerner, *VOYA*

"The glimpses of a society at once fascinating and repelling are unforgettable, and the people who make up the society are real, disturbing, and very much alive. Canadian author Stirling has done a marvelous job with *Marching Through Georgia*." —Marlene Satter, *The News* of Salem, Arkansas

"Stirling is rapidly emerging as a writer to watch." —Don D'Ammassa, *SF Chronicle*

MERCEDES LACKEY

The Hottest Fantasy Writer Today!

URBAN FANTASY

Knight of Ghosts and Shadows with Ellen Guon

Elves in L.A.? It would explain a lot, wouldn't it? Eric Banyon is a musician with a lot of talent but very little ambition—and his lady just left him lovelorn in a deserted corner of the Renaissance Faireground, singing the blues and playing his flute. He couldn't have known the desperate sadness of his music would free Korendil, a young elven noble, from the magical prison he has been languishing in for centuries. Eric really needed a good cause to get his life in gear—now he's got one. With Korendil he must raise an army to fight against the evil lord who seeks to conquer all of California. And Eric's music will show the way....

Summoned to Tourney with Ellen Guon

Elves in San Francisco? Where else would an elf go when L.A. got too hot? All is well there with our elf-lord, his human companion and the mage who brought them all together—until it turns out that San Francisco is doomed to fall off the face of the continent. Doomed that is, unless our mage can summon the Nightflyers, the soul-devouring shadow creatures from the dreaming world—creatures no one on Earth could possibly control....

Born to Run with Larry Dixon

There are elves out there. And more are coming. But even elves need money to survive in the "real" world. The good elves in South Carolina, intrigued by the thrills of stock car racing, are manufacturing new, light-weight engines (with, incidentally, very little "cold" iron); the bad elves run a kiddie-porn and snuff-film ring, with occasional forays into drugs. *Children in Peril—Elves to the Rescue.* (Part of the SERRAted Edge series.)

HIGH FANTASY

Bardic Voices: The Lark & The Wren

Rune could be one of the greatest bards of her world, but the daughter of a tavern wench can't get much in the way of formal training. So one night she goes up to play for the Ghost of Skull Hill. She'll either fiddle till dawn to prove her skill as a bard—or die trying....

Also by Mercedes Lackey:

Reap the Whirlwind with C.J. Cherryh
Part of the Sword of Knowledge series.

Castle of Deception with Josepha Sherman
Based on the bestselling computer game, *The Bard's Tale.* (Available July 1992.)

The Ship Who Searched with Anne McCaffrey
The Ship Who Sang is not alone! (Available August 1992.)

And watch for **Wheels of Fire,** Book II of the SERRAted Edge series, with Mark Shepherd, coming in October 1992.

BUILDING A NEW FANTASY TRADITION

The Unlikely Ones by Mary Brown

Anne McCaffrey raved over *The Unlikely Ones*: "What a splendid, unusual and intriguing fantasy quest! You've got a winner here...." Marion Zimmer Bradley called it "Really wonderful ... I shall read and re-read this one." A traditional quest fantasy with quite an unconventional twist, we think you'll like it just as much as Anne McCaffrey and Marion Zimmer Bradley did.

Knight of Ghosts and Shadows
by Mercedes Lackey & Ellen Guon

Elves in L.A.? It would explain a lot, wouldn't it? In fact, half a millennium ago, when the elves were driven from Europe they came to—where else? —Southern California. Happy at first, they fell on hard times after one of their number tried to force the rest to be his vassals. Now it's up to one poor human to save them if he can. A knight in shining armor he's not, but he's one hell of a bard!

The Interior Life by Katherine Blake

Sue had three kids, one husband, a lovely home and a boring life. Sometimes, she just wanted to escape, to get out of her mundane world and *live* a little. So she did. And discovered that an active fantasy life can be a very dangerous thing—and very real.... Poul Anderson thought *The Interior Life* was "a breath of fresh air, bearing originality, exciting narrative, vividly realized characters—everything we have been waiting for for too long."

The Shadow Gate by Margaret Ball

The only good elf is a dead elf—or so the militant order of Durandine monks thought. And they planned on making sure that all the elves in their world (where an elvish Eleanor of Aquitaine ruled in Southern France) were very, very good. The elves of Three Realms have one last spell to bring help ... and received it: in the form of the staff of the New Age Psychic Research Center of Austin, Texas....

Hawk's Flight by Carol Chase
Taverik, a young merchant, just wanted to be left alone to make an honest living. Small chance of that though: after their caravan is ambushed Taverik discovers that his best friend Marko is the last living descendant of the ancient Vos dynasty. The man who murdered Marko's parents still wants to wipe the slate clean—with Marko's blood. They try running away, but Taverik and Marko realize that there is a fate worse than death . . . That sooner or later, you have to stand and fight.

A Bad Spell in Yurt by C. Dale Brittain
As a student in the wizards' college, young Daimbert had shown a distinct flair for getting himself in trouble. Now the newly appointed Royal Wizard to the backwater Kingdom of Yurt learns that his employer has been put under a fatal spell. Daimbert begins to realize that finding out who is responsible may require all the magic he'd never quite learned properly in the first place—with the kingdom's welfare and his life the price of failure. Good thing Daimbert knows how to improvise!